BEYOND THE WHEAT FIELD

LUCIE JERCH

ISBN 978-1-64300-355-9 (Paperback)
ISBN 978-1-64300-356-6 (Digital)

Copyright © 2018 Lucie Jerch
All rights reserved
First Edition

All rights reserved. No part of this publication may be reproduced, distributed, or transmitted in any form or by any means, including photocopying, recording, or other electronic or mechanical methods without the prior written permission of the publisher. For permission requests, solicit the publisher via the address below.

Covenant Books, Inc.
11661 Hwy 707
Murrells Inlet, SC 29576
www.covenantbooks.com

Prelude

In a desert land he found him, in a barren and howling waste. He shielded him and cared for him; he guarded him as the apple of his eye, like an eagle that stirs up its nest and hovers over its young, that spreads its wings to catch them and carries them aloft.
—Deuteronomy 32:10–11

She swung so high that the chain jerked on her way back down. With her eyes closed and her face turned up toward the sun, her heart was pumping with the rhythm of the swing, the wind pressing against her, lifting up her pretty curly white hair into the sky. Her dress danced, and her feet pumped faster and faster, higher and higher until she could feel the freedom of the air lifting her up.

She wanted to stay in this moment, never to open her eyes again. She wanted the smell of freedom like the scent of wildflowers in spring to soak into every part of her, for this moment to be etched indelibly into her memory. It was one of the very few times she felt safe, a sense of self, of belonging, of total joy. But then she would do the thing she regretted most; she'd open her eyes, and the moment would disappear.

Chapter 1

You will seek me and find me when you seek me with all your heart.
—Jeremiah 29:13

I woke up with a jolt to pounding on the door of the townhouse and the sound of yelling.

"Open the door. This is the police," came the voices from the hallway outside the door of our townhouse.

What on earth was going on? I was totally confused as I looked over to see my boyfriend, Matt, quickly getting dressed. When he saw me looking at him, he put his finger to his lips and said quietly and firmly, "Shhhhh . . . don't move, Sam. I'll handle this." He looked frustrated, cussing softly as he put his pants on.

"What is going on, Matt? Why are the police here?" I asked, looking around for something I could quickly grab and put on. I pulled on a sweatshirt over my pajamas, my hands shaking with fear. I could hear the banging on the door.

"Open up. This is the police. You have two minutes before we bust the door down," the voices kept shouting.

"Shhhhh . . . don't move, I told you. Just get back into bed and stay there a bit," Matt said, holding his hand up to me like a stop sign as he opened the door and made his way downstairs. I don't think he knew what to do either. He kept looking back at me as I looked through the crack of the door.

I went and sat on the side of the bed, terrified, as Matt went downstairs. I didn't know if he was going to open the door to let the police in or try to run out the back slider. I heard the commotion happening downstairs and just froze, unable to breathe. I went to the bedroom door and turned my head to listen through the crack.

"We have a warrant . . ." was all I could hear through the yelling and screaming. Matt was arguing with them, but I couldn't make out what was going on as several people were talking all at once. I wanted to scream out and tell Matt to stop arguing with them, to cooperate with them and give them what they wanted. All I heard was banging around, yelling, the door slamming, muffled voices, then quiet. I waited for a while, afraid. Then I quietly tiptoed down the hall, down the stairs and peaked around the corner past the living room to where the front door was. No one was there. I rushed over to the slider and saw the brake lights of a police car leaving the parking area.

Matt had been acting weird lately, more than his usual weird. He was anxiously looking around, wanting the lights off in the townhouse, which was not unusual since he always wanted it dark, but lately, he didn't want any lights on at all, not even the television. We would spend much of our time upstairs in the bedroom with the drapes closed, watching TV in the dark. He would get up often to look outside, as though he was paranoid that someone was after him. I would ask him several times if something was wrong, but the answer was always no and to stop asking. I had a feeling it wasn't the truth but knew better not to poke a sleeping lion.

Just a few days before the police arrived, I had discovered that I was pregnant, but I hadn't told Matt yet in fear of what he might do or say. I wasn't sure he'd be too happy about having a baby in our lives. I had also found an eviction notice folded in Matt's jean pocket, apparently the second and last notice, indicating we had to be out by the end of the week—and it was now Thursday. I had confronted Matt about it.

"What the hell are you doing anyway snooping around in my pockets? The landlord is an asshole! There was a mistake, I paid the rent." He was livid with me, accusatory; it was never his fault but everyone else's. I knew that he was lying, but I was afraid to call him out on it because he had an explosive temper. I was afraid he would use it on me by hitting me or yelling. I tried to ask him what the plan was. What we were going to do? Where would we go?

"Sam . . . what the fuck! You don't trust me? I'll take care of it. You don't worry your pretty little head. I can handle this," he said, throwing the TV remote across the room, hitting the wall and smashing it to pieces. He swore some more as he left me standing in the room to go to the bathroom.

My best friend and I had met Matt and his brother at a bar. My friend and Matt's brother hit it off right away, but not Matt and I. We just hung out because the other two got together often. We were basically tagalongs. Matt wasn't attractive; he was average-looking. He was six years older, five-nine, with brown hair and blue eyes. But his eyes looked grayish, tired, and he had dark circles under them. After a time, our relationship grew out of convenience, and we enjoyed partying together and doing drugs. Free drugs for me since Matt was a dealer. I wondered if I ever loved Matt, or was it the thought of having someone by my side? I knew I could have done better. I was attractive, never had an issue getting a guy's attention if I wanted to. I wonder if we forced the relationship to happen out of convenience for the both of us, not wanting to be alone.

I was worried. Matt was gone, probably going to jail again. I was beside myself. Twenty, pregnant, and no place to live. To make matters worse, I was unmarried and doing everything my parents disapproved of. Their religion did not look favorably on my lifestyle of partying, drinking, and living in sin with my boyfriend. I shook my head, putting my hand on my still flat tummy, as I thought about the child growing inside of me, trying to remove the memory of a similar situation in my past. I couldn't let my thoughts go there, knowing I couldn't do to this child what I had done to the last. I felt as though I was maybe getting another chance to make up for my previous mistake, even though my life was no better than it had been the first time I got pregnant. My life was still a mess. I couldn't help but wonder how I was going to raise a child on my own.

I felt like I had no other choice but to go plead with my parents to see if I could stay with them for a while, to give me enough time to figure things out. Thankfully, I still had my job working at Re/Max Real Estate in the City of Mississauga. I had not told them about the pregnancy yet either. I wondered how that was going to go, how they would receive the news of my pregnancy. I had a little time since I was only six weeks along. I would have to cross that bridge soon. I packed up my belongings, shoving them into garbage bags, grabbing only the clothes I needed and some personal stuff: my make-up, face wash, hair dryer and curling iron, shampoo, and what cheap jewelry I had. I needed to get out of there quick. I did not want to face the landlord, nor did I want the police to come and get me either. I couldn't take any of the furniture, so I had to leave it behind.

I looked around. *Here I go again,* I thought. This was the story of my life, moving from one place to another, always out of money. I needed drugs to drown it all out—the past, the present, and my hopeless future. I had lost a lot of weight over the years, not eating much, smoking my money away, and not having enough for food. I looked at myself in the mirror. I felt ugly and used up, and I had dark lines under my eyes. At one time, I felt pretty: five feet five, blond hair, big blue eyes, slim, clear skin. Now I looked ten years older, my hair desperately needed a fresh color, my skin looked saggy and tired, and my eyes were red. Too skinny! I cried at the sight of myself. I slid down to the floor, pulling my knees up to my chest, placing my head down and wrapping my arms around my legs. "What am I going to do?" I yelled into the air.

I drove to my parents' house, which was an hour away, wondering what I was going to tell them. Would I tell them I was pregnant? I knew they didn't approve of Matt, and this certainly was going to add to their disapproval. What were my other choices? I had none. Matt had burned many bridges: he hadn't paid back money to his drug dealers and had ripped off our friends, smoking and using the drugs he was supposed to sell and supplying me as well. So here I was, a pregnant, homeless, drug-using loser with a beat-up car filled with all my belongings with plenty of room to spare.

I stopped at the corner of my parents' street, half a mile from their house, not a house in sight. I grew up in the country, five miles from town, on a dirt road. Our neighborhood consisted of seven homes including mine, dotted in the middle of nowhere, between wheat fields and corn fields, miles from other homes. I placed my hands on both sides of the steering wheel, laid my head down against it, and began to weep. "What the hell have I done?" I yelled into the steering wheel. "What do I tell them? What will they say?" It was

May, a week from Mother's Day. I thought, *Great, this is going to be a perfect Mother's Day gift.*

I lifted my head up, my eyes settling on the wheat fields to the left. *Those damn wheat fields*, I thought. They may have looked beautiful to others, their long thin gold stems swaying back and forth with the wind, all in unison as though playing a soft soothing melody, the tops looking soft to the touch. My stomach churned. To me, they represented death of an innocent child. I hated them. It was where I lost her, the child in me, in those fields. It was the reason I was sitting at this corner, in this situation. I sat in the car for some time, cursing at the wheat field. I shook my head, trying to remove the memory, and looked ahead, down the road I had to travel. I was nervous as hell, but I mustered enough courage to go do what I needed to do. I couldn't live in my car. Besides, I didn't know when Matt would get out of jail. He certainly didn't have any money to pay for anything. I would have to figure that out in the next couple days, if I could.

My mother was a beautiful woman of faith. I did not believe in my mom's God, or any God for that matter, but I did love and believe in my mom. She was in her early fifties, short, five feet two, short dark hair with a little splash of gray here and there. I wasn't afraid that she'd turn me away—she would never—but rather I was afraid of hurting or disappointing her, which was almost worse than being cast out. I felt that I was a disappointment to everyone. My mother had been sick all of her life with different ailments, mostly intestinal issues. After giving birth to me, she had a hysterectomy, later having a double mastectomy, an ileostomy, and other procedures, yet that did not stop her from doing things: serving at the church, helping people in the community, and giving so much of herself to others.

It wasn't often, but I remembered times when my mom wasn't sick and in the hospital. I would go with her to help at the Saint Paul's Center. This was a place where people in need could pick up a bag of groceries and a bag of used clothes. I also remembered my mom driving the school bus all throughout my childhood years. When I was too young for school, I would ride with my mom on the bus. I enjoyed watching all the kids get on at school, listening to the chitter chatter around me, even though I didn't talk with anyone, and stopping at each stop to let them off. I sat on the bench behind my mother, wanting to be close.

I didn't speak to anyone because I was so shy, but I loved being around them. It was part of our daily routine. In the morning, we would go to do our bus route. My mom would often stay in bed the rest of the day, then get up in time to go pick up the kids from school. During the day, I often brought my toys into my mother's room and played there as she slept. I didn't understand what was wrong with her or that this was not a normal way of life, for this had been a normal routine for me. Weren't all moms like mine? My neighborhood friend's mom was like that too, but I discovered later in life that it was largely because she often had a hangover.

Besides spending so much time in and out of the hospital and in her bed at home, my mother also had a prayer chair where she spent much of her time sitting and praying. As a young child, the youngest of four, I missed her a lot, her comforting smile, her gentle touch, her good-night kiss, and our reading time together because of her absence. My mom and I read a lot of stories together. My mom was my security. When she was on one of her hospital stays, I felt scared and all alone without her. I would often crawl into my mother's chair feeling the warmth of it wrap around me like a hug. I would run my hand along the soft material, stick my nose against it and smell my mother's scent, lavender.

My dad worked all the time, and when he wasn't at work, he was sleeping. I rarely saw him or conversed with him; he seemed so distant, a foreigner to me, so I spent much of my days alone.

As I pulled into my parents' driveway and shut off the car, it was a little past six in the evening. I walked slowly up to the door, knocked, turned the handle, pushed on the door, and walked in. My parents rarely locked their door.

"Hey," I called, "it's me, Sam." I stood on the landing, nervous, waiting for someone to respond.

"Samantha?" my mother asked as she walked toward the door.

"Yeah." I could feel my heart beating out of my chest. I still didn't know what to say.

My mom appeared in the doorway. "What are you doing here? I didn't know you were coming," she said in surprise as she saw me standing there.

"Yeah, well, surprise," I said, unable to hold back the tears any longer. It seemed that when I was around my mom, I couldn't quite hold it together. My mom brought out all sorts of emotions within me. As hard as I tried to keep them in check, they would explode out of me in front of her. It was difficult to look at her. I felt like I had disappointed her, failed her as a daughter. I wanted to tell her how sorry I was for the things I had done: lying, the drugs, the drinking. I know she didn't like Matt because of the way he treated her little girl; I saw it in her eyes, the sadness. I knew she wanted me to be happy and that it pained her to see me in such turmoil. It was hard for me to look at her eye to eye without feeling as though she could see right through me, beyond the façade to the broken me.

"Hey, honey, what's wrong?" she asked, sadness evident in her voice as she put her arms around me. I shrugged, releasing the hold she had on me.

"Mom, I . . . I . . . really need a place to stay. I'm tired and can't really explain it right now," I said as I looked away from her and stared at the floor.

"Oh? Well, sure, you can stay in your old room. Do you want anything to eat?" she asked, with a worried, questioning tone in her voice.

"I'm sorry, Mom, really, I just want to go to bed. It's been a long, difficult day," I said as I lifted the corner of the area rug with my foot, rolling it up and down. I was not prepared to talk to her about it then. "Where's Dad?" I asked.

"Oh, he went to play bingo down at the church hall," she said, turning around and climbing the three steps that led into the kitchen.

"Oh, okay," I said with a sigh of relief. "I'm sorry, Mom, but we'll talk tomorrow, okay?" I followed her up the steps, walking past the kitchen toward my old bedroom down the hall, relieved to know my dad wasn't home. I knew my mom would talk to him and smooth things over.

"All right, sweetheart, goodnight!" Mom said as she turned toward the sink and began to wash the dishes. I knew she was worried; she didn't say it, but I could tell by the way she looked at me, the way she was fidgeting with the dish towel in her hands.

Later that night, I heard my dad come into the house. Then I heard my parents whispering. The house I grew up in was a small ranch-style home so there wasn't much privacy; the walls were thin. I could hear the frustration in my dad's voice as he asked Mom what I was doing there.

"Not dat she can't stay 'ere," I heard him say with his French accent, "but why is she 'ere? What's going on?" he said to my mom, the frustration obvious in his voice.

"I don't know, but she looked really upset. She was crying," replied my mom in a whisper. "I feel like there's something really wrong." I could sense the concern in her voice.

"Geez, Marge, it's probably dat no-good boyfriend of 'ers. He walks all over 'er. I just don't like him nor trust him," my dad said in a loud, angry voice.

"Shhhh, Albert, you don't want her to hear you," she said firmly.

"For Pete sake, why not? Dat's the truth!" my dad said in a louder voice as though he wanted me to hear. Then I heard my mom whisper something, and they moved into their bedroom and shut the door.

I lay in bed thinking how much this was going to hurt, having to tell my parents. I was also thinking how badly I needed some relief, to smoke some crack. I needed to get my mind off of this whole situation, this mess I was in. Yet I also had a child inside of me to think about. What damage had I already done to it? Was it too late? I didn't know the effects of drugs on an unborn child. I just knew I needed something. I was really beginning to feel the lack of it in my body; the tremors were beginning. I felt hot and sweaty and anxious, and my head was pounding. I had a bit of coke stashed in my purse and took it out. *Just a little shouldn't hurt,* I thought, but it was kind of late; it would most likely keep me awake all night, which I didn't want. I wanted to sleep it all away. Instead, I took out a bit of pot from the baggy I always carried with me and rolled a joint. I was hoping it would tie me over until morning. I opened the window and blew the smoke out into the air as I closed my eyes and tried to find relief with each puff.

The next morning was Saturday. I had not slept well. My body was aching, crying out to be fed what it had gotten used to over the years. I put out a line of coke, trying not to think of the baby growing inside of me, and snorted it, feeling the white powder tingle up my nose. I knew I needed something stronger, like crack, but I couldn't smoke it here at the house. Besides, I didn't have any. I didn't know if I could go on for much longer with the little coke I had left, and I was out of money. I would have to figure out what to do.

The nagging feeling in my gut continued to torture me. I was carrying a baby. I was responsible for its wellbeing. I needed to straighten up, but I didn't know how I was going to do it. How could I stop after many years of drug use? I knew I would go into the shakes and sweats if I didn't use; they were already beginning. The thought terrified me; I was scared. Would that even be good for the baby? At times, the thought of ending my life would enter my mind, but as quickly as it popped in, it flew out. I could never follow through with it. Even though things were a mess and I felt no hope, I was angry—angry at myself and angry at the world. Besides, I had too much pride to do such a thing. I was so determined to prove to everyone that I was tough and could fight through it all.

I would've been content to just hide in my room all day, but around ten o'clock, my mom tapped on the door.

"Samantha, are you awake?" she asked in a soft whisper. I thought about faking it but realized it was going to have to happen at some point, so I better get it over with.

"Yeah, Mom, I'm just lying here," I said. "You can come in." I sat up, my head pounding, and moved to the side of the bed.

My mom opened the door, walked in, and softly shut the door behind her. I knew my dad was not going to come and talk to me. He let my mom take care of the talks in the family. His way of communicating was yelling; my mom was the only one who could talk to him and calm him down.

My mom looked at me, confused and sad. I'm sure it was difficult for her, and she didn't know what to say or do. She sat on the edge of the bed next to me and placed her hand over mine. I couldn't hold it in any longer. I lost all of my courage as I leaned into her and let the tears flow freely. I told her about Matt, about not having a place to live and losing everything we had, which was not much to begin with. I didn't mention the drugs, ever. I had been doing drugs since I was twelve years old and hiding it from my mother ever since. I wasn't sure if or how much my mom knew since she didn't let on that she knew anything. Then I took a deep breath and kept talking.

"Mom . . . I . . . I don't know any easier way to tell you this, but . . . I'm pregnant," I said looking down at her hand over mine as my tears fell on top of her hand. My stomach was in knots as the silence lingered in the room for a few moments.

"Oh, Samantha . . . how . . . I just don't know what to say." She squeezed my hand harder. We sat in the quiet, letting the news settle. I could feel her struggling for words, searching for something to say to me.

"I honestly don't know what to say," she said. "I can't pretend it's good news in regards to this whole situation you're in. Nor my disappointment with Matt. At times I want to shake him to his senses. Yet you are carrying my first grandchild, a child," she said as she turned her head to look at me with tears in her eyes. She placed her hand on my chin and turned my face toward her. "Look at me, Sam, please. I may not fully understand everything that's going on, it breaks my heart to see you going through this. But that does not *ever* change my love for you. I love you so much, Sam. I hope you know that."

"I'm so sorry, Mom, for disappointing you . . ." She put her arm around me and held me as we both cried together. "I just don't know what to do."

"One step at a time, sweetheart, one step at a time. I know you don't want to hear this, but I lean into God more in these times when I don't have answers. I pray for his wisdom and guidance. I will pray for you to find that peace knowing that he has your back," she said, with a tone of hope in her voice.

"Yeah . . . I guess I don't get it. I just don't feel like He's been here for me." Shrugging, I kept talking. "I guess I don't believe like you do, Mom. If it works for you, great. I don't know if I can believe in him." I put my head back down in shame, feeling like once again I had disappointed her.

"Okay, Sam, we will leave it at that," she said. "But that doesn't mean God doesn't still work in your life or love you. He loves you no matter what! You can't make him not love you." With that, she gave me a squeeze and stood up. "When you are ready, come into the kitchen and have breakfast. You need to eat, not only for you, but for your child growing inside of you. This child is innocent and did not make this mess." She opened the door and closed it gently behind her.

My heart went out to my mom. If only she knew how deep my mess went. I couldn't imagine being on the other end, being in her shoes as a mom, and having to hear about your daughter's broken, messed-up life.

I got dressed and went out to the kitchen. My mom made me some oatmeal and tea. She also made herself some tea and sat with me at the table. She was fidgeting with her cup, turning it this way and that, looking down. I could tell there was more on her mind that she wanted to say, but I ate and waited.

"Ummmm, so, there's this thing going on at a church in town, at Holy Cross, Monday night through Thursday, called the Movement of the Holy Spirit," she said. "Sweetheart, I'd love it if you'd come with me." She looked at me with pleading eyes.

"Mom, you know how I feel about church. I don't want to go." I hated church or anything to do with church people or God. I could not understand where God had been all my life. Why would a perfect God, the apparent creator of the universe, full of love, be so distant and not come to my rescue when I really needed him? I had no proof of his existence, only proof that he didn't exist.

"Please, Sam, it's Mother's Day next Sunday, and I'm asking you kindly to please do this for me. I don't know what else to do." My mom stopped to catch her breath, swallowing as if there was a lump in her throat she was trying to dislodge. "I want you there. I'd love it if you came with me. You don't have to do anything. They won't make you do anything, I promise. You can just sit there, but please, I'm begging you to come. For me?" She was looking at me with pleading eyes and tears running slowly down her cheeks.

The event was not at my mom's church, the French Catholic church we grew up in. Rather, it was at another church across town, an English Catholic church she would often attend during the week when they had different events going on. My mom loved this church more for some reason. She said they were more "real," whatever that meant. I knew my mom was trying to "save" me. Save me from me? It was so hard for me to grasp what that meant . . . to be saved. I heard many things over the years of being dragged to church. When I was little, I actually loved being at church; it felt safe to me. There was a feeling inside me that I could not describe. Like a refreshing shower after a long hot sweaty day. I felt light and peaceful. That's probably why I fell asleep often in church. But now, I felt judged. That they would look down on me like I didn't deserve to be there, that I wasn't good enough for them or a relationship with God.

"I'll think about it, Mom," I said, getting up to wash my bowl and cup.

The weekend went by slowly. I stayed in bed most of the time, trying to sleep the days away until I could go to work on Monday. My dad did not speak much to me, and I felt the tension in the house. I did not know how to talk to my dad, to communicate with him, so I avoided him as much as I could.

When Monday evening came, with continual prompting from my mom, I decided I would go with her to church. But I was not going to participate or even listen. I would just go to be with my mom. I figured since I was staying at their house, I could at least do this one thing to please her and get her off my back. For the first three nights, I did nothing but sit. Sure, I listened because there was nothing else for me to do. They sang, spoke about someone called the Holy Spirit, and heard testimonies of people's lives being transformed by God. They were nice stories, but I brushed it all off as a stroke of luck. The people were just fooling themselves if they thought God had any part in their lives going well. I saw things as being at the right place at the right time or being in the wrong place at the wrong time. It seemed like I was at many wrong places at the wrong times. Sure, I had free will to make choices, and I know I've made plenty, yet there were things done to me that were not my choice and God did not, and could not, change it or make it better.

Thursday night, the last night, I was surprised. We were all divided into groups, women with women, men with men, which I was not too happy about. Apparently, the plan was for everyone to be prayed over in order to receive the Holy Spirit, whatever the hell that meant. I had no clue what was in store for me. I tried to get my mom's attention to tell her I was definitely not participating. But my mom was not looking my way and would disappear as if she was purposely avoiding me. A few ladies from the group I was assigned to surrounded me and directed me over to where their group was meeting. I shook my head no, but they smiled and kept telling me it was all going to be great. My face was red from the anger; I was so mad at my mom for doing this to me.

As I made my way over, the aggressive ladies moved me to the chair, although it felt more like a push. Then they wrapped themselves around me, locking me in the middle of the circle. They placed their hands over my head and shoulders and began to chant a prayer. I closed my eyes, trying to hum in my head so I didn't have to listen to them pray. Sometimes I would hear a strange language I didn't even understand, like the jibber jabber of a child who could not talk yet. I just sat and tried to think of other things to distract myself. I felt a sense of comfort pass over me, a warmth, a kind of safety in the middle of these nice older ladies. They reminded me of moms and grandmas, and I was certainly the youngest in the whole group. Their praying went on for quite some time until the announcer asked them to finish up and said that the evening was coming to an end. What? Why didn't the other ladies get prayed over too? I thought everyone was going to have a turn to be prayed for. I became suspicious of their motivations.

I left with a warm feeling within me, but nothing more. I was just mad at my mom. I had been struggling the last few days, feeling shaky, and having really bad headaches. I had tried to go through my stash slowly, but it wasn't enough to keep me going, and now I was facing the beginnings of withdrawal.

"Mom, what was that about?" I said angrily as we got in the car.

"What was what about?" my mom responded with a mischievous grin while looking straight ahead, not turning to look at me.

"You know! You planned this. Did you tell those ladies about me?" I asked her, annoyed.

"They are so sweet, aren't they?" she said. "I'm glad to see that they prayed for you." She smiled, ignoring my question.

"Mom!" *Never mind*, I thought. I couldn't be mad at my mom. I knew she meant well. Besides, no damage done since there had been no conversion.

That night, I couldn't sleep. I thought about my life and what a mess it was. I scratched my head wondering, *How did my life get so complicated, so messed up?* What had happened? It seemed that one day I was swinging on my swing, a child, carefree, and now here I was. I was sweating and in pain for lack of drugs that I desperately needed to keep me functioning. I was slowly poisoning my baby. I was alone. I felt such a deep sense of hopelessness, stuck in this deep hole that seemed to me impossible to get out. I had made a lot of bad choices that hurt many people, including myself. Where were all my so-called friends in my time of need and great distress? When we were all smoking and partying together, we all promised, swore, to be there for one another. We were family! Now that I was pregnant with no money, and Matt in jail, they had abandoned me. Not one called or visited to check in on me. I was all alone with no one to rescue me—again. It was just me. Alone.

At that moment, I thought about my mom's God. I was desperate. My mom had survived some hard stuff in her life. How did she do it without going insane? I thought, *What the heck, if there is a God,* which I doubted, *then what do I have to lose? I could ask him for help, put him to the test, and then I would know for sure if he really exists or not.* So I got on my knees beside the bed, because that's what we did when we were little, and I asked God to please help me as rivers of water began to flow from my eyes. I didn't know how to pray but just told him I needed help, that I was lost and didn't know what to do.

I wept, wanting all the pain and sadness to go away and someone to come rescue me. I wanted my unborn child to live. I again called out to God, louder, the Creator of the universe, to please, if he was there, to hear me calling him, to save me and that I was sorry for messing up my life. I wept alone in the darkness of my room.

My eyes were closed, but I could sense a feeling of warmth and a brightness filling the room. I opened one eye, then two, and noticed a light in the corner. It was so bright that I had to squint my eyes. It shot across the room like a shooting star and entered the top of my head, like a bolt of lightning, moving through my body and out the bottom of my feet. A whoosh, like a tornado, passed through, wiping everything out of its path, clearing the debris, a cleansing of all the crap that had settled in my body for so long. I wept as I felt it move through me, and when it had passed, I sat in shock. *WHAT WAS THAT?* I yelled with joy as I put my hands on my head, "WOW, oh my God, that was amazing!" I said as I looked around to try and find the thing that had just invaded my body.

I felt refreshed, like a new person, clean, free, light, drunk, but without alcohol. Like the best high I'd ever had, but without the drugs. I wanted more. I felt like I was floating two feet off the ground, feeling so much joy, so much love, so much of what I could not describe. Never had I ever experienced anything like it. I thought it had to be God. Was that what it felt like to feel his Holy Spirit that the people at church had talked about all week? Was that it? If so, I was sold on this God. I knew this was beyond anything in this world. My mother's God had showed up. I tiptoed into my parents' room and tried to quietly wake up my mother. I was so pumped, so full of joy and laughter that it was difficult to stay quiet. My mom quietly got up, in her usual flannel nightgown, confused, hair matted to one side of her head. I held on to her arm and led her out of the room and into the hall.

"What is it, honey? Are you okay?" my mom said in a panic, her eyes wide with worry that something awful had happened.

"Mom, something happened!" I said, unable to contain my joy. I couldn't stop laughing as if all the joy was coming out of the dark, deep crevices of my soul.

I hugged my mom, crying, "Mom, something crazy happened to me."

"Yes, yes, I got that, but what? Let's go into the kitchen and talk."

I sat at the kitchen table as my mom made us some tea. I started talking and found I couldn't stop. We talked for several hours about what had happened to me. My mom, too, was laughing and crying along with me, happy to see her daughter this way. Happy that God had pulled through, was faithful to bring her daughter home, not just physically but spiritually.

My mom spoke to me about Jesus, who he was, and what he had just done for me. Even though my mom did not know a lot of my past, she shared how Jesus had died on the cross for me and whatever needed repair, healing, forgiveness, he paid the price for it with his blood. He loved me so much that when I sincerely repented and asked him into my heart, he'd forgiven me of all my wrongs and would begin the transformation of my heart. I had heard this before in church as a little child, but this night, it began to make more sense, and I felt thirsty to hear more. In the past, my heart had been closed. I was too busy running away from myself to see beyond me to this Jesus. I was trying desperately to fill holes that only he could fill. On this night, I felt lightheaded, free, as though a ton of bricks had been lifted off my heart. I wanted more. I wanted to know more about this God who had filled my entire being with so much love and peace in a single moment.

As the days went on, I noticed that I had no desire for drugs, which was a true miracle to me. I had been in rehab before and had experienced severe sweats and shaking, but now I felt none of that. No sweating, no shaking, and no desire to smoke my daily dose of crack. The thought of doing any of it actually made my stomach churn. How did that happen? I could only attribute it to a higher power, to the God I had just encountered, who could have healed me instantly. In a moment of time, he had reached down into the depths of my soul and removed all desire for drugs. What the world could not fix, he fixed in a split second. The idea of this was too much for me to wrap my head around. I had mocked many people in the past for being believers. Called them Jesus freaks. And here I was, wanting to know him, praise him, sing and dance with him, like he was my everything. It was a true miracle. Later on, I would learn that I had a "road to Damascus" experience, like the Apostle Paul in the Bible whose heart was changed by the Holy Spirit.

God transformed me in a single moment. While I was alone in my room, he touched my heart. He filled me with his love and forgiveness and restored hope to me. I knew I still had a long road ahead of me, but I also knew I was not alone. I was no longer living in hopelessness and darkness but in his light. I had hope for a better future and knew he had plans for me. My mother shared a verse with me from Jeramiah in the Bible that read, "For I know the plans I have for you. They are plans for good and not for disaster, to give you a future and a hope." I kept that verse in my mind each day to help me remember that better days were ahead, that I did have a purpose on this earth. I later tattooed it on the inside of my left wrist to remind me of this truth.

Chapter 2

Cast all your anxiety on him because he cares for you.
—1 Peter 5:7

    The day of my salvation, twenty-eight years ago, was as clear in my mind as though it were yesterday. My life had taken many twists and turns before that day and in the days and years that followed. Since my mother's death two years ago, my past had been calling me back, back to the "then." I had avoided it for so long; there were too many memories I could not face, but it was time to take a trip back in my memory to find healing for my soul. I went back to the place where my mother had spent her last seven years, the place where I felt safe with my mom in her little room at the nursing home.

    I could clearly envision myself walking down the hall towards room 6 at Grace Villa nursing home in Hamilton, Ontario, nodding at the residents, who sat in their wheelchairs outside their bedroom doors, waiting for the nurses to clean their rooms or bring them down to the cafeteria for their next meal. The familiar scent quickly filling my lungs, the scents that come with old age: urine, body odor, soiled clothes, aged skin mixed with the smell of bleach that tried unsuccessfully to drown the other smells.

    Sometimes the smell was so bad that I would have to hold my breath as long as I could to avoid getting a splitting headache. I recalled passing by Grumpy Lady many times, trying to avoid eye contact, ignoring the hissing sounds that came out of her mouth when one would pass by her. Or the cute sweet, old couple who, most of the time, forgot that they knew each other. Or the ninety-nine-year-old lady with her walker who was still very sharp for her age, remembering my name each time I visited and every detail I had shared with her about my family. I knew if I stopped to talk with her, I would have to commit to a long conversation. Like many of the residents who dwelt here, Ms. Ellen was thirsty for attention and longed for someone to talk with about anything.

The sounds of cries and screams often pierced my ears and hurt my heart. It was an agonizing journey down the short hallway, which always seemed longer than it should, toward my mother's room at the end of the hall. I approached room 6, a room that was clearly etched in my mind as I entered and glanced at the first bed that Sharon, my mom's roommate, had once occupied. I could still see her asleep in her wheelchair by the bed in her usual spot, slumped over and snoring. But now the room lay bare, with not a trace of a life that had once lived and breathed in this space. Her paintings of flowers and animals no longer filled the walls, and that familiar scent, which each resident bore, had been replaced by the familiar smell of a hospital, cold and lifeless.

I moved across to my mother's side of the room, the curtains partly drawn to separate the two spaces. There, too, was no trace of life. I removed my shoes, climbed into the bed and lay down. I felt the cold seep through my bones and the stiffness of the hard mattress on my back. Closing my eyes, I tried to go back to the place in my mind where comfort dwelled, where my mom once laid, on the days when I would visit from my home in Michigan. I would drive seven hours to Hamilton, Ontario, yearning all the way to lay in this very spot beside my mother. The memories of climbing into the bed, feeling the warmth of her body and breathing in my mama's familiar scent of lavender, warmed me. I sighed as I crossed my arms to give myself a squeeze, feeling the memory of her seep into me, sensing the absence of her and how much I really missed her.

I remember sitting on the steps of our childhood home, where I spent my first seventeen years. I was about five years old. I was crying, waiting for my mother to return from another one of her long-term hospital stays. I sat, every day after school, waiting and hoping today would be the day she would come home. When she did, joy filled my heart from seeing her, feeling her hug me and comfort me. I buried my head in her chest, holding her tight and never wanting to let her go, crying into her. She held me as long as I needed her to, waiting for me to release all my anxieties of her absence, comforting me as long as I needed to be comforted. I would follow her around, afraid to let her out of my sight, afraid of her leaving me again; for as a young child, I could not bear life without her. She was my security, my comfort. Now, in room 6, like that child waiting on the steps, I longed for her to return. I longed to smell the lavender and to feel her comforting arms around me and to hear her tell me everything was going to be all right. But the moment never came.

I came often when my mom was alive, when I needed to get away, to feel the comfort of my mother's touch and her words, "I'm so proud of you, honey." I longed to hear those words now. On those nights, we would cuddle, talk, laugh, and cry, spending hours sharing our hearts' deepest pains and struggles, and also the victories. We'd empty our hearts out into the room. The walls were good at holding in the secrets we shared. It was a place where heaven came crashing down, invading our time together, healing our souls. It was a place where my mom and God dwelt in one spot together, for the two most influential beings in my life were together in this place.

Pictures of all the loved ones my mom had cherished—her four children, grandchildren, and great grandchildren—covered the walls; they were smiling back at me, but there were no voices to speak of the lives that lay beyond the smiles. I had come to understand why my mom loved her room at the nursing home so much. It did not make sense in the midst of a place filled with sickness and death just beyond the door of her room. I believe my mom needed a release from her many years of suffering with illness, pain, and hardship, not only of her own life journey of trials and past pains but also of the trials and hardships her children were going through: marriage issues, addiction, money problems, raising children. I also knew my mom needed an escape from my dad. Their marriage was a difficult one. The nursing home was the one place where people were taking care of her, and she wasn't forced to take care of anyone else.

I thought that I too wanted a room where I could hang pictures, only the nice ones, of beautiful, happy faces of my loved ones and pretend all was well. I only wanted to embrace the joy displayed in each of the pictures, not the hardships or challenges of life. I deeply longed for those times with my mom, where for a moment, the world would go away, where her tender touch and words would bring healing to my sometimes-broken heart.

I was often strengthened by my mother's faith, her love of the Father, her Savior. I thought that I myself was weak, struggling to deal with raising my children, not really knowing what I was doing, even though I'd been given the role of motherhood. It was unlike anything I had ever experienced before, and even though I'd had many struggles and challenges in my life, dealing with my own issues was completely different than watching my children in the midst of their own battles. Oh, I deeply love my children. I'd do anything for them, but they were now following their own journey of discovery, trial, and error, and I tried so hard not to interfere. That certainly wasn't always easy though, especially when I myself have struggled through what seemed like every kind of struggle known to man: fear, insecurity, low self-esteem, sexual, mental, and physical abuse, suicide attempt, abortion, etc.

I remember the last ten or so years of my mom's life. I had watched her as she struggled with her own demons. I knew that the medications she took didn't help her think and process things clearly, yet I saw the turmoil deep within her as she battled for her soul. Watching her in the final season of her life wasn't easy. When I was young, I thought my mom was ten feet tall and could save me from anything and anybody; she was my hero. Yet in reality, my mother was only five-feet-two, a petite woman. Throughout my childhood, I could only remember my gentle mother yell twice. In one instance, my two brothers, my sister, and I were all in the kitchen sitting around the table eating; my mom was standing at the kitchen sink doing dishes. I could not recall the conversation or the reason my mom did this, but she picked up a plate, yelled, and threw it across the room where it hit the wall behind us and smashed into pieces. We all sat quietly staring at mom in shock; tears streamed down my face. Barely moving and paralyzed with fear, I picked up my blanket, the one I carried with me everywhere I went and draped it over my head to hide my trembling body. I was afraid that the woman I admired so deeply, my hero, my only safe place, had lost it.

There was another time when my mom let out a high-pitched scream as she was doing the dishes. She smashed several glasses, one after another, in the sink, as if each glass represented something or someone she hated. Then a moment later, she quickly collected herself, cleaned up the broken glass in silence, and carried on as though nothing had happened.

Looking back at my life, I could honestly relate to the sudden outbursts of frustration and rage. I had no clue exactly what my mother had endured in life or everything she had to deal with behind the scenes, but as a woman who had done some growing up, lived a little, and had a family of my own, I now understood how life could get overwhelming. I too had lost it a time or two, screaming at the top of my lungs from a combination of defeat and frustration, only to fall into bed at night feeling the guilt wrap itself around me, smothering me, for once again failing as a mother, for losing control of myself.

I believe that there was so much more to my mother than she let on. There had been a lot of pain from her own childhood that she hadn't faced: her father's rejection, drunkenness, and selfishness. My mom did not speak of these things until we were all grown and gone, maybe as a way of protecting us from her pain or trying to suppress the memories that were too difficult to face. That was my mom: thinking of others before herself, not wanting others to go through the pain she had endured throughout her own life, yet suffering in silence.

I knew very little of my mother's life story as a young child, but what I did know was that at one point, her family had been quite wealthy. My mom grew up on the eastern part of Canada, in a town called Dalhousie, New Brunswick. They were French-speaking folks. It was a pretty town with rolling hills, rivers, and many lakes, along with the permeating smell of fish in the air. My father also grew up in New Brunswick, further east on an island called Lameque. It was a small town with a little over a thousand people, most of whom I am related to. My parents both migrated to Ontario, where there were more opportunities for work. My dad got a job and retired from working on the production lines of Chrysler. My parents met through a friend of a friend, married, and raised us four kids. Our first language was French. As a child, the kids would make fun of me because of the way I spoke. I'd say many things backwards, like paper toilet, which would make the kids break out in laughter. I was always embarrassed to talk because of it.

My mother's father, my grandpa, made and repaired leather shoes and purses. His business grew as did their possessions. They lived in one of the biggest house in their community and were well respected because of their success. My grandpa also enjoyed drinking and entertaining businessmen and women. But eventually, the drinking got the better of him, and he lost everything. The family had to move out of their large beautiful home to a small townhouse, which was quite a drastic change from the lifestyle they were used to.

I only knew my grandparents when they lived in the old green townhouse where the paint was faded and chipping and the siding was missing a few wooden slots. I remember our visits once a year. My parents would load us four kids up in the brown station wagon and make the twenty-plus-hour trip to Dalhousie as we all slept sprawled out in the back seat most of the way there. Once I spotted Sugar Loaf Mountain, I knew we were only a few hours away. The beautiful scenery of the mountains and rolling hills began to unfold before our eyes. From the flat, boring landscape most of the way, the road began to wind around the lakes and mountainous hills.

When we arrived late in the evening, past our bedtime, we were sent downstairs to sleep in the cold, musty old unfinished basement. Two steel queen-size beds sat in the middle of the room surrounded by boxes and junk that had been stored there, probably since my grandparents had moved in many years ago. My two brothers, Jacque and Ronald, slept in one bed while I slept in the other bed with my older sister, Rachael. I wasn't very close to my sister, maybe because she was six years older than me. I think it was more that she didn't like me. She probably still held a grudge against me for being her only present when she turned six as I had been born the day before her birthday. While we slept, a broom was placed against the headboard so we could swat away the cobwebs and the occasional mouse that scurried across the floor. Sleeping down there, I always felt as though something was crawling on me, and I would often wake up with a scream if I felt anything brush against my skin. Of course, my brothers, who constantly teased me, would make up scary stories about the many kids who had once slept down there and who had disappeared by the next morning. I was terrified and worried about monsters coming to take me away, so I stuck very close to my sister. I didn't like staying at my grandparents' house; the basement gave me nightmares—I called it the dungeon where spiders, rats, and monsters lived.

My grandfather would mostly sit in front of the television, smoke, and go to work on occasion. He had a little leather shop in town; he made shoes and purses and did repairs to keep him occupied and bring in a little money. Sometimes Mom would take us down to the shop. I loved the smell of leather. We'd watch him work the leather and sew his creations together. Grandpa was not the kid-friendly type; he would not talk to us much and tell us often to go away and play, but we had no place to play. There were no toys, except the few we'd brought, nor did my grandparents have a yard for us to play in. The townhouse was stuck to a dozen or so other townhouses with the sidewalk only feet away from the front door. The inside of their house was always filled with smoke as though we were living in a constant fog. I couldn't recall my parents ever smoking, even though my sister said she remembered my dad smoking once. The smoke bothered me, and when we left, the smell followed us for the twenty-hour car ride home.

My grandpa talked often about how bad smoking was and wanted to teach the kids a lesson. In his rough smoker's voice, he called the four of us over.

"Here," he said in French as he handed us each a cigarette. "You want to smoke? Smoke as much as you want." He stood up, threw the rest of the pack on the floor, and sat heavily back in his chair as though making a statement. At the time, I didn't understand why he would do that, give a bunch of kids under the age of twelve cigarettes.

"What? Really?" My older brother Jacque's eyes lit up, his lips curled into a big happy grin. He looked like he'd just won the lottery.

"Yes!" my grandpa said, nodding towards all of us. "Go ahead, try it out."

My brother Ronald, who was three years older than me, kept looking at his cigarette then at Grandpa, not sure if this was for real.

My mother said to her dad in an angry tone, "Dad, you can't give the kids cigarettes at their age, or ever!" She stood up, one hand on her hip, staring at him.

"Yes, I can. They need to learn a lesson. Jacque has been staring at me ever since he got here. He wants to smoke, so let him." Grandpa reached over to pick up his lighter from the end table beside his chair. "Put it in your mouth, and I'll light it for you." He flicked the lighter and lit Jacque's cigarette while staring at my mom, telling her he had the authority to do what he wanted. Jacque began to cough, but he continued to puff on it and eventually got the hang of it.

"Samantha, come here." Mom called me over and took my cigarette. I could tell she was mad but didn't say anything else to her father. "You are way too young to have this." She threw it down on the table in frustration. She wanted no part of this whole thing, and she left the room. We could all hear the door to her room slam shut behind her.

I didn't smoke, but I was curious, so I stayed and watched my brothers smoke. My sister, Rachael, took one puff, coughed her lungs out, then gave the rest to Jacque. Ronald smoked one and said he had a headache. I couldn't stand the smell of the smoke that lingered in the air and on my clothes. I pinched my nose to stop the smell and the smoke from invading my lungs.

I went to bed that night while my brother was still puffing his third or fourth cigarette. When I woke up in the morning and came upstairs, my parents were not there. Rachael was sitting in the kitchen with Grandma, eyes all red from crying. When she saw me, she said, "Mom and Dad took Jacque to the hospital late last night."

"What? Why?" I said as I made my way over to her. She picked me up and sat me down on her lap. I didn't want to look at Grandma; she intimidated me.

"He smoked too many cigarettes, and it made him sick," my sister said as she wiped her face with her sleeve. I stared at my sister for a long time, not sure how to react. Was this serious? If she was crying, then I should be crying because my sister seemed to never cry. Fear started to well up in me. Rachael held on to me; I'm not sure if it was to comfort herself or me. My brother almost smoked himself to death. I didn't understand all that had happened or why, but I knew that we had to stay there a few days longer—a few more days in the dungeon. Secretly, I was afraid the smoke in the house might kill me too. My mom didn't talk to my grandpa, only to say goodbye; she was so mad at him. My grandpa said he didn't mean for my brother to get that sick but that this surely was going to do the job and keep all of us away from ever wanting to smoke. Grandpa never lived to learn that he had been wrong that day; both my brothers began smoking in their early teens and never stopped.

The last time I saw my grandpa was when I was twelve. He was laying in his bed, skinny from the disease that was eating away at his body. I did not want to be near him because he looked too scary. His skin was loose and gray, his eyes had sunk into his head, and he spoke with a deep raspy voice that was hard to understand. The cancer had taken away what dignity he had left as he lay in bed unable to take care of himself. My grandpa died shortly after our visit.

Grandma Melody was the complete opposite, a tough, sturdy woman with a deep faith. I did not know her well either, but what I did see of her was a woman who had lived a difficult life as well. When we went to visit, she was all business, cleaning and preparing food. She intimidated me, so I tried to keep my distance, but I watched out of the corner of my eye; I was in awe of her. I was fascinated by her little stature, four feet eleven, yet she exuded boldness and strength as though she plowed through life, ready for the next challenge.

I believe my grandpa was the weaker of the two. I could not understand why my grandma put up with him for all of those years from the stories I had heard. He had brought such hardship into their lives by his own bad choices and made her life more difficult. Even though I could not fathom or understand why my grandma did not leave him, I admired how she honored and took care of him to the end. She was a powerhouse of a woman for all that she'd endured. She never raised her voice nor did I ever see her disrespect her husband. But I did hear her often in the quiet of her room, shouting and praying to her God.

Thinking of Grandma now, I remember two things about her: the first was the statue of Jesus she kept by her side and talked to often. It cracked me up. It was about five inches high and four inches wide, and she would have conversations with it in French, *"Jesus, je t'aime beaucoup."* Grandma would tell Jesus about her day and what concerns she had as though the statue was alive. Maybe it was not just a statue but something she could see and touch in order to envision the real Jesus clearly in her mind.

The other thing about Grandma was the fact that she always wore high-heeled shoes and a dress everywhere—when she was in the house, when she went for her daily walk, shopping, everywhere. Even at age ninety. The little woman with little feet. I would often stare at her feet, wondering if it was really comfortable or if her shoes were glued on, if she was unable to remove them. I never saw my grandma without them on, nor did I ever see her put her feet up to rest.

Of course, as a child, you only perceive things through a child's eyes. I did not see what happened behind the scenes of Grandma's life either, only what was presented to me. I watched at a distance as a young child and only really got to know her later as a young adult. It was then that I saw a softer side of her, gentle and loving. I remember her laughter, that sweet joyful laughter that made you laugh along with her. I loved being close to her, feeling that life had come around full circle for her, that she had reached a point of peace within herself and how her faith had carried her through times that would have been unbearable without it. She spoke about her Jesus with such love and admiration, like he was hers and she his. At the time, I did not understand that relationship between my grandma and Jesus, but in years to come, I too would hit a road that would lead me to discovering God in a deeper, more intimate way. I would then remember my grandma and her Jesus and understand.

Often after visiting my mother's parents, we would head further east to visit my father's side of the family. It was like visiting the olden days. The farmhouse where my dad was raised still stood alongside the old, now dilapidated, barns where they used to raise animals to feed the family. My father was one of eleven children, which meant I had many cousins.

As we drove up the long two-track driveway to the house, which always seemed like it was leaning more to one side and badly needing a few coats of paint, I could feel my excitement rise the closer we got. It was a whole different part of the world that seemed separate, a whole different kind of life than my other grandparents and myself. I felt rich compared to these folks, yet they seemed more content, more joyful and welcoming. I felt loved every time we visited. My many aunts, uncles, and loads of cousins would gather for large seafood cookouts by the ocean's edge with big pots filled with lobster, crab, and oysters. We would stay up late around the fire and play with our gazillion cousins while the adults caught up with their lives.

My grandma often sat in her rocking chair on the porch. Grandpa had long ago passed away and was buried in the field behind the house. My grandma, Anastasia, was old. She always wore a scarf around her head, and her face looked like an old dried-up, wrinkled apple. I loved my Grandma A; I had a special bond with her. I looked forward to playing Parcheesi with her and hearing her laughter. Grandma A would cover her mouth when she smiled or laughed because she had no teeth and she was embarrassed. I thought she was so cute; her eyes danced with joy.

There was no electricity, and the house was only heated on the main level by the wood stove, which they also used for cooking. When it was bedtime, rocks were heated, wrapped in a towel and placed at the bottom of the beds in the second-floor rooms. I would climb in the bed and feel the warmth of the rocks. Unlike my mom's parents' house, this place gave me a sense of belonging. I loved the simplicity of life there, even though it seemed like a hard life, at best.

Lying in the bed at the nursing home, things that had been neatly locked away had begun to seep through the cracks, loudly calling me to come visit. These memories of my life had been aggressively stalking me since my mother's death two years ago, on January 24, 2014. In the months leading up to her death, something inside of me began to stir up many thoughts and revelations, some good, some not so good.

I had a deep love and admiration for my mother for the way she had suffered all her life with illnesses, a difficult marriage, and the struggle to raise four kids, but persevered through it all with such courage and strength. Yet I harbored so much anger toward her. I felt robbed of a mother. It was not the fact that my mom did not love me—on the contrary, I knew my mom loved me and my siblings more than anything. I never felt anything but love from my mom. My mom gave life to us; her family was her everything. But I had held so much resentment and bitterness for being abandoned and left to raise myself, angry at the illness that had robbed me of a mother. I was just a child left to try and make sense of all that had happened to me. My father, whom I was not very close to, was someone I was also angry with. He was never there for me. I felt unprotected. Then I felt shame and guilt for being angry at them, being angry at all. But these feelings were real to me as a child, and they had cost me a lot of pain.

After a life-changing encounter with Jesus in my early twenties that began my journey toward becoming a new creation, no longer living a life of addiction and promiscuity, happy to leave the old me behind, I did not think the past mattered anymore. That was the old me, and apparently, according to Jesus, it had been crucified on the cross. Gone, thank God! That ditch that I dug to separate the then and now, which had turned into a river had, over the years, forced a little stream to form off the main river that began to flow into the now side. It trickled memories into my being that I could not ignore. Ignoring the past did not prove to be a healthy thing to do.

Sure, it was great for a while, not having to face that awful part of myself, pushing her back behind the line to the "then." What good would it do to go there anyway? There would only be pain and sorrow. Plus, it was not just about myself and my bad choices but also the injustices that had been inflicted upon me. I would have to confront some hard stuff that I felt were better left alone. Had I not forgiven? Forgiven them, forgiven myself? Had Jesus not forgiven me? Thrown it into the sea to never bring it back up? Often, these struggles happened within my mind. Did I really want to go back? I knew the answer was no, but was it necessary to go back to the land of "then" even if every part of me didn't want to face those hard places? If I didn't, would I be stuck in a place of fear, fear of the past chasing me down?

Why, after all these years, did I still suffer from the wounds of my past? It was long ago. Should we not all just pull up our bootstraps and get on with life? Suck it up? I didn't want to reach old age just to fight with the demons in my past, and I wondered if my faith was strong enough to resist the calls from "then" or maybe my faith was not strong enough *to go* to "then."

Thinking of all that lay on the other side of the line, into "then," I thought of how much of it had crossed over into the "now" already. I had been running all my life to get further away from it, but when I turned around, why did it seem as though the line was right behind me? There were my fears, the way I pulled away from things that reminded me of "then," my struggle of self-worth and self-like. How I felt dirty, used. How it all affected how I raised my kids, having a deeper intimacy with my husband, trusting others. As much as I had grown over the years, the secrets that held me captive lay deep within me. As though it owned part of me, owned a large piece of my heart, a piece of my inner me that I needed to claim back.

Chapter 3

*Come to me all you who are weary and carry
heaven burdens, and I will give you rest.*
—Matthew 11:28

The loss of my mother released the flood gates of my memories, and they began to pour out into room 6 like a pungent mix of sweet wine and vinegar. I didn't know why now, after all those years of suppressing them. Maybe I had been given the permission to let them out since I didn't have to worry anymore about hurting my mother with my past because she was no longer alive. I had questions that dwelt in the back of my mind that I'd never asked my mom, that I dared not ask, in fear that my mother wouldn't be able to withstand the pain her daughter had to endure as a child or that she'd worry that she hadn't been able to protect me from it. My mother wasn't a weak woman, but because her love for me ran so deep, the news would have crushed her.

My siblings and I hid many things from our mother and father. We wanted to protect our mother, knowing she had enough problems to deal with her illnesses. We never saw our dad much, did not have much of a relationship with him, so we never felt safe telling him anything. I knew my past wasn't all my parents' fault, yet I had paid a heavy price because of my mother's illness and my father's absence. Everyone did. How could I ever share that with her? The burden and heaviness would have killed her long ago. I knew too that my father had worries of his own; he worried about being a single dad, that his wife would die too early, about being left with four kids he didn't know how to relate to and raise.

I did not understand many things about my dad, except the fact that he was distant and angry much of the time. But I remembered the one thing my dad loved to do was to fish. His love for the water was evident. He was born and raised along the shores of the Atlantic Ocean where they fished for lobster, crab, and other fish starting at a very young age. My father told many stories to his grandkids that I had never heard before about his times on the water as a little boy, how he had been tied to a pole at the stern of the boat by his brothers in a storm to keep him alive. He was the youngest of eleven.

My father went often to a lake up north from our home, Lake Simcoe, to fish. In the winter, he loved to go ice fishing. I went ice fishing with him once. We were dressed in layers of clothes; my dad was wearing his Carhartts. I was scared walking on the ice in the middle of the lake, let alone driving a car out there. We parked and unloaded the hut from the back of the trailer. I was fascinated by the way my father cut a hole in the ice with an auger and put the hut over the hole with a wood stove to keep us warm. We would sit on buckets, stick our poles in the thick hole in the ice, hearing the plop of the lures in the water, and we would wait. My dad caught the first fish, and as he pulled it out, he unhooked it and placed it on the ice where it began flopping around wildly. I got a huge kick out of watching the fish trying to escape by wiggling its body toward the hole. I was eight years old then.

After an hour of fishing, I got bored. I never caught any fish, but only my dad did. He had horseshoes tied around his neck; luck was always on his side. I got really cold, my hands stiffened from holding the pole. I didn't want to tell my dad. I played outside on the ice a bit, trying to move around and warm up, but that didn't last long either. I was getting anxious and asked my dad several times how much longer we were going to stay. I could tell that he was getting irritated with me. My dad was planning to stay all day, but after a few hours of listening to me moan and groan, he packed up angrily, and we left. He wasn't happy about it and never asked me to go with him again. Thinking back on it, I felt bad that when I had finally had the chance to hang out with my dad, I blew it. If I could do it again,

I would have stayed close by him and soaked in his presence. That was the only time I recall ever spending that much time with him.

Fishing was probably my dad's escape, his place of solitude and peace from a life that he didn't know how to deal with. A sick wife, four kids, working more than fifty hours a week, trying to get as much overtime as possible to be able to pay the bills. As I grew older, I began to understand more about that, to see beyond my pain to the pain and hardships of others. Of course, as a child I saw with child's eyes; my perception of life was different than adults. I didn't realize my dad was human, that he had feelings and emotions like me. I saw him more as angry, short tempered, and that he didn't love or care for me. But he had trials that were difficult and brought stress to his life; he needed an escape from it all, to unwind and regroup, or else he would have drowned in it all. I tried to process the things happening around me, why my mom was sick and absent, why my dad was emotionally detached, why I was left in an open field to be abused. But it was difficult to piece together as a child.

Both of my parents came from a religious Catholic background. We attended church every Sunday growing up. Both my parents were also French Canadians born and raised in New Brunswick, so it made sense that they went to a French Catholic Church. I learned French before I knew any English. Being raised Catholic was all I knew about religion and watching my mom live it out, which was different than what I learned in church.

Some of the things I learned as a young child were that my sins could only be forgiven through a priest, the mediator between me and God. Once a month, my dad would drag us four kids down to the church for a time of confession. We would sit on the bench and wait our turn, oldest to youngest, so I was always last. To pass the time, I would count as each of my two brothers and my sister went in to the confession booth to see who took the longest. I concluded that the longest time meant the more sins to confess. The priest would say hello while he passed by the bench we sat on waiting to enter the confession booth for our penance. When it was my turn, I would pull back the thick black curtain and sit down. The priest would say hello again through a little screened window that divided the box in two, the priest on one side of the wall and me on the other side. I didn't quite understand why it was set up this way or why such secrecy when I knew the priest and the priest knew me.

The first time I had ever stepped foot in the booth, I didn't know what to do. I had often wondered what happened behind the curtain. I couldn't wait until I was old enough. The priest walked me through the routine, step by step. He talked about sin and what it was, anything that was against God's will and ways. He helped by naming a few: lying, disobeying my parents, and hurting others. When it was time for me to confess, I repeated the sins he had just listed to me. I heard him chuckle softly.

"Say ten Our Fathers and five Hail Marys, Sam. Go out in peace. Your sins are forgiven in the name of the Father, Son, and Holy Spirit," he would say through the screen window. I could see him smile, then close the little black curtain covering the hole.

"Thank you, Father," I whispered. I stepped out of the box after he said my sins were forgiven, thinking, *That was easy.* If I sin, all I have to do is confess, and I'm done. Until I fully understood the complexity of how my actions actually had an effect on others, hurt others, and had consequences, I used the confession booth as a way to continue my life of sinning. I could pile them up, and in a month, I would be forgiven and set free once again. It was harder to try to be good, to be nice to my brothers, to not lie, to listen to my parents than it was to allow myself to let sin control me and fall into it.

After confession, I would kneel to say my Our Fathers and Hail Marys while my brothers and sister were sharing with one another how many they'd each had to say. It became a game; who could get the most penance. The one who had the most would have to do an extra chore. As I got older and felt the weight of sin, understanding its effects on my life, the confession booth became a welcoming sight. From the day I stepped out to the day I returned a month later, I lost the feeling of freedom as my sins began to accumulate once again. I had to carry them around with me every day until confession booth time. Sometimes, I had some hard, deep stuff that I wanted to get off my shoulders, and it almost killed me to wait, especially when it happened shortly after the last confession. Then I would have to wait another month to confess in order to feel light again after unburdening all my sins onto the priest. In my mind, I believed the priest was pretty cool to be that close to God, that he was the only one we could go to for any kind of relief.

The other thing I learned was that when someone died, you had to pay and pray them out of purgatory. I did not quite understand the whole concept of purgatory, but it sounded to me like a waiting room in the doctor's office where you had to wait your turn to be called in to be seen. I did not like it when someone we knew died, a long-lost aunt, third removed.

At nine years old, I worked for a farmer two miles down the road from our house, picking asparagus in spring, as well as strawberries and apples. My dad would come around the house collecting from everyone because he said, "Everyone is a part of this family, and that's what families do, help each other." Then he would put the money in a card to pay for a special mass, dedicated for the person who had passed so we could pay and pray them out of purgatory and into heaven with Jesus. I kind of thought it was really mean of Jesus to do that. People waited all their lives to get to heaven, and then they had to wait some more? What if no one had money to pay for a mass to be said on their behalf? Would they just stay in the waiting room forever? This bothered and confused me, which only added more to my confusion about what kind of God my parents believed in. I was driven by guilt, feeling as though I would rot in hell if I didn't do what was asked of me.

I was the youngest of four in my family. I spoke very few words and saw few faces for the first seven or so years of my life because I spent most of my time hiding behind my mother or my blanket. But I did have my little friend next door, who was only a few months younger than me. I felt safe with her, and we shared secrets together. I could not look anyone in the face without feeling insecure and afraid. My very best friend and constant companion was my animal blanket, which went wherever I went, with no exception. It was part of me, and being without it was like leaving a piece of me behind, the braver part of me. It saved me from the dark, from looking at the faces that wanted to speak to me, and from the world that might swallow me up if given half a chance. Many people would look and comment on what a gorgeous little girl I was, with my long pale blond hair with little ringlets and big blue eyes and dimples when I smiled. They said it was a shame that such a beautiful child would hide herself from people who desperately wanted to connect with her. As I remembered it, I never thought of what I looked like or how others saw me; it was more the fear that dwelt within me, the fear of people, the fear of everything. I wasn't sure where this fear stemmed from, but I couldn't remember a time without it.

The first day of school for most children was usually a moment to remember, a huge milestone in a sweet way, fostering a sense of independence. For me, it was a nightmare. On my first day, I stood with my brothers, my sister, and my mom in front of our house waiting for the bus to come pick us up. My siblings were talking to me, excited that it was my very first day of school. It seemed as though they were waiting for this day to arrive more than I was. I was holding tightly to my mom's hand, shaking and crying, telling her I didn't want to go to school. I wanted to stay home with her. I could see the yellow bus coming in the distance, making its way closer and closer to where we stood. I began to cry harder and harder, trying to run back home as my mother's grip got tighter and tighter.

"Mommy, I don't wanna go. Please don't make me go!" I screamed. I could barely breathe as I thought of letting go of her hand and going on the big scary bus. The bus stopped, and my siblings got on along with other neighborhood kids. But when it was my turn, my mom lifted me up to put me on the first step of the bus, but I spread my legs apart and put one on each side of the door while my mom tried to push me in.

"Sam, stop, it'll be okay," my mom said, trying to pry my feet off the sides of the bus.

"Nooooo, I don't wanna go!" I said, crying and screaming.

I had a lot of strength when I was mad and afraid. I held on to my position, and my mom was losing the battle. I remembered the bus driver giving my mom a look of sympathy and telling her she needed to move on as she pulled the bus doors closed. It wasn't as though I was scared of riding the bus—I had ridden on a bus with my mom ever since I could remember since my mom was a bus driver too. I was scared of being on the bus *without* my mom. I didn't want to feel the loneliness again. I didn't want my mom to go away, and I was scared to be without her.

I remember riding with my mom on the bus, sitting right behind her. We'd pick up the kids from their homes in the country and drop them off at school. I could specifically remember this one dirt road where we passed a farmer's place. His chickens often ran out into the road, and my mom would slow down, trying hard not to run any of them over. Once, my mom killed one. The farmer was so mad he came out screaming at her, cussing up a storm. My mom didn't want to open the door of the bus, afraid the farmer was going to hurt her, so she drove off as the farmer ran after the bus screaming. He called the bus garage, cussing at my mom's boss. Every day, when we had to drive by the farmer's house, I crossed my fingers and prayed that we would go by without incident. I'd see the farmer stand out on his front porch waiting for us. I felt the sting of his glare come right through the bus.

There was also a time, although I was too little to remember the details, that our bus was hit on one side by a large truck. I remember the sudden impact that threw me against the side of the bus, hitting my head against the window hard. I remember the truck driver banging on the door that was jammed in, yelling at us, asking if we were okay. I was conscious, but my mother was not. She was slumped over the steering wheel. The fire truck and ambulance came. After prying the door open and getting my mother out, they took us to the hospital. I sat beside my mom in the ambulance. She was lying down with stuff all over her and a man talking. I didn't understand all that he was saying. I was scared. I didn't want my mom to go away again to the hospital. She stayed in the hospital for several weeks, but I don't recall what the extent of her injuries were. They checked me out, said I had a few good bumps and bruises but that I'd be okay. Years later, in my mid-thirties, after suffering from headaches and jaw pain, apparently caused by the accident, I had upper and lower jaw surgery to reset my jaw and alleviate the pain it had caused me for many years following the accident.

So on that first day, I didn't go to school nor on the second or third. I don't remember how long it went on for, but I could tell my mother was getting really frustrated as she held on to my hand tightly, pulling my arm as she walked briskly toward the house, mumbling to herself. Day after day, my mom tried her hardest to get me on that bus to no avail. I could still hear the laughter flowing out the windows as the kids on the bus watched this same routine every day. Back then, most families only had one car. My dad worked different shifts, leaving my mom with no transportation in the daytime, in the afternoons, or sometimes even in the evenings. It was a week or so until my dad was on a different shift, and my mom could finally drive me to school herself. Eventually, I did get on the bus, after several weeks of acclimating to my classroom. When I got on the bus, I sat right by my sister, never leaving her side. I didn't think my sister liked that very much. Whenever I began to cry at school, they brought me into my sister's classroom so I could sit with her and stop crying. My sister's friends thought I was cute, but my sister did not think it was cute at all. She would look at me with her lips puckered, her eyebrows drawn together and her arms crossed. She'd whisper to me to stop being such a crybaby and getting sent to her class; it embarrassed her.

Growing up, I cried many nights because I desperately wanted friends. Someone to be able to have conversations with, but everyone thought I was weird because I was so shy and never spoke. I'd often hear kids ask the teacher what was wrong with me. This only pushed me deeper into myself, separating me further from my peers.

We also lived among an interesting mix of neighbors: five French-Canadian families, one mixed couple with two kids, and one British family with accents that made me laugh. Our house was situated right in the middle. The neighbor to the left had a large family, but my parents did not like them. Really they just hated their lifestyle. They were drinkers and partiers. There seemed to always be a fight outside their home with yelling and screaming every weekend. The kids had friends over who liked to hang out there because they allowed anyone to drink at any age, including anyone in the neighborhood. That's why my mom did everything in her power to keep her children away from there. Of course, my siblings and I did not understand why; we thought the neighbors were so cool, they were allowed to do anything. We thought my parents were just jealous that they were so popular.

I once overheard my dad say to my mom that the house next door was the house from hell. I did not understand why he thought that at the time. It was confusing to me because sometimes the older teens from the "hell" house would babysit me and my siblings. Why would my parents allow them to take care of us if they tried to keep us away from them? I was too little to remember, but my sister told me that she would often lock us both in the bathroom to protect us. I didn't know why that was, only when I was an adult did I understand the reason.

I called the house to the right of us the plastic house. Sometimes, when my mom was in the hospital, I had to walk over to the plastic house after school until the babysitter was able to come get me. When I walked into the house, everything was covered in clear plastic. There was a plastic runner that went through the kitchen that led you into the living room. The furniture, the lampshades, and the pillows were all covered with plastic. I would sit on the couch and wait for my sitter to come. I hated going there. It was eerily quiet, and the lady hated kids touching anything. It was difficult to figure out why the lady in the plastic house loved plastic so much. It was cold, sticky, and made lots of noise. I was afraid to move and used to pray for someone to hurry and come save me from that dreadful place.

Next to the plastic house lived my mom's best friend. She had many kids, much older than me. My friend from the "hell" house and I were the youngest in the neighborhood. This house to the far right held many secrets behind its four walls. This was also where my mom's best friend, and cousin, lived. My mom's friend came over often crying about something. Her children too spent lots of time at our house, staying over because of the chaos in their house. Often, my mom would be talking to and comforting one of the girls, holding them as they cried. I did not know all that was going on in that house because I was too young to understand it, but I did know it wasn't good. I would hear a man's voice ringing in the neighborhood, yelling at one of his kids or his wife. It was not often that I was allowed to go over. They had many problems.

There was a time their dog attacked our dog and killed it. The neighbor's dog was big, and our dog was little. I screamed when I came home from school and saw the blood from my little dog spread out on our lawn; my mom told me what happened. I was in shock. I stood staring at the spot and cried and cried. Princess was my one and only dog.

Shortly after, I heard a gunshot from the neighbor's house and started running toward it. When I got there, I saw the neighbor's dog lying dead on the grass next to their house. I stood staring at it in shock for a long time. Then I turned around and screamed all the way home. I did not understand why they had to do that. Two dogs dead. Two traumatizing events in one day. It was too much for me to handle. I did not like the man who killed his dog at the strange neighbor's house. That memory stuck with me my whole life.

One day, I was going to town with my mom, and along the way we saw a car in the ditch on the other side of the road that collided against a telephone pole. I was little, only four years old. I heard my mother gasp as she pulled over and told me to stay in the car. My mother ran over to the car and tried to open the driver's side door. I heard my mom screaming, "Mariette, wake up, Mariette!" She pounded on the window, trying to open the driver's side door.

I stood up on the seat to see what was going on. I remembered seeing my mother's best friend from the weird house slumped over the steering wheel with half the car wrapped around the pole. My mother turned around and ran back to the car. We drove to the nearest house to get help. The police and ambulance came. When they arrived, my mom took me to the plastic house so she could go back and help Mariette. After weeks in the hospital, healing from the accident, my mom said Mariette went to another hospital where she could get more rest for her mind. I realized later that my mom was talking about a mental hospital.

Two doors to the left was the house with the mixed couple. I didn't know them for too long. They had two girls whom I got to play with for a little bit, but they didn't stay in the neighborhood long. Apparently, the dad was very violent, and one day, his wife took their two girls and left him. People in the neighborhood were scared of the dad. He was a big man, but he eventually sold the house and left.

In the house to the far left of ours lived the British people with funny accents. My mom and dad liked them, and I liked them. I loved hearing them talk, and they were really nice and funny. Their kids were way older than everyone else in the neighborhood, so I didn't see them much or know them. My parents and the British people liked each other. They often took vacations together and went over to each other's houses to play cards. There didn't seem to be too much excitement going on at their house. They seemed to be the more "normal" family in the neighborhood.

In the house right behind ours lived the farmers. They farmed all kinds of vegetables. They had lots of kids too. I didn't know how many; I just played with the twins. They were two or three years older than me, a boy and a girl. My oldest brother would often go into their fields to shoot frogs. He'd bring them home and make fried frog legs. Even though my brother said they tasted like chicken, I never had the desire to try them.

The neighborhood was quite a mixture of different families and lifestyles. At the time, I did not understand the complexity of it all or the depth of brokenness in our little country community. Only when I was older did the whole picture make more sense and the events that happened began to bring clarity to my mind, putting the puzzle pieces together.

My friends from the neighborhood and I often played hide and seek and hopscotch. We spent lots of our time outside. I was very shy, and sometimes they would make fun of me because I would carry my blanket around and suck on my thumb. I always felt like the odd one out.

For me, there was no escaping the chaos of my life. Outside was where my mixed bunch of neighbors lived and where confusing, bad things happened. Inside was where loneliness dwelled when my mother was not home and the fear of my father lay. It was a place of pain and fear. I could not find peace in my mind as life whirled around me. There were many things I did not understand and could not put into perspective. To me, life was scary, and there was no way of escaping it; there was only falling into it and allowing it to take me along on the journey it chose for me.

Chapter 4

If a man has a hundred sheep and one of them wanders away, what will he do? Won't he leave the ninety-nine others on the hills and go out to search for the one that is lost?
—Matthew 18:12

"Sam?" my mom called as she knocked on my bedroom door.

"Yes? What, Mom?" I answered. I was lying in my bed, listening to the Bay City Rollers on my record player. They were my favorite group.

"Can I come in?" she asked, yelling over the loud music.

"Yup, just a sec." I got up, pulled the needle up from the player, and moved it to the side. I walked over to the door and opened it. "Hi, Mom. What's up?" I leaned against the door, waiting for her to talk. I did not want her to come into my room; I wanted to be alone.

"Well . . . I spoke to Mrs. Godin on the phone today. Lucille wanted to know if you'd like to go to her house for a bit after school tomorrow?" she said, looking me in the eyes.

I looked at her, confused. "Why would Lucille want me to come over? I'm not friends with her, Mom. I don't even really know her." I didn't want to go to Lucille's; she never paid any attention to me. We went to a French immersion school together. I was twelve years old. She was a grade and a year older than I was. Why would she want to hang out with me?

"Well, she wants you to go over. I think it's a good idea, she's a nice girl," my mom said, more telling me than asking me. This was all too strange. Something was going on that she wasn't telling me. Why would this girl randomly ask me to go over?

"Fine, if that's what you want me to do," I said, slowly shutting the door as my mother moved out of the way.

"Samantha . . . it will be good to make some friends," she was saying as I closed the door. I could hear the worried tone in her voice. I knew she wanted me to have more friends, to get out. I was very introverted. Besides my neighborhood friend, who had moved away, and my friend from elementary school, which I no longer attended, I had no friends.

I was not too happy about it, embarrassed that my mother had to arrange for me to have friends, but I decided that this was going to be my chance to turn my life around. I was going to prove to my mom and everyone else that I could make friends. I made a conscious decision that this nonsense of being shy was going to stop and I was finally going to have a social life and friends.

The next day, after school, I walked home with my new friend, Lucille, excited but scared. I had known her for a long time, her family attended our church, and her mom was friends with mine. But I had never really talked to her. On our way to her house, I had a hard time coming up with anything to say or talk about, which made me feel anxious and sweaty. I remember this as if it were yesterday. Lucille was a popular, beautiful tall brunette who lived in an old beige stucco townhouse; it was possible that it once was white. We entered her house; no one was home. I thought it odd that her parents or older siblings weren't there, that it was just the two of us.

Shortly after we got to the house, other kids from the neighborhood complex started coming over too. It seemed like it was part of their daily after-school routine. I don't remember the faces or names of the kids, but I remember the details of the night because it was then that my life shifted several degrees in the wrong direction. At the time, I thought it was the right direction. Maybe I was so pre-occupied with my shyness that the world around me and the people were just a blur. I couldn't help wondering if I'd made a terrible mistake. I did not know that there would be other kids there. It made me feel really uncomfortable to the point where I had knots in my stomach. We all sat cross-legged in a circle on the floor in the living room. My head was tilted down, eyes staring at the shaggy carpet as I picked at the little green threads, heart pumping hard, afraid to say a word.

"Look what I got," said one of the guys as he pulled out what looked like a cigarette, but different, and lit it. I watched him inhaling in, blowing out, inhaling in, blowing out, then passing it to the next person. As this thing was moving in my direction, I was ready to pass it on to the next person. As I took it and proceeded to hand it over to the person to my left, everyone in the circle started chanting

"Take a toke, take a toke, take a toke." I'd never heard that term before. Sure, my family and friends smoked, so I had seen it before, but this looked and smelled different. The smell was strong and powerful. The cigarette-looking thing was thinner; it wasn't smooth like a cigarette and had no spongey thing at one end. I shook my head, wanting so badly for the kid next to just take it from my hand. The kid started getting mean.

"What's wrong? Are you too chicken to try? You a goody two shoes?" he said with a sneer.

Then the kid next to me turned to Lucille and asked why she had invited me. "Is she going to snitch on us?"

"Oh . . . she's all right. My mom told me to babysit her after school today for a few hours. I'm sure she won't tell," she said, turning her head to me and giving me a threatening look as if to say, *You better not snitch!*

What? I thought. I was livid, so mad that I started shaking inside. How dare my mom ask Lucille to babysit me? That was her way of getting Lucille to be friends with me? I wanted to get up and run, but instead, I stayed frozen in my spot. In a split-second decision, out of pure anger, I put the joint in my mouth and took a puff, inhaled, then coughed my lungs out for a good minute. The kids laughed and cheered. I looked over at Lucille with a smirk on my face. She smiled back at me, raised her hand, and gave me a thumb up and nodded. That made me feel real good inside, like I was accepted into their group.

Another joint was lit and another, going around several times. Each time, I got better at keeping it in, then exhaling it out without coughing. It was becoming a game for me to see if I could get through one puff without coughing, not aware of the effect it was having on me. When it was all gone, I realized that my shyness was too. I was feeling so good, so free, so happy. I was laughing, cracking jokes, and talking. I discovered I was soon the life of the party, that they liked me, including the boys. Joy filled my heart at that moment as I finally felt that I fit in. It was a time I remembered clearly because it was the first time I ever felt good about myself and that the kids actually liked me. Up to that point, I had felt like an outcast no matter how hard I tried to fit in. I'd felt so empty, broken, and alone. But the drugs made me feel free from the pain that lived inside of me, removing any thought of pain, an escape from it all, and I really liked the feeling of freedom.

I thanked God, whom I barely knew, for giving me this miracle. I truly thought that this was the best day of my entire life . . . until the next day came, and the old me had returned. This time, I cursed God for doing this to me. The thought that entered my mind then was, *How could I feel like that again? How do I get back to that moment?* The obvious answer was to get more of the stuff I'd had the night before.

When I saw Lucille at school the next day, I asked her where I could get some of what we'd had. She was more than happy to introduce me to a guy who could set me up with some. The guy she introduced me to became a big part of my life as the years went by. Because of one choice, one moment, and a deep hatred for a little part of myself, my life changed in a dramatic way. Did I know this was going to lead to almost ten years of drug addiction, partying, and abuse? The addiction of not wanting to feel, to remember the things that had happened to me at a very young age, that memory I tried to bury, was buried with the drugs. The comfort I got from my blanket had been replaced by the drugs I consumed to numb all my painful memories of my childhood years.

After the encounter at Lucille's house at the young age of twelve, my need for weed grew stronger and stronger, and my obsession for it did too. I wasn't just satisfied with a joint or two; I needed more. After some time, weed wasn't enough. I began to crave more and more to make sure the old me wouldn't surface. I began to redesign my outer shell from a shy timid girl to a tough, strong one. I tried so hard to run away from myself, from all the things I hated about myself. I believed that eventually my exterior image and attitude would flow inside me and there would be no more room for the old me to live, that I would push her right out.

At fourteen, I started getting into bars with a fake ID that I obtained from a friend of a friend. Looking back later and thinking of what I did at fourteen and what my own kids were like at fourteen, it shocked me. I was way too young to be drinking, let alone going to bars. How did I get away with it? How did the people at the bar not know I was many years short of drinking age? Where were my parents? I was sure I didn't look that old, but I had an advantage. The guys who worked at these places were the same guys I bought some of my drugs from and who were part of the circle I was beginning to fit into. They were family, they said, as they turned a blind eye and let me slip on by. I truly felt like part of a family, that they cared about me, and I knew they would protect me. I longed to feel safe, to be protected. It seemed as though, so far in my short life, I had been in the wide-open field, making me vulnerable to be taken advantage of like I had been when I was a young child.

Carl, one of the bouncers whom I formed a close bond with, was much older than I was. It seemed he worried about me and took me under his wing as his little sister. He was a huge guy with arms the width of my waist. I felt like a princess around him. He was handsome, six feet tall, with a head of blond hair and blue eyes. Everyone respected him because of his size, but he also had a gentle spirit. The fact that he cared so much about me made me feel special. I did believe that in a strange kind of way, these people I hung out with really cared for one another, for me. It was a type of brotherhood/sisterhood thing, a strange bond we had with one another. We all seemed to be in the same boat, dealing with the same things and pulling on each other as though we all didn't want to be alone in this war we were in. Nobody wants to be alone no matter what you are going through. The crazy thing was that when you are drowning, you tend to grab onto someone else who is also drowning when what you really need is someone who knows where to find the life jackets.

This didn't make sense to me at the time; although we somewhat understood each other, we did not know how to save one another. Instead, we traveled the road of self-destruction together, pulling one another down.

There were unspoken words, loud but silent. Funny how each of us had pain stuck deep inside yet stayed silent, keeping it locked away from one another. Friends? In an odd sort of way. Each trying quietly but loudly to destroy the inner pain that laid deep in the darkness of our souls. We had an unspoken language. To help one another, we fed each other drugs and alcohol to try and kill the thing that we all so desperately wanted to be rid of. I didn't know what most of my friends' demons were. Maybe if I had, my own problems would not have seemed so big. I found out much later, when it was too late for some, what their lives had been like after several had committed suicide.

There were many times when there were some close calls with the law. One time, some friends and I had just come from a pick-up, each of us loaded with something on our person. I had several sheets of acid in my purse worth a few thousand dollars on the streets. We heard the police siren behind us. In a panic, we quickly tried to stash our stuff as we pulled over to the side of the road. For me, it was the first time I'd had a run in with the police. I was only fifteen. It had been close to the beginning of my drug-dealing days. I was so nervous but was trying not to show it. I could feel the beads of sweat trickling down the side of my face. I was sure the police sensed my fear. Everyone was thoroughly searched, including me, and everyone was put in the police car and brought to jail. Everyone was charged except me. I was brought to the police station, but I did not have my license, so they called my parents to come pick me up. I was by far the youngest of them all. They had not found anything in my purse; I could not figure out how that happened. There was no way I could hide large sheets of acid that easily.

When I checked my purse later, they were all there. They would have to be completely blind not to have seen them. As for my parents, I found it odd that nothing happened. My dad did not say a word when he picked me up; it was silent on the car ride home. My mother wasn't home; she was having one of her frequent hospital visits. At the time, I was elated that I did not get in trouble, but deep down, I felt as though no one cared about what happened to me. Looking back, I wished I'd been disciplined, that my parents would have been stricter.

I often wondered why I was spared from so much more trouble than I deserved and could've been in. Many years later, I credited it to my mother's many nights of prayers. I thought my mother didn't know anything about what was going on in my life. She never indicated anything to me, and I thought that she was totally naïve and did not care. I later realized that my mom probably knew more than she let on but could not do anything physically. My mom was very sick in those days, and my dad was always at work. She hung on to her God and knew he could do way more than she could have done herself. Prayer was my mom's only weapon, and a good one at that. There were many more similar incidences where things could have been much worse for me and I didn't know why I was spared from them.

Once, my friend Val and I were driving down a dirt road. Val had just picked up her niece, who was seven at the time. Val was driving too fast. I saw a car ahead of us go over a hill in the road and disappear. A thought, or warning, rang in my mind to tell Val to slow down as we approached the hill, but I didn't say anything. We flew over the hill at a high speed, and when we got over the top of the hill, the car ahead of us had stopped to turn into a driveway that was right on the other side. Val quickly turned the wheel to go around on the left, but we were going too fast. The car caught on the gravel, rolled several times, eventually ending upside down in a five-foot-deep ditch. The driver's side was trapped by the ditch, my side window broke and had a three-foot opening to the outside. All I could remember was Val's body coming across me and out the broken window in a split second. She was screaming and trying to get me and her niece out. In that moment, everything happened so fast, panic set in, and escape was on our minds. We all had a good number of cuts from the broken glass and bruises, but other than being shaken up, we were fine.

Even though my mother's prayers protected me from many dangerous situations in my life, they did not protect me when I was young and innocent. I had a hard time understanding why God would protect me from getting into worse situations than I was already in, by my own choice but didn't protect me from those who had done injustices to me, which weren't my choice.

The parties were endless. I did not know how I got through high school. I was high most of the time, high or hungover. Many nights, I would pass out wherever, places I did not know. As time went on, I noticed that not only did I lose my shyness but also any respect I ever had for myself. I lost the innocence I had as a little girl. I was afraid of the world then, and bad things that were out of my control happened. The light was still visible within me, but as time went on, the light began to quickly dim, and the darkness seemed to be taking over.

There were times when the light would try to come back in, try to show itself to me, that it really did exist and, if I let it, it would push out the darkness. I did not know it at the time that I was being invaded by darkness; it had slowly snuck its way inside of me. I did not know such a thing existed, an enemy, that invaded one's soul, that wanted to steal, kill, and destroy everything, whose sole purpose was to crush me and steal my identity. Yes, I knew of the light of day, the dark of night, sadness and joy, but I never really equated it with being a battle between good and evil, fighting for my soul. Nor did I realize that I was giving in to it, that I was allowing the enemy, Satan, to take bits of me, one bite at a time. I did not believe in God. I did once, when I was little, but not then. I didn't believe because he allowed my innocence to be taken away from me, ripped from me against my will.

What kind of God would stand by and allow such things to happen to a young child? Nor did I believe in Satan. Life was about good people and bad people, good and bad luck, good and bad choices. I believed there were evil, mean people in the world, the same way there were good people. I just saw what I was doing as trying to fit in, trying to be part of the world around me, to be loved and accepted, not meaning any harm to anyone. I was just trying to figure it all out myself. And one day, God, in a crazy kind of way, introduced me to the enemy, to the darkness that lingered in the world.

I had a small pick-up to make at a guy's house. I was accompanied by two guys my boyfriend Carl had sent to go with me. The relationship between Carl and me that had been like a brother/sister relationship when I was fourteen changed to a boyfriend/girlfriend one when I was sixteen. Carl was thirty-two. He was a big-time dealer, huge and strong, and everyone had respect for him. Walking up toward the door, a very strange feeling came over me. I thought it was just my nerves. The closer I got to the door, the heavier I felt; it was as though someone was pressing against me, pushing me back away from the door, not wanting me to get closer. I was trying to reach the door, but it felt as though I was swimming against the current, each step heavier than the last.

Not understanding what was happening, I pressed on, trying to ignore the invisible warning signs. As I raised my hand to knock on the door, an alarm inside of me rang out, warning me to turn around, and a sudden churning in my stomach began. The door opened, and this young man was standing before us all dressed in black with a hood over his head. I remembered his eyes were so dark and scary. I quickly looked away and noticed the other two guys with me were staring at him with suspicion. My heart was racing, and I was wondering what we should do. Should we turn around and leave? I thought maybe if we just told the guy to give us the stuff Carl sent me to pick up, we could quickly get out of there. I threw around Carl's name, reminding everyone who sent me and what my purpose was, using his name as a protection, a warning, that no one messes around with Carl's girl or his friends.

As we stepped into the house, I noticed several other people sitting in the living room around a small table, everyone dressed in black. Spread out on the table was what looked like a Ouija board. I was confused, the whole atmosphere felt dire. The guy, Dave, was introducing his friends to us, but all I heard was a bunch of muffled sounds. I didn't care who these people were; I just wanted to quickly get out. I knew we were safe though because Carl was a higher-up in the drug world and could do real damage to these guys if any harm was done to me or the other two guys, and Dave knew it. But I couldn't get rid of the weird, sick feeling that was stirring up inside of me. I felt like a volcano was forming, bubbling, raging, preparing to erupt from within me.

"Hey, I wanna show you guys something really cool!" Dave said with great enthusiasm as he walked toward the stairs. "It's upstairs in my bedroom. Follow me." He was so excited about it and said it would only take a few minutes, then we would be on their way.

I was hesitant, insisting that we were in a hurry to get back, but Dave was persistent. We followed him up the stairs. Each step I took up to his bedroom felt heavier than the last. When we entered the room, it was dark, all painted black. I was holding onto my stomach, trying to keep what lay at the bottom at the bottom. I had never felt like this before. It was different than being sick with the flu or eating something that didn't agree with me. It was an invasion of some sort, heavy, dizzy, difficult to breathe, a darkness pressing in.

As we all entered the room, Dave pulled back the black curtains that hung as doors to his closet. Along the back wall of the closet sat a long black table with candles, books, and other paraphernalia that I couldn't quite make out.

"This is so cool," Dave said as he pointed to the table. "So last night, I placed a Bible on top of the satanic bible, and when I woke up in the morning, the Bible was facing down underneath the satanic bible." As he was talking, I felt the bile within my stomach churning and making its way up to the surface. I had little time to think. Turning around, I quickly ran out the room, down the stairs, and out the back door in time for the volcano to erupt all over the back steps. Everything I was feeling moments before emptied itself right there, all the heaviness and darkness making its way out of me and onto the steps before me.

That day is etched in my mind as though it happened yesterday. I thought a lot about the feeling of heaviness and darkness that had come over me that day. I had never felt it before, and it changed me. I didn't completely understand at the time, but I knew there was a presence in that place, a presence of evil that I did not want to meet again. I could not define it then; only years later did I come to understand that I had brushed against the forces of darkness, Satan, that this young man, Dave, had sold his soul to the devil.

It was a first introduction for me into the spiritual realm that, in later years, I would come to understand in a deeper way. I believed God had given me a gift: he had revealed to me the reality of the spiritual battle that existed in the world. He clearly drew a picture for me of the darkness that represented Satan and the light that represented God, such a contrast from one to the other. I wish I could say that, at that moment, my life turned around and I began to search for the light, for God, but I did not. I still had many storms to walk through before coming face-to-face with God. But it was another seed planted along the path to him.

From the age of twelve to the encounter with Jesus at twenty, my days were filled with drugging and parties. Bars and bush parties, band parties, rock concerts and parties for no reason but to get loaded. There were many people who crossed my path in those days, so many that it was difficult to recall each one, yet each affected my life in some shape or form. If just for a moment I could have opened my eyes to the reality of life that surrounded me, things might have been totally different. How many people suffered with such deep inner pain and tried to kill themselves or drowned their sorrows by using drugs or drinking alcohol, injecting their veins with poison, hoping it would remove the depth of their pain, if only for a moment, only to return with a vengeance, starting the cycle all over again? Did I, in the midst of my own drowning, miss the possibilities of the people who may have spoken a word or two of warning and truth into my life? Or was I afraid of facing the possibility that no one cared?

When I first started using drugs, it was in small amounts, but the more I used, the more I needed for it to have any effect. It was mild stuff at first; then I worked my way up to the harder stuff: mescaline, coke, and crack. Of course, it cost money, so I would make up lies to tell my mom: *I need new shorts for gym, I need lunch money, etc.* Then I would steal from her purse. But as I got older, my addiction was fed by taking advantage of my gender to get free drugs and date guys that were dealers.

As my relationship with Carl grew, he would take me to parties where coke was prevalent. He took care of me with whatever I needed. There were many times when I could not remember a thing that happened; I'd been so wasted. I would wake up in unfamiliar places but knew I was protected. No one would mess around with him, even when he wasn't with me. I also began to sell drugs at school and would make pick-ups for him. This lasted about a year until one day, Carl just disappeared. No one knew where he went or what happened to him. I was devastated. I went back to feeling vulnerable and unprotected. I fell deeper into my black hole, caring less and less about myself. I felt like everything I ever cared about had been ripped from underneath me: my innocence, my mom, my boyfriend. I never saw or heard from him again nor found out what had happened to him.

My life during those years was filled with so much chaos, pick-ups and parties, and times of lost memory. There were many parts that were blank, times I was thankful I did not remember, but there were also times that I forever lost. I didn't go to prom. I missed out on most fun normal teen experiences and much of my childhood for that matter, and that is what I regret the most.

Chapter 5

He measured off another thousand, but now it was a river that I could not cross, because the water had risen and was deep enough to swim in—a river that no one could cross.
—Ezekiel 47:5

When I look back to the path I took, I cannot help but wonder what drove me to make the decisions I made. When I reached a fork in the road, what made me choose one way over the other? A few weeks after my encounter with God, I remember hitting one of those forks in the road when I had to make a really hard decision. Matt was in jail, I was pregnant, twenty, and living at my parents' house for the time being.

Mike was a childhood friend of my older brother, Jacque. When I was younger, I had a major crush on him. He was always so sweet to me. Mike eventually moved across country to Vancouver, British Columbia. When I came home from work one day, Mike was at the house visiting my brother, who still lived at home.

"Mike!" I cried out as I ran over to him and gave him a hug. He was still so good-looking. Tall, slender, with shoulder-length golden brown hair and tanned skin. He looked like a Californian surfer.

"Oh my gosh, Sam, you're all grown up. It's so good to see you," Mike said, hugging me back with a tight squeeze.

"What are you doing here?" I asked, my eyes dancing with excitement. I missed him so much.

"I'm here for a wedding. My aunt is getting married Saturday," he said pulling out a chair for me to sit at the kitchen table. He sat back down next to me. My heart melted, what a gentleman. "It's so awesome to see you. You are still so beautiful."

I blushed as he said that. I never thought I was beautiful. I had many people say this to me in the past. Sure, I had nice long blond hair and blue eyes, and I was slender. Never had any issues with pimples. But I never felt as though I was anything special; there were a lot of other girls who were way prettier than me. I just didn't feel special. But Mike always seemed to make me feel good when he was around.

"Thanks, you were always so nice to me. So, how are you? Do you like it in Vancouver?" I asked, smiling at him. He was so handsome. I knew my cheeks must have looked flushed.

"I'm doing great. I love Vancouver. It's perfect weather, and you get both the mountains and the ocean. What more can you ask for? It's beautiful," Mike said. "Hey, I don't have a date for the wedding Saturday. Would you like to be my date? Then we could catch up. It'd be fun to hang out with you, an old friend, you know, since I can't technically invite your brother here," he said as he pointed to my brother Jacque who made a weird face back at him. My brother was four years older than me. He was about five feet ten, a little shorter than Mike and filled out more; he often worked out.

I stared at Mike for a few minutes, not knowing what to say. I wanted to go. I missed him, yet I was in such a mess. I had not made a decision on my future with Matt yet, and besides, I was pregnant.

Mike picked up on my hesitation, "Sorry, I know I threw this at you, but think about it. It's just a fun night out with an old friend," he said with his beautiful, perfect smile.

"Okay, fair enough, I'll think about it and let you know in a couple of days. In the meantime, if you find another date, that's okay," I said, kind of hoping he wouldn't. I felt a pang of jealousy already.

"Oh, I wasn't really looking for one until I saw you. I thought it'd be fun to hang out and catch up," he said, looking at me with gentle pleading puppy eyes.

"Thanks, Mike. I'll get back to you in the next day or so. Just leave your number by the phone," I said, getting up from my chair. I wanted so much to jump in his arms and tell him to take me away, to be my prince. What was wrong with me? I was pregnant with another man's baby. My heart was racing a mile a minute; my palms were sweaty. Oh my gosh, I had it bad for him.

"Sounds good!" he said and got up and hugged me. I turned around and walked back to my room at the end of the hall.

That night, I lay on my bed thinking about Mike. He was the same as I remembered him: handsome, nice, and sincere. He always seemed to be compassionate toward people's feelings and would take the time to sit and talk. I didn't know what to do. Matt was in jail. Would that be like cheating and unfair to him since he was behind bars? But, I thought, he put himself there; why should I suffer for his stupid, idiotic mistakes? I was the one left behind to deal with the broken pieces. I needed a distraction from my thoughts and to have some fun. Besides, Mike was just a friend. He would be leaving in a few weeks to go back west and who knew when I would ever see him again?

I called him the next day and told him I would go with him to the wedding.

"That's awesome, Sam. I'm so excited. Thanks! I'll pick you up at four o'clock," Mike said, his voice radiating happiness.

When Saturday came, I had a hard time finding something to wear. Everything felt tight and uncomfortable around my waist. I finally settled for a loose dress that had a simple rope belt. When Mike picked me up, he looked so handsome in his suit. I kept stealing little glances at him when he wasn't looking. My heart was stirring inside of me, and I was beginning to think that it might have been a mistake agreeing to go to this wedding with him. Many mixed emotions were battling inside my head. I was thankful he couldn't see the tug of war that was happening inside me. He had asked me as a friend, and that was all, I kept saying to myself. Then I would shake my head to try and get the crazy thoughts out. *What was I thinking? How awful was I to think of another man besides the father of my baby?*

That night, we talked about a lot of things: our younger years, his life in Vancouver as a firefighter, his parents' divorce, my life with Matt. We danced and had a good time. I felt so safe and comfortable around him. He treated me like a princess, opening the doors, pulling out the chair, getting me a drink—he was so attentive to me.

Matt had never treated me this way. I felt that I could be truthful with him, so I poured out my heart to him and told him about the pregnancy. Mike was so compassionate through it all and listened. I felt so good to just be able to talk with someone and share my feelings of uncertainty and fear and not be judged. I was sad when we pulled into my parents' driveway at the end of the night.

"Thanks so much, Sam, for the wonderful evening. I had so much fun with you and really enjoyed talking to you," Mike said as he turned to look at me with tenderness in his eyes.

I was looking down at my hands folded on my lap. "Me too, Mike. Thanks. I really needed that. It's been a long time since I could just let go of it all, even if it was just for one night." My heart was leaping out of my chest, it was pounding so hard.

"Listen, Sam, I'm not going to pretend. I really like you. I've liked you since the first day I met you. I had a crush on you, but we're adults now, you know. I know this is so sudden, but I've thought about you often, and now after seeing you again, those feelings have come up again, stronger this time," he said as he reached over to put his hand over top of mine.

My feelings were jumping all around inside of me as his hand sent tingles all over my body. How could such a nice, good-looking guy like me?

"I want you to come back home with me. I mean to Vancouver. I would take care of you, Sam, and the baby. I don't care if it's not mine. I'll make it mine. That boyfriend of yours doesn't seem like he's taking really good care of you."

Wow, I was overwhelmed by what he was asking me to do. Move? Go with him?

"Mike . . . I really like you too. I had a crush on you too, but I just can't pick up and leave," I said as quiet tears ran down my face. I desperately wanted to go, to leave and never look back.

"Why not? What do you have here that's holding you back? Do you love him?" Mike asked. I felt his green eyes piercing the side of my face.

"I don't know, Mike. I'm so confused right now. I need time to think. I'm really flattered, really, that you would be willing to take care of both me and my child. I don't even have the words to say how I feel about that. I've made so many bad decisions, choices. I just want to make the right one now," I said, turning to look at him, my heart ripping in half. "I'm confused as to which is the right one."

Mike leaned over and gave me a kiss on my cheek. "I'm fine with that, Sam. Just know that I really do want to take care of you. I know we would make a good team," he said, gently putting his hand on my cheek where he'd just kissed me.

"Thanks, Mike, I'll talk to you soon," I said, opening the car door and stepping out. "Thanks again for the night out." I shut the door and headed into the house, my heart beating fast. As I entered the house and shut the door, I stood, breathless, thinking of Mike and the night we had. He wanted me. He seemed to really love me. My heart was torn. "God, please help me. Please give me the wisdom to do what is right because I don't know what to do. I can't think straight or clearly. I need you to guide me. I've messed up my whole life, and now I want to do it your way," I said into the air while I removed my shoes, climbed the three steps that led into the house, and made my way to my bedroom.

It was a struggle for the next several days. My mind was in a constant battle. Mike had come by several times to visit my brother, yet I knew it was really to see me. The offer tempted me, calling me to a new life, a redo, leaving all this behind me. But deep inside, as much as I wanted to run, which I was good at, I felt that I needed to face the here and now. Even though I didn't know what the future held for me, even though I was afraid, I just couldn't bring myself to leave. Running away was tempting, but something inside of me kept telling me to stay.

I called Mike four days after our date. I couldn't face him; it was too hard and tempting if I had to see him again and look into his beautiful, trusting green eyes. My heart tore in two. I did really care for him and wondered often if I had made the right decision.

"Mike . . . I . . . I am so sorry, but I can't go with you. I really do care about you, but I know I have to stay and deal with Matt and our situation before I can jump into another relationship," I said, my voice trembling and every part of my body screaming to go.

"Okay, Sam, I understand," he said, pausing for a moment as I heard him sigh. "But if you change your mind, Sam, you know how to reach me. The offer still stands," he said quietly. I could feel his disappointment through the phone. We said our good-byes. I cried as I hung up. A dream had just slipped through my fingers. My heart wanted to follow him.

Often, in the years that passed, I would sometimes regret the decision I made. Two years after Mike left, I heard he'd died in a car accident. I cried for him, for us. I wondered what it was that made me stay when he asked me to go with him. Was it God? Did he hold me back? At the time, I so desperately wanted to go, but I felt something stronger than my own will that stopped me from going with him. For a long time, my heart yearned for a "do over," for the chance to change the decision I made because my life after Mike left was nothing short of sheer hell.

When Matt was released from jail weeks later, he came looking for me, which wasn't too hard since he knew where my parents lived. I had not spoken to him since the night the police came to our door. He begged me to give him another chance, that he couldn't live without me, that he had changed while in jail. He was sober now. When I told him about the pregnancy and my newfound faith, he said he was ready to have a family and that we should get married. The time in jail seemed to have sobered him up, and I felt he deserved another chance. Besides, I thought, now that we were having a baby, that was motivation for him to change and want to provide for us. I didn't know how to fix all the messes in my life, all the mistakes I had made. I believed that because it hadn't worked out with Mike, maybe this was where I was meant to be, with Matt. It seemed like the right thing at the time, to marry the father of my baby. I'd always wanted to get married and have a family, the kind of thing most girls dream about and want. I wanted so badly to believe he had changed, that maybe through my influence with my newfound faith, God would change him and we could make it work. Anything was possible with God's help, right? Once the baby arrived, he would fall in love with fatherhood and see how great it was to have a family and want to do everything he could to take care of us.

Taking a leap of faith, I married Matt. It was a hot, humid day in July. I was a little over four months pregnant but didn't show. Just a handful of people knew I was pregnant. I walked down the aisle with my dad at my side looking dapper in his tux; for a moment, I felt joy walking beside him, my arm looped in his. But as we walked toward Matt, who was standing at the altar, he turned and whispered in my ear. "Sam, it's not too late, you can turn back any time now. You don't have to do this. The money doesn't matter."

I looked at my dad through my veil, in shock. "What? Are you serious? Oh my gosh, Dad!" I said through clenched teeth. I was so mad. My eyes scanned the area around us to see if anyone else had heard. How could he say such a thing now? He had never said anything about it prior to this day, not a word, and now he chose to say this. I tried holding the tears back, thanking God that the veil was covering my face so no one could see the shock and hurt I was feeling. I did not want to look at him for the rest of the night. I felt such anger toward them both for not believing in me and encouraging me. I knew that they did not want me to marry Matt, and that knowledge hurt me. But on my wedding day, how could my dad have the audacity to humiliate me like that? I wanted to hear the words that any bride wants to hear, words like, "You're so beautiful," "I love you," "I'm so proud of you." But instead, my heart was broken. I was determined to prove them wrong. I was determined to have a good time considering all that had happened. This was my wedding day, the one and only one I would ever have.

The night went well; we danced and had a great time. I saw a childhood friend that I had not seen in years. She was my only friend in elementary school that I had spent a lot of time with—we stayed at each other's house almost every weekend. She wasn't popular either, so it was no surprise that we connected. I was pleasantly surprised to see her at my wedding with her dad. I admired the relationship she had with her dad. I looked up to them both and often wished I had that relationship with my dad growing up. When I was at her house, he treated me like a daughter and took us out to places: skating, horseback riding, the store for candy. He showed me what a true father-daughter relationship was, and I was forever grateful for the time I spent with them. It was a place where I felt safe, an escape from my neighborhood and the abuse that happened in the wheat fields.

"Mary, wow, it's so good to see you! How long has it been, seven years?" I asked, giving her a hug and turning to her dad, Bill, and hugging him.

Mary handed me a present; it was heavy. "I think so. Congratulations! Dad and I got this for you," she said with a mischievous grin on her face. "Go ahead, open it." I opened the card first, which had some money in it. Then I unwrapped the gift and saw that it was a case of canned French pea soup.

"Oh my gosh, I love pea soup!" I said with a silly grin on my face and laughter in my voice. It brought back some good memories.

"Yeah, I didn't wanna do it, but Dad insisted. He just gets a kick out of it every time we eat pea soup. He'd say, 'Remember the time when Sam . . .', and we would all laugh and say, 'Yup.'" Mary looked over at her dad as they both chuckled.

"Sam, I enjoyed the times you spent at our house. We had lots of fun," Bill said, reaching over and putting his arm around my shoulder, giving me a side squeeze. Tears came to my eyes. I felt the love and safety from him that I had when I'd visited as a young child.

At one of my first sleepovers at Mary's, they'd eaten French pea soup. I had never heard of it, and by the look of it, the rich thick yellow texture, I didn't think I'd like it, and it must have shown by the expression on my face. They laughed at me and said that it was okay, that I didn't have to eat it. Mary's family loved pea soup, and they kept asking me to just try it. After many promptings, I broke down and decided to try it. To my surprise, I loved it! Every time after that, when I went over, I would ask them if they could make pea soup.

"Thanks, Mary. It is so good to see you," I said, and it was. I had so many fond memories with her. On their farm, they had cows, goats, chickens, and other animals. I loved going and seeing the animals. It was where I had tried goat milk and hated it, but I did learn to try new things after the pea soup incident.

"It was really good to see you too. Congratulations," she said as we hugged and said our good-byes.

Seeing her and her dad reminded me that there had been some good times in my life as a child. That I had a safe place to go and be a kid. Mary's place was one of them. They seemed few and far between, but I did have a place to escape to, to be a child and feel safe, tucked away, if only for a little while.

I looked over and saw my mom dancing the night away with her friends. It was good to see her having fun. I liked my mom's friends—they were all crazy old ladies. There was a gang of them, women friends, a sisterhood who had met for coffee more than twenty years ago and remained friends to this day. They knew a lot about each other, more than anyone else, even their own husbands. They experienced the hardships of raising a family together, defiant children, some of them passing away too early at the hands of cancer, death, depression. There was much laughter mixed in with many tears and secrets held within the walls of their hearts.

I was jealous of the relationship they had with one another, but in a good way. I knew my mom needed them. Still, I wished I had friends like that. They would drink wine, giggle like teenage girls, and share their frustrations with one another. I knew the times when my mom had spent time with her friends, and I also recognized the times when she needed to. It was like an addict needing a fix. If it went on too long, my mom would become anxious, snappy. They gave their hearts to one another, and I knew that these friends were a life jacket for my mom, one that saved her many times from drowning.

The women encouraged me as well. Sometimes I joined them as they gathered for their weekly coffee time. They had seen me in all stages of my life, yet when I was with them, my soul was filled with acceptance and love. Their smiles filled me with joy, and their hugs were like tender squeezes to my heart, pumping life back into it. Their words of encouragement sat with me through many years of hating myself. They often told me that I was beautiful, so beautiful, when I only felt ugliness. Even though, at the time, I thought they were just being kind, there was a sincerity I felt about them. They were real.

I felt so full of joy and life for the first time in a long time. The room was filled with laughter, and many people danced the night away. Many times, I would stop to soak in the moment. It was hard to believe this was my wedding night. It wasn't often that my family was in one place all together. Life seemed to have scattered us in all different directions, and I haven't seen my two brothers in a long time prior to my wedding. We weren't really close; our lives didn't cross much except on special occasions like Christmas.

My brother Ronald, the one closest to my age, came walking toward me with a big smile on his face. He was with Angie, an old neighborhood friend that we'd grown up with. My brother was five feet eleven, tall, slender, and muscular. He was twenty-four and worked for a steel construction company putting up steel beams for tall buildings. In school, the girls loved him, his freckles and beautiful ocean-blue eyes were a big hit in attracting the girls. He was also quiet and gentle. Angie and my brother were always together growing up. Angie was from the troubled house where her mother spent much time in the mental hospital. My brother and Angie were inseparable. I think they liked each other. I really liked Angie; she was always so nice to me and would sometimes play with me. Angie had beautiful thick long brown hair. Now it was shorter, shoulder length. My brother and Angie handed me a large wrapped box. The two of them watched with big grins on their faces as I unwrapped the box and opened it to find a bunch of chocolate bars.

"What's this for?" I asked, looking at both of them with a confused look on my face.

"It's all the chocolate bars I promised you when we were kids if you'd give Angie your swing," my brother said with a chuckle.

"Oh my gosh, right, you guys owe me a whole load of them!" I said as I looked down at the box of chocolate bars laughing.

"Well, I hope this will do," said Angie. "Thanks for giving up your swing for me all those times your brother bribed you, and sorry it took this long to repay you." She came over and gave me a hug. "Sorry," she whispered in my ear.

We all laughed, and Ronald joined in on the hug. I thought it was so sweet of them to do this; it filled my heart.

"No worries, I forgive you both," I said, recalling the many times I had swung on the swing in the yard of my childhood home.

I was often alone as a child, playing in the yard. I loved the feel of the wind against my face and the freedom I felt as I tried to swing high trying to touch the sky with my feet. When my brother Ronald and Angie would come into the backyard, I would often be swinging on one of the two swings. Ronald would say, "Sam, I'll give you a chocolate bar if you give Angie your swing." I believed it every time and gave up my swing to Angie for a chocolate bar I was promised but never received. Time and time again, the promise was made, but no chocolates were ever exchanged, until now.

I didn't want the night to be over. It was the most fun I'd had in a long time. I loved being around my family and seeing them celebrate, leaving their hardships outside if only for an evening. I felt more happiness for them than for myself. Gatherings brought people together, and for one day, all our troubles and the outside world went away. We were here with the people we knew and loved and wanted to be with, even though the very people, outside this day, were the ones that hurt each other. It was like we wanted to forget, pretend that everything was good between us all. Yet I knew there was an unspoken silence that would one day scream loud to escape.

I hadn't seen Matt much, but I felt full of joy regardless. I was sad when the night was over, to see the fun end and everyone leave. I wanted to hold on to it a little longer, to dance with the joyful sound of laughter and the love that filled the room. I didn't know when I would see everyone again, and I was afraid the feeling would not last, the closeness, the connection I felt with family and friends. It was the first time I felt an overwhelming amount of love poured into me, and I was afraid to let it go. I wanted to stay in this moment, the feeling of being surrounded by a rosy glow that warmed my heart.

Chapter 6

Where then is my hope—who can see any hope for me?
—Job 17:15

The week after the wedding, I felt happy and peaceful. Matt was off for the week. He had been working for a company that made airline service trollies for the last several months. Surprisingly, he had kept his job this long. We hung out together, which was unusual, but it gave me hope for our future. When Matt returned to work, things began to slowly spiral downward. The old Matt began to creep back in. He started drinking again. I would find hidden bottles around, which was never a good sign. Besides, he was a whole different person when he drank, even after one drink. He became mean and aggressive.

He also didn't like the new me. The me that didn't do drugs and didn't party anymore but went to church and attended AA meetings, the me that worked and went to school part-time. He tried everything for me to change back into the Sam he once knew, but after some time, he gave up. Instead, he would come home drunk, and if I said anything to him, he would grab me by the hair and drag me back into the bedroom, telling me to shut up and to mind my own business. I tried hard to be silent, but even that wasn't enough to placate him. He would come into the bedroom, wake me up, and make me have sex with him, forcing himself on me. He acted as though he had a right to do whatever he wanted because I was his wife. I hated him when he drank; he was volatile, spewing hateful words at me and slobbering all over me. I hated his body against mine and the scent of his breath, the stench of alcohol flowing out of his mouth.

He would often disappear for days at a time to strip joints and parties, never holding a job, and spending all our money, my money. I did not mind when he failed to come home and often prayed that he would just disappear. I hated the thoughts that crossed my mind when he left me to go and watch other women strip before him, drinking himself to oblivion and coming home all hot for sex. It made me feel physically sick. I often wished something would happen to him on the way home since he often drove drunk. Nothing ever did happen, except being pulled over by the police several times and losing his license, which never stopped him from driving anyway. I was always anxious, never knowing what state he was in when he arrived home or *if* he would arrive home. Often, I was left at work with no ride home or at the apartment with no vehicle.

Even though my life was a mess, I continued to work on myself. I attended AA, trying to work on all the years of bad choices I had made that had some lifelong consequences. God was peeling the onion one layer at a time. It was painful and hard. I felt like I was in the battle alone, no one to share with, no one to talk to. I felt like it was my problem to deal with, and no one really cared. No one really knew what was happening behind the four walls of my heart or my home, how bad it really was.

"Matt, come on, wake up!" I yelled. I had been shaking his body for the last fifteen minutes to try to wake him up. I was having bad pains, but the baby wasn't due for another three weeks. Matt had come in late again, drunk, and wouldn't wake up. I had to get him up, and there was no way I could drive to the hospital. I didn't know what to do. I was panicking, and the pain was really bad. Hunched over and grabbing my stomach, I went into the bathroom, having to stop between contractions until the pain subsided, and grabbed a cold glass of water. I returned to the bed and dumped the water on Matt's face. He shot out of bed, his arms flailing wildly. His hair was a mess, and his eyes were bloodshot.

"What the fuck!" he said in confusion, jolting out of bed. I stepped way back to get out of the way.

"Matt, stop! You have to wake up. I think the baby is coming," I said, keeping my distance from him, nervously not knowing what he would do.

"What? It's not even time yet," Matt said, mad and looking at me like I was crazy.

"I don't know, I'm just having some really bad pains every few minutes. You gotta bring me to the hospital. Pleeeease, Matt," I said, crying. What I really wanted to do was strangle him. He was such an ass. I had to tiptoe around him for everything. I was the one pregnant. I was the one sober and trying my best to take care of the child growing in me. He didn't seem to care. All he wanted to do was drink, party, and watch women strip. I wanted to attack him, punch him, but I knew that would only make him mad and turn around and hit me. I was mad at myself for stooping so low in allowing a man to treat me like this.

"Shit! Are you sure, or are you just having those fake contractions?" he asked, mad that he might have to get up.

"*Yes, I am sure!*" I said. Now I was really frustrated and didn't care anymore what he would do. But I was also aware that if it turned out to be a false alarm, I would pay for it dearly. I had been awake a long time, and it was getting worse.

"Yeah, yeah, give me a minute," he said, trying to get his mind on the task of finding some clothes.

We lived thirty minutes from the hospital. Matt thought having a baby gave him permission to go through all the red lights and go over the speed limit. I thought this alone would make the baby come out right there in the car. I was so scared of how crazy Matt was being, driving so erratically. I believed he was still hungover from the previous night. He could have killed all three of us. Thank God, it was early in the morning and the traffic was light.

We arrived at the hospital, and the nurses got me settled into the birthing area, hooking me up to the machines. The doctor came in to check how far I had dilated, but I was only at four centimeters. I was surprised I was only that far along. I was in so much pain. My back was killing me. I laid on my side, holding tightly to the railing of the bed, squeezing hard with every contraction, internalizing the pain. I never imagined that it would be this painful. I was only twenty-one and, of course, had never experienced childbirth. I kept telling the nurse that my back was hurting me so badly. The nurse sent the doctor in to check on me again. He said that the baby was breeched. I had no clue what that meant.

"It's when the baby is face up instead of face down, and butt first," he explained. "I cannot seem to get her turned around. That is definitely why your back is in so much pain. Would you like an epidural?"

"What is that?" I asked, feeling so stupid I didn't know anything. We had not gone to any birthing classes; our lives were a complete mess. I didn't have the baby's room ready or anything. I wasn't due for another three weeks.

"We inject a needle with a line in your back and feed medicine into you to relieve some of your pain."

"*Yes!*" I yelled before the doctor said anything more. Why hadn't they said anything before all this? Meanwhile, Matt was already asleep in the chair next to the bed, oblivious to all that was taking place.

I could hear someone screaming down the hall. I asked the nurse if the woman was giving birth. The nurse laughed and said she wasn't; she was only a few centimeters dilated. That made me even more fearful.

A few hours later, I gave birth to a precious little girl we named Lauren. She was perfect. I couldn't keep my eyes off her. The delivery was hard, but after the medicine was injected, I felt much better, exhausted, but better. The doctor took a while to sew me up after such a hard delivery; apparently the birth tore me up pretty good that the doctor had to put many stitches in. But the minute Lauren was born, it was amazing how all the pain was lifted and so much love filled my heart. I already loved and adored her so much. Her face was so cute, pink and round. She had no hair; she was completely bald. When she opened her eyes, they were big and blue. She weighed eight pounds and one ounce. Nice and healthy. I counted her toes and fingers, all there.

My hospital stay was lonely, but I was glad for the help. Matt barely came to see us. I felt such a deep loneliness within me. I began to honestly hate Matt and regretted marrying him. I wondered if I ever did love him, or was it just the thought of having a man by my side that would take care of me, us, that made me do it? I wanted to be taken care of, to feel loved and wanted, but that certainly was not the case with Matt. The regret of not taking Mike's offer to move with him to Vancouver often filled my mind, clouding it. I so desperately wanted to turn back the clock and be given another chance to make the right decision to go with Mike. I often would wonder what it would be like to be with him instead of Matt. At the moment, anything seemed better than my life with Matt.

    The nurses at the hospital did not care for Matt at all. The times he did come in to visit, he would come with his brother, and they would just sit in the chair sleeping off their night of partying. Once, when they left, they exited the emergency exit, setting off the alarm. I was so embarrassed. I was afraid to go home, not knowing what our future held. Plus, how was I going to protect Lauren when I couldn't protect myself? I wanted to stay where it was safe. My parents often came to visit me in the hospital. They were so in love with Lauren, their first grandchild, even under the circumstances. Each time they came, I wanted to beg them to take me and Lauren home with them. To save me from Matt, from the miserable life I was living. But I kept silent. I felt like this was my mess, my battle to fight, not theirs. I didn't want them to think of me as a failure, a loser. My parents had been clear before I married Matt that they didn't think it was a good decision. I hated to admit it, but my dad was right. I thought about when he walked me down the aisle and told me I could change my mind about marrying Matt. At the time, I had been so mad at him; but now, I knew he was right. He saw things I was too blind to see. I wanted to replay that day, to turn around, but it was too late.

    I held and cradled Lauren often; being with her filled me with so much love. She filled one of the empty holes in my heart. I couldn't stop staring at her. She was so beautiful, and I was scared. I didn't know how to take care of a baby, but I didn't want to let her go. I was also scared of the situation I was bringing her into. The guilt and shame often rolled in and spoke to me, telling me how awful a mother I was. It would fill my mind with so much debris that I felt numb, as though I was just going through the motions to keep myself and my baby alive. I now had someone I needed to protect no matter if I was a bad mother or not. I loved her so deeply.

That time in my life was difficult. A few times, when it got really bad, I called the police. They would arrest Matt and keep him in jail overnight to sober up; then he'd return home. A few times, Matt went to rehab. Sometimes by his own choice, and sometimes, it was the courts that made him go. The first few times, I had hoped he would come home and go to AA. He would do well for a few months. Then he would meet some new friends, and they would go off drinking and partying, and the whole cycle would start again, crushing all hope that Matt would ever change, that he would ever become sober and the man I wished he would be. Several times, I left and moved, unable to deal with all the emotional turmoil. But in time, Matt would find me and threaten to kill me and himself if I ever did it again.

I lost count of how many times we moved because we were unable to cover the rent. When I lived on my own, I had managed to pay my bills, but with Matt, we never had any money. He would spend it all on drugs and alcohol. He would steal my credit card, checks, and any cash I had. Many times, I tried to stop him, but of course, I paid the price for it. The physical abuse got really bad at times.

I remembered the first time I experienced abuse, before we were married. He came home one day, mad as heck. I hadn't done anything wrong, but I figured he probably owed someone money. He grabbed me by the hair and dragged me up the stairs of our basement apartment and out to the car while I was kicking and screaming, trying to break free. He shoved me into the car and drove and drove like a mad man into the middle of nowhere. I had no idea where we were. I was disoriented and terrified. He was driving really fast, going through red lights, stop signs, and down dirt roads. Music blaring. I kept yelling, "What's wrong? Where are we going?"

He just yelled back, "Shut the fuck up!" He went on, telling me what a good for nothing bitch I was, and why did he ever hook up with me?

Both of my hands were holding tight to the door handle, trying to stop them from shaking. Tears ran down my face, my whole body shaking. Then he stopped. He sat for a minute, cussing. I was trying to be quiet when he ordered me to get out of the car. I didn't move. I was scared and didn't know where we were. He got out, came to my side of the car, opened the door, and grabbed me. I was kicking and punching out at him. I was not going to go without a fight, but he managed to get me out of the car and throw me into the ditch. He was cussing up a storm as he walked over to me. I put my arms over my head and curled up as he lifted his foot and kicked me several times, then got back into the car and drove away.

I laid in the ditch in shock. I did not know what to do nor did I know what I did for this to happen. I cursed at God. I did not believe in him at that time, but I yelled at him anyway. How could he do this to me? Strangely, I felt a presence surround me. I felt a peace that it would all be okay. I had never felt that way before. After a while, I got up and started to walk, having no clue what direction to go. I did not have any money; everything I owned was back in the basement apartment. I walked for what seemed to be several miles until I came to a bridge and saw two guys fishing. I must have looked a mess with a dirty tear-stained face and dried snot stuck to my face. I screamed for them, crying in relief. They saw me, dropped their poles, and came running over to see if I was okay. They were older gentlemen, maybe in their forties, tall, one with a nice beer belly, the other was skinny with a mustache and beard. But I noticed that their eyes were kind, soft.

"Please help me! If you can just tell me where I am?" I asked, seeing the puzzled but tender looks on their faces as they tried to figure out what happened, if I was okay. I stared at them with pleading eyes. I was desperate.

"You are south of Highway 5. Do you need a ride somewhere?" they asked.

I bit my lip, afraid, not knowing if I should trust them. *What if they were crazy and wanted to hurt me?* I laughed inside. *Like, really, look at me now and look who just threw me in the ditch. Who cares anymore?* I just wanted to get home.

"Yes, please!" I gave them my address. One of the men pointed to his truck down the road as they went to collect their fishing gear. I jumped in the back of the truck and waited for them to return, wondering if I was doing the right thing, letting two strange men give me a ride home. The ride to my apartment was awkward and quiet. They were very kind and many times asked if I was going to be okay, if they maybe needed to bring me to the police station. I shook my head no, looking down. They were probably wondering what on earth happened, who did this to me. Then I wondered, what would I tell the police? I was embarrassed and filled with shame. When they dropped me off, Matt wasn't home. I was so relieved. He was nowhere to be seen for three days after that incident. When he did return home, he was so apologetic, crying and promising he would never hurt me again. I never did find out where he went, and he had broken his promise over and over again. I never believed him again.

That was the first of many moments of abuse. I had been thrown down the stairs, dragged by my hair, punched and kicked. These incidents happened when he was out drinking, which was often, leaving me by myself. I could not go on like this. I had a beautiful daughter I tried to protect, but I was stuck in the middle of this chaotic lifestyle.

Finally, four years after we married and after several attempts of leaving, one night after Matt didn't show up for several days, I went down to the police department and got a restraining order because of the abuse, the threats, and the danger Lauren and I were in. I then had someone from my work change the lock on the apartment door. When Matt came home several days later, in the middle of the night, he was mad and screaming when his key would not work and he could not get in. He started kicking the door and calling me all kinds of names, threatening to kill himself but me first. The neighbors called 911, but before the police came, I was on the other side of the door crouched down with my head in my knees, crying and praying for God to help me, for this all to stop. I so desperately wanted this to be over, to be done with all this.

Lauren, who was almost four, had woken up from all the noise and sat by my side. "What's wrong, Mommy?" she asked, crying. "Why is Daddy screaming on the other side of the door?" Looking at

Lauren, in that moment, made my heart hurt more for putting her in this situation. She didn't understand the extent of it all. She was so beautiful. She looked a lot like I did at that age. Long blond hair, big blue eyes, round face with a few dimples.

"It's okay, honey, it'll be okay. Your dad is sick and needs help." I thought that was the stupidest thing I could say, but I did not know what else to tell her. Everything was a mess, and I didn't know where to begin repairing it all.

The police came and arrested him, and all I could hear was Lauren screaming and kicking for her dad and at me for what I had done to him. It broke my heart. Lauren did not understand the severity of the situation. She just saw her dad get dragged away by the police. She didn't experience the abuse or the emotional turmoil of our lives. I did the best I could trying to protect her from it all. I was sure that Lauren must have felt and heard a little of it but probably wasn't sure what the extent of it was. At least that was what I hoped.

Eventually, I found another place to live with the help of my church friends. The strange thing was that in time, Matt slowly began to back off, as if he'd lost interest, but later I found out why: he had a new girlfriend. I was relieved and knew it was God protecting me and Lauren from his constant harassment.

I had lost my job at the real estate company. They had closed their doors months before this happened. I decided to enroll at the university to work toward a psychology degree. I collected unemployment, and as a single mom, the province of Ontario helped with school expenses and day care. Life as a single mom was difficult. I barely had two pennies to my name; our main staple was macaroni and cheese with ketchup. But the freedom I felt inside was priceless. Lauren and I were inseparable. We saw many *Disney on Ice* shows, and almost every Sunday, we went to the ice rink to go skating. I spent hours with Lauren on the ice holding her up as I taught her how to skate. I enjoyed this peaceful time with her.

I was growing in my faith and depending more and more on God's provision. I went on a few dates but knew in my heart that I was not ready, nor interested. I had had enough of men and relationships to last a while. I needed time to heal, to discover who I was, and to spend time with my daughter. I made an agreement with God that I would not date for at least five years. I didn't want to look at another man anyway—I hated them, and I put them all in the same category as Matt. I saw them all as Matts. Selfish and mean, fulfilling their own desires and needs. I needed some work done on my heart.

The court granted me full custody, but Matt had weekend visitation, which he hardly showed up for, and when he did, I worried the whole time. I had no clue where or what he was doing with Lauren, nor did I want to question Lauren and put her on the spot. She was just a little girl. I was careful not to put my daughter in between us. Yet I did not want harm to come to her. So I began to do what I could, what I saw my mom do many times when she could do nothing else: I prayed for God's protective hand to be upon Lauren. Matt was ordered to pay child support, but I never got a dime from him. He would work for a while but not long enough for the government to catch up with him to garnish his wages. Even though the money could have been very helpful, I was okay with eventually severing all ties with Matt. I did not want Lauren in that kind of environment. Matt was just not responsible or safe.

Chapter 7

Awake, O sleeper, rise up from the dead, and Christ will give you light.
—Ephesians 5:14b

A short time after Matt and I split up, I found a job at a family-run business, wholesalers for hunting and fishing equipment. The family I worked for was very kind. After several months, I learned a lot about each of the family members, the owners, their daughter, son, and son in-law. They all worked at the business except one son, Brad, whom I had never met, but I'd heard many things about him like how much he and I apparently had in common. The family was a little different than my own, a little more reserved, so I wasn't too convinced when they tried to set us up. Besides, I figured I was done with guys. I didn't want to hook up with anyone for a long time.

After almost two years, I had grown closer to the family, and I felt like part of their family. Lauren and I were invited to their homes for dinners. This made everyone even more determined to try to match their son with me, but I didn't want any part of it. One day, while visiting my neighbor who lived in the same building as I did, the phone rang. My friend answered it, looked at the receiver with a puzzled look, and handed it to me.

"It's for you," my friend said, shrugging.

"Really? Who is it?"

My friend shrugged again, saying, "I don't know."

"Hello?" I said into the receiver, confused.

"Umm, hi! My name is Brad, and my mom gave me this number. Is this Sam?" The man's voice sounded crackly, like he was nervous.

"Yeeees," I said, again confused because I didn't know any Brads. Why was this guy calling me on my friend's number?

"Well, I know this is kind of awkward." I nodded as if Brad could see me through the phone. "But you work for my parents, and I'm calling you to see if you'd like to go out for a beer and maybe some wings?" I could feel the question ringing in my ear. Was this for real?

"Huh? I mean, wait. You're John and Silvia's son?" I asked, surprised.

"Yup, that's me," he said. I could feel his smile through the phone.

"Okay, so pardon my shock, I was totally not expecting your phone call," I said. I didn't have a phone but used this number in case of emergencies. I had not given permission for anyone to give it out to potential boyfriends.

"Umm . . . my mom," he said with a half-nervous laugh, "and my sister, they told me to call you."

"Oh reeeally?" I said. The phone went silent for a moment as I was pondering what I was going to say to those two women.

"I'm sorry. I thought they would have told you. I feel really awkward now. Thank God you don't know me or where I live," Brad said with an embarrassed tone in his voice.

"No! But I'll deal with them later," I said with a little chuckle. "And I'll go out for a drink with you and some wings."

I couldn't believe I was actually agreeing to this. I had made a deal with God that I would wait at least five years, enough time to get my life straightened out. I didn't want to get into another relationship. I had been in too many that had broken my heart and my spirit. I was torn. I thought after a year and a half of the family bugging me, I knew they had good intentions, and they had been good to me. I felt honored that they thought I was good enough to go out with their son. I could at least honor them and do this one-time thing and hope this would be the end of it. I thought if they really knew me, my past, they wouldn't be so quick to set their son up with me.

"Oh, wow, okay, how about Saturday?" Brad said excitedly. "I'll pick you up around six, and we can go to Kelsey's or something." Kelsey's was a restaurant with a variety of choices from burgers, chicken wings to salads and pasta dishes.

"Okay, sounds good. Do you want my address, or do you already have that too?" I asked, unable to keep the smile from my voice.

"Uhhh, I already have it," Brad said with a little chuckle.

"Okay, see you then," I said as I hung up and looked at my friend. "I guess I have a date with the boss's son," I grinned. I was going to have a few words with my boss's family, those sneaky people. I thought it was kind of cute though, and I felt honored that they would go to this extent to set us up.

On Saturday, I was nervous all day waiting for Brad to pick me up. I checked my hair over and over again and changed my clothes too many times. When I heard the knock on the door, I checked in the mirror one last time before opening it. I tried not to look surprised when I opened the door to find what was on the other side. He certainly was cute but in a geeky way. He had big eyeglasses on, and he was shorter than I expected, but not shorter than me, and skinny, with a cute head of blond hair. He was nothing like the guys I had dated. He looked so young, like he was twelve years old. I noticed later, after a few sneak peeks, that he did have a muscular build and a cute butt, which certainly was a plus.

I smiled while turning around to grab my purse and grinning thinking, *Here it goes*. When we got down to the parking area of the apartment complex, Brad headed towards a beat-up gray Ford pick-up truck.

"Wait . . . this is your truck?" I asked, unable to keep the note of surprise from my voice.

"Yes . . . sorry, you don't like it?" Brad said, apologetically.

"Sure, I like it. It's just that it's . . . so different from what the rest of your family drives, like Cadillacs, Lexus, Mercedes, you know . . . fancy cars," I said, shrugging my shoulders.

"SOOO does this mean it's a deal breaker? You don't wanna go out with me 'cause I don't have a fancy car?" Brad asked, confused.

"Oh, no, no, that's not it." I slapped my forehead with the palm of my hand. "I guess I'm just surprised, that's all. No, I'm not like that. I didn't wanna go out with you, remember? I mean . . . okay, forget it, I'm putting my foot in my mouth." I felt my face turn red in embarrassment. What I'd wanted to say had definitely turned out completely wrong. I felt like sticking my head in a hole and hiding.

"Naaah, that's okay. I think I understand," he said, with a little half chuckle, which sounded like half the truth. "I'm a little different than my family," he added.

I was sensing that. I was not against having money or nice stuff, but with all I had gone through, what I desired the most was a sincere heart, one who was honest and true to who they were.

We drove to Kelsey's just a few miles from my apartment. After we sat at a table, we ordered chicken wings and beer. I didn't really care for beer but decided to get one anyway so it wouldn't be awkward for him. Brad was the sweetest thing. Sure, he was different than any of the guys I had dated, but that was probably a good thing. Since my past relationships weren't anything to brag about, why not go to the other extreme? He was intelligent, fun to talk to, and very polite. He opened doors for me and pulled out my chair for me to sit. It wasn't that he was ugly; he was just a little awkward or maybe it was I who was awkward around him. He wasn't like any guy I had gone out with. He wasn't tall and muscular. He seemed quiet, gentle. He reminded me of the "nice guy next door" type that the girls liked to talk to, wanted to get advice from, but was too nice to date. I was surprised how different he was from the rest of his family too. His family was more reserved, stuffy. Brad seemed laid back. He liked sports and loved to ski, boat, water ski, and camp. I don't think the rest of his family was like that. As the night went on, I felt a little butterfly, just one at first, fluttering around in my stomach.

We spent several hours just talking. I found out that he had been married and that it had been bad from the beginning. I wanted to know why he had married her, even though I had done the same thing.

"We were . . . very different from one another," Brad said, crinkling up his face.

"In which way? I mean were you just not compatible? Did you not know this when you married her? Were you drunk?" I laughed. Brad laughed too.

"No, I wasn't drunk, just stupid, I guess. I didn't see the clear signs that were flashing all around me. I wanted to get married, but it just wasn't easy for me to get a date, you know," he said, as he pointed to himself as if to say, *Just look at me, right?* "So when I met her in a bar and she paid attention to me, I decided to ask her out. When she said yes, I jumped at the opportunity." He looked down at his beer and took a drink.

"Sooo it sounds like you were surprised? Like no one else would like you so you kind of took the first one and ran?" I asked, confused.

"Weeell, I guess now that I said it out loud, it sounds like that, huh?" he said with a thoughtful expression on his face as he worked on peeling the label off the beer bottle. He seemed to be in deep thought about his past relationship, a little uncomfortable talking about it. "Maybe I did."

"So what happened?" I asked, curious.

"Well, she had mental issues that I was unaware of. She also had an eating disorder, which I was willing to support her in getting the help she needed to overcome it, but she didn't think it was a problem. I'd find food hidden all over the house. She did nothing but sit around, watch TV and eat. I tried everything, even wanting to go to therapy with her, but she wouldn't. She made it seem like I was the problem. After some time, I just gave up and couldn't deal with it anymore," he said, with a sense of deep sadness as he took another swig of his beer. "How about you?"

I was not ready to share my life with him. It was more complicated than his. I didn't really know this guy, if I could trust him. There were still some deep wounds and fears I had to work on. I still had a thing about trusting a man. "Maybe another time." I said. "I'm sorry, I'm just not ready. My marriage was . . . difficult. It's hard for me to talk about it. I'm still working on a few things." I felt bad that he had shared his heart and I couldn't.

"Okay, hey, no problem, really," Brad said, waving me off. "Don't sweat it. When you are ready, you'll know."

That definitely gave him extra points for not pushing me and for being understanding. He did have an awesome smile, and I felt comfortable with him. He was easy to talk to.

As we were leaving, Brad casually asked, "Next Saturday, would you like to go out mini golfing and maybe get some pizza?" He looked down shyly, kicking a rock with his shoe.

"Okay, sure, sounds good! I love mini golf. I just need to find a sitter though, but let me call you to let you know for sure," I said, surprised he asked me out again. I was excited. I liked him, and I was looking forward to getting to know him more as a good friend.

We walked out to his truck. "So what's up with the truck?" I asked, laughing out loud.

"Oh, if you haven't noticed, I'm kind of a little guy, and I feel way bigger and taller in that truck. Kind of boosts my manliness," Brad said with a laugh. "I just like trucks. I'm kind of a country boy at heart. Trucks and country music."

I thought that was funny and cute. I really liked him. It felt good being around him. I felt relaxed and that I could be myself, and not have to prove anything. He seemed down to earth and simple. I could do simple—I didn't need anything complicated right now in my life, or ever again.

Of course, when Monday came and I went to work, all eyes were on me when I came through the door. They were all waiting, anxious to hear about how our date went. The minute I walked in the door, they were hounding me with questions. I had to laugh. I told them I thought he was nice, that we were just friends, and that we were going to hang out a bit next Saturday if I could find a sitter. Brad's sister piped up right away and said she would take her and that Lauren could hang out at her house while Brad and I went out.

"Oh, okay, thanks," I said, looking at her with a grin, knowing what she was up to. She was more than willing to help Brad and I hook up. "You're awfully quick at offering to take her! You guys are cracking me up!"

I was swept off my feet. I fell in love with Brad. I loved his company and his gentleness. He seemed so genuine and so different from any guy I knew. I tested him often, asked him about his job, how long he'd been working, what were his aspirations for the future, where he saw himself in a few years, how he was in the company of friends and family. I wanted to see if he truly was who he said he was and if he really loved me and was devoted to me and me alone. I let him chase me; I did not push the relationship. I was scared. I had been hurt so many times, and my self-esteem was not too high. I was scared to let my guard down, to be taken advantage of, to be vulnerable.

I saw so much in Brad that I longed to be a part of his life forever. He may not have been the tall, muscular, long-haired hippy type I was used to, but I liked this new kind of man. He was stable, smart, and a hard worker. After each date, we grew closer and closer to where we saw each other daily. It was harder and harder to be apart from one another. Brad seemed to be a part of me now, and I eventually moved in with him and broke the promise I had made to God. It was supposed to be his way, his timing, and no dating for five years.

For many years, I struggled with this. Not the decision to marry Brad but the decision to move in with him. How I so easily dismissed in my head what I swore I would never do again. I wanted to live the dream of one day doing it right, walking down the church aisle to marry my true soul mate in a white gown with family, close friends, and God as witness to a beautiful union between two people in love becoming one. I accepted the fact that that dream would never happen. We were married in Jamaica with Lauren as our witness. Even though it all worked out, I felt ashamed that I did not trust enough in God and had not been patient with him. I had to grieve the loss of a wedding day I had so longed for, I so desired deep in my heart. Not for the dress or the people or party, but for myself, my desire to be pure and whole for my husband. I did not stand whole before him; many pieces of my heart had been given away. Everything in my life so far seemed to have happened so quickly, and I got caught in the whirlwind of events. I had allowed my feelings to take over rational thinking, only to fall into unhealthy, broken relationships, giving pieces of myself away to each, bit by bit.

I knew that God knew my heart and that the gift he gave me in my husband, Brad, was huge. I was truly grateful for that. Brad was an amazing husband, father, and best friend. We couldn't have been a better match for one another.

It was difficult to share my past life with my kids; it still brought shame and embarrassment. I knew I had made mistakes and that there was a cost to my choices. I wanted my children to experience what I hadn't but had longed for, the beauty of marrying their soul mate, of walking down the aisle in white on the outside, and on the inside, the white standing for purity of heart and soul, not leaving parts of them to someone else. I wanted them to be whole to the one they married. I knew I had little control over them understanding that because they had not lived and experienced what I had experienced in my life.

They did not understand the fact that with each relationship, I had given a part of myself away. I did not feel whole, pure, or clean when I married Brad. I did not tell him this, but I felt it. I had left much of myself behind the "then" line. The shadow of every relationship I was in attended my wedding with Brad. They stood there with me as I took Brad as my husband. They came into the bedroom with us. They followed me around, reminding me that I was broken and unclean. Even though this wasn't true in God's eyes, that I was his child, cleansed in the blood of his son, I still felt the effect of my past. No one could understand the pain, hurt, and loss I felt within me.

There were many "in hindsight" moments for me in my life. I saw myself as a baby Christian, so new to the faith, relationships, and really to the whole idea of a new life. I wasn't really good at always seeing the whole, overall picture. I did a lot of what felt right at the time and not so much of what was right and good overall. Complicated. I grew spiritually and moved away from the "then" part of my life. My thoughts and actions changed as my mind was being renewed. God spoke about baby Christians drinking milk at first, the first steps before learning how to eat more solid food. Looking back, I saw the immaturity in my spiritual walk. As I moved closer to it, I realized how little I knew and how thirsty I was to know more of his ways and for him to purify my heart.

Life got more complicated as I was raising my kids. I didn't want them to do what I'd done. I didn't know how much or how little to tell them of my past. I didn't want to give the impression that what I'd done was okay. I wanted so much more for my children.

It was hard to explain to them when I had done the exact opposite of what I was trying to teach them to do. They could use my past against me, and I wished I could go back and do it over, but then I also knew I wouldn't have met Brad. My life worked out with Brad, yet I spent many years trying to erase the past and be able to be fully there for Brad. It wasn't easy. It made me feel guilty, not being able to give him my full self.

During our honeymoon in Jamaica, we'd sit by the pool or on the beach and Lauren's voice would keep ringing in the air around us. "Mom, mom, watch. Brad look at me. Mom, Brad, Mom, Brad." We tried to put her in camp at the resort one morning, but Lauren cried and complained about it, not ever wanting to go back, so she ended up being the center of our attention all week. It wasn't something we had planned on doing. We picked this particular resort because of the kids' camp, so Brad and I could have alone time together. We never did have alone time or strolls on the beach or dinner by candlelight. It made me sad in a way. Torn. I wanted Lauren to be there, but I also wanted to have time alone with Brad.

The wedding was beautiful, simple, and I was so happy marrying Brad. He truly was my soul mate, and we certainly could not leave Lauren out of it. But again, I missed out on my perfect wedding, perfect honeymoon. We had two random hotel employees, I think a gardener and a cook, as our maid of honor and best man. Their faces ended up in most of our wedding pictures. Lauren never left our side too. We first planned a wedding at home surrounded by family, but it was filled with many opinions of how we should do it or not do it. The fact that we had both been married, even though it was different this time for us, it felt as though others didn't feel it was as special. My relationship with Brad was not like the others; it was a two-way deal. We loved doing things for each other, cooking together, cleaning. I felt cheated that we both didn't get a do-over, a special wedding, our wedding, because we had done the big deal once before.

To say our beginnings were without challenges would be lying. We had challenges of a blended family. All of a sudden, Brad had not only a wife, but a child as well. He had missed the first five years with

Lauren. He treated her like a daughter, but I could see the challenges of raising another man's child while her father popped in and out of her life. The few times Lauren went to visit her biological father, she came home with an attitude and treated Brad poorly. I knew it must have been hard for Lauren too. I didn't know how to handle it. I was already feeling plenty of guilt for what I had put Lauren through during her first several years of life. I did a lot of the parenting through guilt and allowed Lauren to have pretty much what she wanted, which ended up putting a huge strain on my relationship with Brad.

I saw Brad step back many times, and as I recall those times, I knew what I had done wasn't the best choice. But I didn't have a crystal ball to look into and ask what the right thing was. I knew for sure that I deeply loved Lauren and that Lauren loved me and I wanted all the good things in life for her. It was a struggle and a deep sense of guilt that I carried for a long time, and it did have consequences for them as time went by. I learned that parenting was the hardest thing I ever had to do in life. At times, it could be the most rewarding, the most fulfilling, and at other times, it was full of the deepest pain, hardship, and a keen sense of failure. Most of all, I could not do it alone. I needed my God to help guide me through each step. I knew I didn't know what I was doing most of the time, and I would have given up a long time ago because of the failures I'd previously experienced, yet my God pushed me through, and I was forever grateful to him.

Besides our challenges with Lauren and raising a family, Brad and I had so many things in common. We got along really well and grew strong together; we became a team. We felt comfortable with one another and were excited to see what the future held. It was as if we fit together like two puzzle pieces, and Brad's family jokingly reminded us often that they were the ones who had put us together. We would smile at them and nod our heads, bow down, and thank them profusely for the wonderful act of kindness of putting us together.

Chapter 8

*We can rejoice, too, when we run into problems and trials,
for we know that they help us develop endurance.*
—Romans 5:3

A few days before Brad and I were married, Brad's company announced that it was closing its doors. It was quite a shock to us both and not a great beginning to our new lives together. It was terrible timing, a week before we were leaving to fly to Jamaica to get married. I knew that there was no way I could support us both on my income. Brad worked as an engineer designing gear couplings for steel mills. He had a lot of skills he could lean on while seeking another place of employment, but it would probably take some time. The week before leaving was a very stressful week, and we were wondering if we should still go, what we would do, and how we would pay our mortgage.

Two days before we were to leave, Brad received a call from a company in Michigan, a competitor, looking for an engineer. We couldn't believe it! It was crazy what had taken place in just one week—losing a job unexpectedly and being offered another. They told him they were interested in offering him a position. They had done some business with Brad before and knew his credentials were solid, so the job was his if he wanted it. They asked Brad not to make a decision until he took a trip to come and check out the company. Brad told them he would consider going to visit and would talk to me about it.

Brad also shared the fact that he was going to Jamaica to get married in a few days. Garret, the owner, said that Brad could come the week after we returned. Brad asked me what I thought about moving to another country. Even though it was right underneath Canada, it still felt so . . . foreign.

"Michigan? I mean isn't it dangerous over there? I hear of so many shootings happening in Detroit. And what about Lauren? I don't know if I can take her out of the country." I had many unanswered questions. It was hard when I didn't really know anything about the United States. All one really heard about the country to the south of us is that there were lots of violence.

"It's on the other side of the state a few hours west of Detroit. The owner says it's a small town right on the edge of Lake Michigan. You know, I love small towns. I really hate it here in the city. Burlington is getting bigger, more populated. I don't like it," Brad said. "Remember I'm more the truck and country guy."

"Ha-ha . . . yes, dear, I do remember. I hate the city too. What's the worst thing that could happen? We hate it and just don't take the job? Right?" I said, looking at him with excitement. "We really have nothing to lose. It'll be a nice adventure for us to take a drive and look."

"Yeah, thanks, Sam. If we're interested in the job, we'll look into all the other stuff we need to check into first to see if it's possible. Let's just keep an open mind about it." We both agreed to take a trip to check it out when we returned from Jamaica. We'd be officially married. I was excited! Things were coming together. A whole new adventure with my new husband.

The trip to South Haven, Michigan, took almost seven hours. After crossing the border into Detroit, we must have taken a wrong turn, which ended up taking us to an unsafe part of the city. Brad stopped at the first gas station, which was run down, and got out of the car, locking it as he exited. I watched Brad approach three guys standing outside of the station. He spoke to them briefly then returned quickly to the car.

"What did they say?" I said, feeling anxious and in a hurry to get on our way.

"'What the hell you doing in this part of town?' That's what they said," Brad said as he quickly got in the car and locked the doors. He started the car, hands shaking, and drove out of the parking lot. "They pointed to where the highway was and told me to get the hell out!"

"Well, this makes me feel a whole lot better about moving to Michigan," I said, feeling more anxious now to get out of there quickly before anything happened to us. I hoped this town we were going to was much nicer than this place.

Brad didn't say anything except shrug and grin at me. I'm sure he was thinking the same thing. When we arrived in the town of South Haven, we went directly to the office. The owner, Garret, and his wife, Mary, were there to greet us. They were so sweet. They welcomed us with open arms. They had also booked a special honeymoon suite at a hotel for us. When we checked into our room, there were flowers and a fruit basket congratulating us on getting married.

"Oh my gosh, that is so sweet! I like them already," I said, so touched by how they welcomed us.

"Yeah, me too. I feel good here. It feels like home already," said Brad with a big smile.

We freshened up. Garret, Mary, the plant manager, and his wife all came to pick us up in Mary's Toyota minivan. They drove around to show us the town, the lake, and beaches. There were two beaches, the North Beach and the South Beach, which were divided by a river in between. Down the river was where the boat slips were and the boat house. They parked the car, and we walked along the beach for a bit. Brad and I kept stealing glances at one another, our eyes filled with awe; we were falling in love with the place. It was so beautiful and quaint. The town sat right along the shore of Lake Michigan. The sand was like none I had ever seen, almost pure white and soft. The sound of the water coming onto shore was soothing to my ears. I loved being close to the water. It was in my blood; both my parents grew up by the water.

At dinner, they talked about the company, what their goals were, and the family-like environment they had and continued to strive to maintain. Brad and I felt that immediately. Everyone was so kind. Each in our own thoughts, Brad and I felt in our hearts that this was the place we wanted to be, to work and raise a family. To move away from the hustle and bustle of city life, the stress of traffic, and the fact that it took so long just to go to the store five minutes away. It wasn't the life we wanted, living in the city; we both wanted a more laid back, relaxed life, a new beginning for our life together, and I loved the idea of leaving my old life behind, moving further away from the "then" in my mind and in physical distance. I wanted to put the people and places that continued to remind me of "then" farther away from me. This was the perfect opportunity to do it.

On the drive home, Brad and I talked about the pros and cons of taking the job and moving. We both ended up with more pros than cons and decided to take a leap of faith and accept the offer. Brad would be making more than his last job, plus all his medical expenses would be paid. We still had a few bumps to go over: getting a work visa, getting permission to take Lauren out of the country, and selling our house.

Going through the courts to have permission to move Lauren out of the country took a little time. Since Lauren's dad, Matt, never paid child support nor showed up for visitation, it made it much easier to get the courts to terminate Matt's parental rights to Lauren. Matt lost all rights of opinion and decisions pertaining to Lauren, which gave me the freedom to move anywhere I wanted to, including another country.

It was not something I wanted to do to Lauren or Matt, for that matter. I wanted Lauren to know her dad and to have a good relationship with him. But over time, it proved to be very unhealthy for Lauren. Matt was not responsible and only broke Lauren's heart by not showing up and breaking many promises to her over and over again. It also broke my heart in so many ways as I wanted the best for both of them. Even though Matt hurt me in so many ways, I still cared about his well-being. I wanted him to have a good life, to get clean, but I knew that I had no control over that. Matt had many opportunities to change his life, and I knew I had to move on with mine. I had made the mistake of feeling sorry for him too many times; he took complete advantage of me and never followed through with his promises to change.

The whole process of moving took several months. It was a learning experience for us both as to what was needed to move across the border to a new country, a country just hours west of us. Brad had to apply for a green card, which would allow him to work in the United States. The company had to put ads in three different papers to advertise the job, giving those in the United States a chance to apply, giving the American citizens opportunity to get a job in their own county, before employing someone from another country. Because of the uniqueness of the job, there were only several people who were qualified in the world, which was an advantage for Brad. There were no qualified people who applied for the job, so it was his.

The house sold within days after we put it up on the market, and by the time the closing day came, Brad and I had everything ready for the move. We were both excited and nervous for our new beginning together, a fresh start. The moving truck came and loaded all our stuff. Brad would drive his truck, and Lauren and I would follow behind in my car.

It was difficult leaving my family, mostly my mom and sister, Rachael. We were close, but I felt that Brad and I needed a fresh start to our lives together. I didn't want to leave my family, but I knew that we could often visit each other since we were only seven hours away. But I was a little concerned about Lauren. It was a big change in a short amount of time, on top of moving away from the two people she loved more than anything, her grandma and grandpa. Lauren was also close to her aunt, my sister, and cousins. My mom and dad had helped out a lot, helped take care of Lauren. They took her when I was running from Matt, which were some tough years. My parents were a safe haven for Lauren and for me too.

My dad, whom I was never close to, had a special bond with Lauren. I saw him pour so much love into her, a love I, myself, had never experienced. I would watch my dad with Lauren, the way he was so gentle with her and so protective. He often got mad at me about Matt, concerned about the situation I was putting Lauren in. Yet it was confusing to me because my dad had never given me that protection or the love he so freely lavished on my own child. I was jealous yet happy that Lauren was so loved by him. I wondered what had shifted in my dad. Why now? After many years, I sought his love and approval. Maybe he was repaying me through his love for

Lauren. I sometimes saw it in his eyes when he looked at me, the sadness and guilt. Lauren could do anything to my dad—she had him wrapped around her little finger.

We said our good-byes to family and friends, mostly Brad's friends. I didn't have many friends since I left them all behind after my life took a turn away from the drug and party scene. I had met people at the church I was attending, but I wasn't really close to any of them. When I went to church, Brad would often tag along. I wasn't sure if he was a believer or not. He didn't seem to participate and didn't talk about his faith or lack thereof. I didn't want to bring it up because I wanted him to go along with me. I enjoyed his company. I felt safe and secure, and I was scared if I confronted him he would stop going with me. I sensed that he loved me very much and that was why he went to church with me, but I thought I'd pray for him and just leave the converting to God. As much as I desired Brad to experience what I had, I knew myself that no one had convinced me to believe. I had to find my faith and own it for myself. I had an encounter with God that was personal, that opened my eyes to his love and truth. I know that Brad would have to have his own encounter with him.

All was packed up and ready to go. After crossing the border into Michigan, I really felt the realness of it all. I felt my life physically crossing the line into a new beginning. I felt such a freedom come over me as if the "then" was really behind me for good.

I had passed Brad on the highway after Brad got stuck behind a truck. I tried to keep an eye on him, hoping at some point he would pass me and be in the lead again. After a few miles, I lost track of him. I didn't know the way since I had only been there once. I panicked and pulled over on the busy highway to wait for Brad to pass me. After twenty minutes, there was no Brad. Back then, cell phones weren't available without paying a high cost to get one installed in your car. A police car pulled up behind me, and the officer got out of his car and walked over to my car. I cranked the window open.

"Everything all right, ma'am?" he asked, concerned.

"Well . . . yes. I just lost my husband," I said, a little worried.

"Well, ma'am," he said with a little chuckle, "most women would be happy about that."

I laughed too; it did sound funny. "I'm not to that point yet. I'd like to keep him a little longer. I passed him a while back but not sure where he is."

"Okay, be careful and good luck finding him," he said, turning around and going back to his car.

My heart was pounding fast—I was getting more worried as the time ticked away. After another twenty minutes, Brad pulled up behind me. I sighed in relief. He walked over to the car.

"Where did you go? What happened? I was worried," I said, trying to calm my breathing.

"What?" Brad asked, confused. "Didn't you see me pass you? I drove for a while and noticed you weren't behind me. I pulled over to wait, but you never came so I turned around. I'm so glad you're both okay. It scared me," Brad said in a frantic tone of voice.

"Me too! That was scary. Okay, so I promise not to pass you again. I will follow you closely," I said as Brad bent down to give me a kiss and waved to Lauren.

When we arrived, the moving truck had already arrived. It was late afternoon. We were moving into a beautiful new home that Brad's new boss owned until we searched for a home of our own. I wished we could have purchased it, but it was beyond what we could afford. The home had never been lived in; we were the first. It had two stories with three bedrooms, two on the second floor and the master on the main floor. The living room was large with cathedral ceilings and a large stone fireplace. The kitchen was large with an island and granite countertops and dark mahogany cabinets. It was amazing. We settled in, and Brad began his new job the following Monday. It was early October, and by early November, we had already received an invitation to join Brad's boss's family on a skiing trip to Colorado. Brad and I had never been there, but we loved to ski. We caravanned down to Colorado together, which took two days. It was a boring drive, flat lands most of the way until we reached the beginning of the mountains just east of Denver. It started with seeing little peaks way on the horizon, but as we continued driving toward them, the mountains grew and grew and grew. What began so small, unrecognizable, grew into a beautiful picture. The pictures I saw of the mountains in magazines did not do justice to seeing it with my own eyes. It was the first time I had ever seen mountains.

I could not get over how beautiful it was in the mountains of Colorado. The first few days though, I had altitude sickness. It was awful. I was dizzy, light headed, and threw up several times. I stayed in bed for the first few days while everyone else went skiing. I was sad missing out, but I was in no shape to even get out of bed. After a few days, I was good to go. We skied down a mountain each day and swam in the outside heated pool surrounded by snow and mountains. I loved it. I found out what an amazing skier Brad was and that he had gone on many ski trips over the years, not always on the trails but sometimes flying up to remote areas to ski down steep parts of the mountain. It was interesting to me how I continued to learn more and more about Brad, especially the fact that he seemed to enjoy taking risks. I was careful not to share too much of my past; I wanted to leave that part of me behind. It was enough to have shared my previous broken and abusive marriage with him, let alone the details of my broken, chaotic life prior to that.

A little over a month after returning home from our trip to Colorado, I wasn't feeling well. Everything I ate would come right back up, and the smell of food nauseated me. I had a feeling I might be pregnant and went to the store to purchase a pregnancy test. Brad and I stared at the wand, nervously, as we waited for the results. When the lines turned up red, we both jumped and yelled at the same time. We were so excited. Tears filled our eyes as we just stared at the results. I could still remember the feeling of elation I had at that moment. It was another step further away from the "then" into building a new life I so yearned for. There was now hope for the home with the white picket fence, the happy marriage, and the wonderful children.

I was sick throughout most of my pregnancy. My parents came to stay with us that Christmas to help us out. I could hardly stand up due to nausea. My sister, Rachael, and her two children came for a short visit too during the Christmas holidays. The kids had fun, and they all played games as I spent most of the time lying on the couch. On New Year's Eve, we played the game Gestures. We took turns standing up and acting out the words on the card, trying to get our team to guess as many of the words within a minute and to accumulate as many points as we could. We laughed so hard. We had never seen our dad be so silly and such a good sport; we all had tears running down our faces and hurt bellies from the laughter. It felt good to laugh, to feel happy and free.

By New Year's Day, I was feeling a little better, the days were up and down, so we all decided to go skating. We called a place in the next town over to see what the skating times were: two to four o'clock. We all loaded up the cars with our skates and headed out. When we all arrived at the rink and looked around, we saw people going in. We grabbed our skates and headed in to find out that it was not an ice rink but a roller rink. We all looked at one another and busted out laughing. When you say *rink* in Canada, it's an ice rink, but apparently, it's not the same in the United States. They clearly weren't as fond of hockey as Canadians were!

No worries, the gang decided it would be fun to go roller-skating. We rented roller skates, put them on and headed to the rink. My mom and dad made their way to the little practice rink on the side. I wasn't too keen on Mom going skating or roller-skating, but she insisted. She said she did not want to miss out on the fun. We had not been there long when my dad was waving and yelling to us all to come over.

"Mom 'urt herself. I tink she broke 'er leg!" Dad said frantically, his French accent deeper and harder to understand when he was scared or stressed out. "They are calling the 'ospital to send an ambulance." French people don't pronounce their *H*s where there is one and put an *h* where there isn't one. So, your hair is 'air' and the air is 'hair'.

"Dad, breathe. What are you saying? What happened?" I asked him as I reached over the wall and grabbed his hand.

"Mom . . . she fell! She's 'urt!" he said as he kept looking in the direction of where my mom was laying on the ground, people surrounding her.

"Oh crap!" I said making my way around the wall along with the others.

"Kids, go take your skates off and meet me over there." I pointed toward the crowd. "Nanny hurt herself, and an ambulance is coming."

Rachael and I rushed over to where our mom was laying in the middle of the rink holding onto her ankle. It did not look good—it was twisted in a weird way. The man next to her said an ambulance was on the way. They brought her to the local hospital to take x-rays of her foot. She had broken and fractured it in several places. They had to do surgery to repair it and place some pins in her leg. She was for sure going to spend a few days in the hospital depending on the severity of the injury.

My dad, sister, and I stayed at the hospital while Brad and my sister's boyfriend took the kids back to my house. The surgery took several hours and went well, but it would be a long road to recovery; there had been lots of damage done to her ankle.

"I knew she shouldn't 'ave gone," my dad said, in a voice full of regret.

"Well, Dad, we can't change it now. I know it's too bad, but we gotta deal with the situation the best we can," Rachael said, glancing at me as she gritted her teeth. I could tell she was a little bit frustrated with our dad.

"It looks like you'll be staying in Michigan a little while longer, at least until Mom gets a little better. Well, enough to travel back and see her own doctor," I said with compassion, putting my arm around my dad. "It'll be okay, Dad."

"I guess," said my dad, not looking too happy about the situation. He always looked like a lost puppy when my mom was not around. He didn't seem to know what to do, how to take care of himself.

We stayed at the hospital with our mom for several hours and then left for home. My sister was leaving the next day; she and her boyfriend had to go back to work. She was feeling bad about it. I reassured her that I would take care of mom and dad.

"Sam, I know you can take care of her, but you're not feeling well yourself," Rachael said patting me on the back and looking at me with confidence.

"We'll manage. Dad and Lauren can also help," I said with a grin.

"Yeah, okay, good luck with that!" Rachael said, rolling her eyes. "I'm sure Lauren will be a big help." We both laughed, knowing that our dad was going to be lost, not knowing what to do.

My mom stayed in the hospital for three days until the doctor said she could come back to my house. Everyone was good at helping and pitching in. I was still nauseated most of the time, and my mom felt so bad about ruining everyone's holiday.

"Mom, stop," I said. "It's not something you planned on doing, breaking your ankle. It just happened."

"But I shouldn't have insisted on roller-skating when you all told me otherwise. I just didn't want to be a party pooper. Seems like I always have to sit out of everything," my mom said, feeling guilty for breaking her foot.

I knew what my mom meant. She had many things physically wrong with her, and she had dealt with these things all her life. She was tired of all her limitations. She wanted to, for once, do something spontaneous and fun. I sat by her and just held her. We sat quietly together, each inside our own thoughts, not needing to say a word; there was already an understanding between us. After a month at my house, my mom was released to travel back home to Canada. I was glad she was recovering, but I knew I was going to miss them. I enjoyed their visit, even under the circumstances. I missed home and my family.

The months passed, and my belly grew. We didn't know what gender the baby was; we wanted it to be a surprise. We were working on names for both a girl and a boy. We had bought a house and moved in a few months before the baby was due, which allowed us a bit of time to get the room ready. The due date was the end of July, and when June arrived, I started craving watermelon. I would send Brad out to get me one and then sit to eat half of it in one sitting. I remember my craving with Lauren was ice cream sundaes with pineapple and strawberries.

The last two weeks of my pregnancy, I was miserable. I just wanted this baby out. My neighbor friends, whom I had met when we moved in, took me down to the lake a few times, hoping the crashing waves would help hurry the process along. They tried everything: took me on many walks, the beach, going for a car ride down a bumpy road. I was happy I had friends who cared so much about me, and I didn't want to tell them when I had enough. Finally, several days after the due date, I started having hard contractions late at night. I lay in bed, trying not to wake Brad up, staring at my watch every time I had a contraction to see how far apart they were and how long they lasted. The time in between got shorter and the contractions got stronger and stronger. We had a plan to send Lauren down to the neighbors. I decided at six in the morning, when I couldn't wait any longer, to wake Brad up and tell him it was time.

"Brad, wake up," I whispered as I shook him gently, not wanting to startle him.

"Mmmmmmmmmm," came out of Brad.

"Brad," I said a little louder with a harder shake, "it's time!"

"Time? Time for what, honey?" Brad said half-asleep.

"Time for the baby to come out!" I said louder as a contraction went through my body.

Brad shot out of bed like a madman. "Really, let's go, oh my gosh." He looked around, not knowing what to do.

"Brad, you need to put on some clothes," I said, kind of laughing between my contractions. "I'm all ready to go, got my bag. Just waiting on you to bring Lauren down the street and bring us to the hospital."

"Okay, okay, I'm getting ready," Brad said as he walked around looking for his clothes in the wrong places. I had to point him in the right direction and keep reminding him of what he was supposed to be doing. It was quite a humorous scene that I wished could have been caught on video.

Finally, he managed to get dressed, bring Lauren to the neighbor, and get me into the car and to the hospital. When I was nearing delivery, they gave me an epidural, and at eleven in the morning, we gave birth to a beautiful baby girl. Brad got to see the whole thing and cut the umbilical cord. I remember how overjoyed Brad was. I was too, but to see Brad experience it for the first time was precious. He held his baby girl and cried like a baby himself. We named her Alissa. She was perfect! Nine pounds, three ounces, twenty-one inches long. Ten toes and ten fingers. No hair, like when Lauren was born. She also would be a towhead, completely white hair. Looking at her, I wondered how that huge thing had even come out of me.

The hospital pretty much kicked us out the next day, which was okay with me. I wanted to go home anyway. The days and weeks after that seemed a blur with getting used to another child, a baby. I had a really hard time trying to breastfeed. I was sore and in agony, which took away from enjoying Alissa. Brad was frustrated because he didn't know how to help, and of course, he couldn't breastfeed her himself. Life was a little chaotic. I didn't like the first weeks of adjustment. Lauren was six and a half, more independent, and to me, it was like starting all over again. I felt depressed and struggled with my feelings because I loved Alissa so much; she was such a sweet baby, yet I was exhausted and just felt like a milking machine. The first month felt long until things slowly started to feel like we were getting into a routine, and Brad and I felt more comfortable with our new baby and parenthood in general.

The memories of those times are so fresh in my mind, and it all seems like it was just yesterday. I remember holding my babies, their smells, good and bad, their little feet and hands—the first coo, their loud cries, their first words and first steps. Then, their busy two's and their sassy three's, their blankets they loved so much and their sweet, deep laughter when we tickle them. I enjoyed being a mom. I wanted to savor every moment. In time too, Brad adopted Lauren after we lost contact with her biological father. Brad wanted to make it official and for us to be a family.

Things were going well. We were attending a new church, Christian Reformed, a little bit out of town in the middle of nowhere. It was unlike the traditional Reformed Churches. We had been going to the Catholic Church in town, but it didn't really feel like home; it felt stuffy and full of traditions. I knew that Brad was still struggling with his faith. I wasn't even sure if he really believed or not. He would go through the motions, but I didn't feel that there was a connection there. Brad was an amazing person, honest, loving, giving, hardworking, but I knew there was more to life than that. I wanted Brad to experience God the way I did. I was so in love with Jesus that I wanted him to have that same experience, for us to grow together in our spiritual journey.

A few months after Alissa was born, my neighbor friend invited me to a women's Bible study at her church. I had never really gone to a Bible study before, and I was excited to try. I loved it right off the bat and found myself thirsting for more. I didn't really know my Bible or have one of my own. The Catholic Church I had gone to had never really discipled me. The lady who was leading the study, Karen, had such a different vibe about her. I could not describe it. She wasn't old, maybe a few years older than me; I was thirty-three. She was short, stout, kind, loving, and compassionate. I felt drawn to her and her faith. I asked her where she went to church.

"Oh, it's this little old church a few miles outside of town. My family loves it because it's an outreach church serving the community around it. We get really poor people, actually all different kinds of people who come. You can join us one Sunday at eleven, if you'd like?" she said. "But it's nothing much to look at. It's in this old grange hall," she explained as though she was a little embarrassed to invite anyone.

"Okay, I'd love to," I said. The next Sunday we went and liked it; even Brad liked it. It was different, small, and quaint, and I loved the pastor, Pastor Ed. He preached with compassion, and I just felt drawn in. Pastor Ed reminded me of an old southern preacher. Slick black hair greased back, medium height, skinny, but loud. When he preached, he jolted you out of sleep as your spirit was drawn in to his message.

That week, Pastor Ed came to visit us at our house. I had never had a house call from a priest in all the years I had gone to the Catholic Church, and here was this pastor we'd just met showing up at our house. He sat with us on the front porch of our home in town for over an hour. He asked us all kinds of questions, where we were from and about our family. He never pushed us in believing what he believed but allowed us to ask questions. We had lots of them. Eventually, Brad and I began to attend regularly and were drawn in to attend Sunday school Bible study before church. It was a Bible-believing church, and Pastor Ed was a Holy Spirit–filled man. We learned many things we didn't know and asked many questions. God was changing us and teaching us about himself.

Over time, Brad gave his life to Jesus, and I really saw the transition in him. Brad began to understand the difference between religion and relationship. Before, it was about trying to do the "right" thing, being good. But as he grew, he watched others and how their lives were different, more peaceful in the midst of chaos. They failed at times, but he watched how they got back up and continued to fight, to move forward, to persevere in the midst of trials. Everyone had problems; it was a matter of how we all dealt with them, if we laid down and gave up. It wasn't about just being good, but it was about giving our lives to the Creator, the one who knew us inside and out. Exactly how we wished our fathers to be. Loving, patient, encouraging, full of wisdom. Even though Brad's father and mine were severely flawed, we had a perfect Father in heaven who desired a relationship with us. Our desire was to completely trust in him. I saw Brad gave more and more of himself to God.

CHAPTER 9

I am the Bread of Life.

—John 6:48

    I thanked God for the day of my salvation as it permeated the atmosphere of room 6. I felt its warmth envelope my body, like a blanket covering me, pressing down. I felt safe. I envisioned what the room was like when my mother occupied the space—the beautiful light-green dresser in the corner where the small television sat, often with Joyce Meyer's voice shouting into the room, the angel figurines staring down at me. The pictures filled the wall with four generations of faces, and in the middle was the portrait I had painted of my mom, which looked ginormous compared to the rest of the pictures.

    I smiled as I remembered painting that picture many years ago after I saw my mom suffer so much physical pain after going through surgery to remove part of her intestine. She returned back to the hospital shortly afterward, sick with septic shock caused by a leak in her intestine that had filled her body with waste and poison, almost killing her. The doctors had to perform an ileostomy, a surgical procedure creating an opening through the side of her lower stomach where the intestinal waste passed out and into a pouch, which was adhered to the skin. That was one of my mom's "nine lives" taken away.

    That was the first time I thought my mother would surely die. The doctors and nurses had called the family to say this could possibly be her time to go. My mother had had many procedures in the past, but none threatening death like this one had. I drove from my home in Michigan. I had gotten the call while at a horseshow with Alissa. I had been with my mom just the week before to help move her into the nursing home and then to stay with her for her surgery. She was then moved back to the nursing home, and I thought all was well until I got the call. I left right away. When I arrived at the hospital and walked into her hospital room, I saw her lying on the bed. She was down to seventy-two pounds. The shock of seeing her that thin took my breath away. I could not maintain my composure. A sound came out of my mouth, and I had to lift my hand to cover it. My hand muffled the sound that my insides were making as I wept into it. I sat in the chair next to her bed watching her sleep, her body consumed by the bed. She looked like a little child wrapped in a cloud. I was not ready for her to go. I wanted to crawl into bed with her, to hold her, but was afraid I would break her small fragile body.

I sat staring at her and praying. When she woke up, she turned to me and smiled. That was a tough moment for me, trying to be strong for her, yet inside I wanted my mom to comfort me, to tell me it was going to be all right. I had to be on the other side now. I needed to comfort my mother. I needed to be the strong one now. My mom was the pillar, the one you called for advice, for encouragement, not the other way around. My mom was the strong one, wise one, the one that was the glue to the family. She kept everyone connected. The roles had shifted the last few years, and the transition was not an easy one. From mother caring for daughter to daughter caring for mother. I realized that one day death would happen, but I was unprepared emotionally for that day. All the years of knowing my mom, she was there for me, strong, maybe not physically, but mentally and spiritually. She was a powerhouse. My precious momma who prayed me out of danger and out of the hands of the devil.

My mom, even though she was physically sick, would sit in her prayer chair, which she saved her money for many years to buy. I could still see it clearly in my mind. It was soft beige with a round high back that hugged you when you sat in it. This was my mom's chair, her special prayer chair. She seemed to have had much to pray about because she spent many hours in that chair, occasionally pulling all-nighters. Sometimes, as a teenager, I would come home late trying to sneak into the house without making a noise, hoping my parents wouldn't notice that it was past my curfew. Trying to go past the living room to get to my bedroom was quite the challenge, slowly creeping by in the dark, thinking all was good and lights were out. Then, as I passed the entrance to the living room, I would hear a soft whisper, "Goodnight," which always scared the wits out of me. I would leap two feet off the ground, my heart almost jumping right out of my chest. My mom never said anything else. The silence was painful enough, and the guilt would come in and fill me up.

My mom wanted to take a shower. She asked me in her weak voice if I would take her to the shower room to wash her up. She had not been washed in days and felt dirty. I was scared. I didn't want to break her; she was so fragile. But I asked the nurse for permission, and the nurse nodded yes. I gently helped her into the seat of her walker, feeling how fragile and light her body was, and wheeled her to the shower room down the hall, afraid of any little bumps along the way that would jolt her delicate body and hurt her. I positioned her under the showerhead and locked up the wheels.

I began removing her nightgown and was taken aback by how skinny and sick she looked. It was as though no one had fed her in months. I also tried to hide my unexpected reaction to seeing the discolored pouch stuck to the side of her stomach. I wanted to break down and cry for her. I was sure my mother saw me turn my head quickly away, trying to hide my feelings and disgust for the foreign object. I hoped I would never be the one who would have to empty it. My mother's skin was gray and shook from the cold, which was no surprise since she only had skin over her bones with no muscle in between. I removed the showerhead from the wall and began to wet my mother's skin gently. Tears were running down my face at seeing my mother so weak yet so strong. My mom did not say a word as she sat with her eyes closed, soaking in the warmth of the water.

I took the sponge, squeezed some soap over it, and began washing her body as though washing a fragile child. This was my mother, broken and dying. What was she thinking right at that moment? This woman had given life to four children and lost several in between, had climbed many mountains, fought many battles, and now could not do a thing without help. How did it come to this? How did life get here, to this place, this time? My mom had washed me many times, and now I was washing her. Something about it seemed wrong.

Tears flowed from my eyes like rivers for I did not see a weak woman but a woman of strength and courage. Even though her body was weak, she had more strength than most people I had ever known. I knew this was hard for my mom, letting others serve her, take care of her. As I washed her, she too cried. I believed that my mom needed the shower for two reasons: so she could feel the warmth and cleanliness of the water and she could let her tears flow along with the water. It was a place of releasing, letting go of all that had built up in her and mixing her tears with the water to hide the deep pain that lay within. My face was blank, trying to pretend I didn't notice her tears, her pain, flowing out of her. I was giving her this time to herself to release it all along with the water.

No sound came out of my mother. Her eyes stayed closed while the rivers met one another and washed the pain down the drain. I gently washed her hair, massaging her scalp. I knew my mother liked her head massaged. No words were spoken between us, each lost in our own thoughts. My heart filled with the love I had for my mom and the overwhelming honor I felt in those moments of intimacy with her.

The memory faded. I recalled the picture I painted that hung boldly on my mother's wall. I painted it shortly after the episode of my mother's near-death experience. The bright and colorful painting was of my mom floating in the clouds with wings attached to her shoulders and a new body representing the day that she would finally bury her old broken flesh and receive a new one. My mom often talked about the day she would be whole after so many parts of her body had been surgically removed. When my mom first saw the picture, she insisted on hanging it up right in the middle of her wall, even though I thought it was silly. My mother was proud to share with everyone the story behind it, the colorful lady, with a green polka-dot dress and wings, flying in heaven with her new body.

Often, when I visited her, she would be sleeping, but when she woke up, she would open one eye and say, "Oh, I guess God's not ready for me yet. I'm still here." Once when my husband and I, Brad came to visit, Brad joked with her about the best way to know if she was in heaven or not—before even opening her eyes, she could put her hands on her chest to check and see if it was flat or not. We all laughed so hard at that. Years ago, my mom had a full mastectomy, leaving her chest flat and a little sunk in. She often dreamed about having a new body with beautiful breasts. She would joke about it often that when she got to heaven, one of her rewards would be a pair of nice big fluffy ones.

The picture made me laugh, knowing that God would honor his daughter and give her her heart's desire. After my mom's passing, I envisioned her dancing and singing with her newfound body, her new breasts, no more pain and no more sorrow. Yet even though I knew my mom was where she wanted to be, with her Savior, I still felt the absence of her in my life. I had no place to escape to, no one to crawl into bed with, no one to cuddle and talk to. I could no longer hear her say, "I love you, I'm so proud of you," and that left a hole in my soul. There is nothing more fulfilling than hearing words of encouragement and affirmation from your mom.

I cried and emptied myself once again, remembering room 6 of the nursing home, the place where my mother no longer inhabited. The empty space beside me in the bed had now been replaced by God's comforting presence. My heart ached as I told him about all that weighed me down, all my hurt and sadness. Even though he knew, it felt good to say it again. My heart ached for what I had lost, not just my mom but for so much more, what the enemy continually tried to take away from me. My daddy, Jesus, held me, listened, and comforted me. I told him I longed to be done, longed for heaven where there was no more of this pain or sorrow, to be dancing with my mommy. But he told me it wasn't my time, that I couldn't stay in the room much longer. He held me tight, and I felt safe.

"Why do I have to go?" I asked, sadness filing me with the thought of leaving. "I don't want to go out there." I pointed outside, into the world.

He didn't answer but held me tighter. Deep within me, I knew why. I was tired and needed to rest a little longer before heading back into the world where I had to face so many hard things.

I looked around the room some more as so many memories of my mother were everywhere. Looking out the big window, I saw the birdhouse she had hung on the tree. The bench outside, where my mom loved to sit when she was able to get out of bed, was one of her favorite places to get away to. She had one of the best window views in the nursing home. It faced an open field, where trees stood tall and grass grew, not like the other residents who had views of the highway or other buildings. I recall my mom's beige rocking chair and ottoman beside the window. On the floor beside it sat her knitting basket, which held knitting needles, yarn, and other things needed to knit socks, hats, and mittens. The last year of her life, she could no longer knit. It was too hard for her to see, and her hands no longer could move with the flow of the needles.

Watching my mom in her final years, I learned about the difficulties of getting old in intimate detail. It wasn't just about physical aging, but it's also the things that she lost and was no longer capable of doing. My mom loved to knit and sew, but she hadn't been able to sew in the nursing home. While I was growing up, she made many outfits for me and my sister, and she made many quilts too. It was difficult to watch her struggle more and more, trying to move her hands to knit and becoming frustrated at not being able to complete something she so enjoyed doing. She'd finish a project but cry at the imperfections of her work, when once it was near perfection. To lose another thing that meant so much to her, she must have wondered, *What now?* She also loved to read, but eventually that too was taken from her because her vision was growing weak. I often wondered what my final days would look like as I watched my mom try to maneuver through hers.

During my mother's last days, I remember sitting next to her bed, holding her hands in my own. She was incoherent. My mother was lying on her side, hands always in motion as if she were dreaming of knitting. She would reach out to me, running her hands up and down my arm and grabbing onto my sleeves. She would begin to move her fingers up and down as if she was holding yarn and knitting. She would begin to knit . . . knit one . . . pearl two . . . then her hands would rest for a bit and start all over again. She would do this with her eyes closed. Her hands were warm and soft against my arm, pulling against my sleeve.

Once my mom grabbed my arm, she'd roll my sleeve up my arm as far as she could manage. I wondered what she was doing, what she was working on. Her facial expressions seemed to say that she was working on something special—her look was so intense. The touch and the movement of her hands against my body brought warmth to my heart, and I wanted her to keep going. The hands that had comforted, served, and healed so many. The hands that cooked so many meals, wiped many noses and tears, prayed for so many souls. I remember often looking at and touching her hands in years past, looking at their beauty and feeling their warmth. They had worked hard, yet they still looked beautiful to me.

It was hard not to think about what the last years would look like for me. I'd watched my mother's journey through life's ups and downs, building a life then having it torn down again, one hard layer at a time. She had to let go of so much she had worked so hard for, only to spend her last years in a nursing home. It made me think about my own life, what was important and sacred, and look at the things I collected or thought important when, really, they were fleeting, dust in the wind. The last several years of my mother's life were an opening into the future for me. My mom was my lens to seeing what mattered to me most, and it began, for me, as a journey of internal cleansing.

I took a look at my life, took out the things that only hindered me, that kept me away from the people that mattered to me the most. I decided not to be so focused on things and accomplishments to prove my worth but on people. I decided to focus on family and friends, to live in the moment and cherish the memories that were made. My mom had nothing, only what was left in her room, but she had more than most: she had love to give and people who loved her in the final years of her life. They were there because of her, not because of what she was or had, but because she gave herself to them. She loved deeply, and she said often how filled she felt in her ten-by-ten space.

CHAPTER 10

No one is righteous, not even one.
—Romans 3:10

As I lay in my mother's bed, my life was being poured out into room 6. I recalled memory after memory and released them into the room, along with the others that the walls held captive. They were like a web of events all interweaving in and out of each other, creating knots of deep wounds within me. I would recall a memory, and it would trigger another and another, an event here and an event there. For many years, I had pushed the memories away, wanting them to stay behind the line into "then." But as I walked through life's journey in room 6, parts of my past would continue to creep up behind me, tugging at me and calling me back, wanting to be released and set free. As more years filled the gap between "then" and "now," it didn't seem to push it further back, but as I grew older and lived, more of my past seemed to float closer and closer to the surface.

I had kept so many secrets from Brad, my husband, that I was ashamed of. I didn't mean to keep these things from him. I just didn't think that the past had anything to do with our future. When I had my second child, Brad's first, my heart was aching and yearning for the other child I had lost. I couldn't get my mind off of it, and it seemed like everywhere I went, there was something that would bring me back to that memory. Just watching my own baby was a huge trigger or when someone asked me how many children I had.

Sometimes I would be sitting in church, and a word would stir it and push it to the surface, causing a flood of tears to start. Brad would look at me to see if I was all right, and I would just brush it off as a happy feeling, thinking about God, but I was really experiencing deep sorrow and shame. He didn't know the turmoil that was going on deep within my soul, for I had never shared that part of my life with him. I was no longer that person and didn't want Brad to think differently of me. Nor did I want to ever face that "old me." I wanted to leave that part of me behind.

But as hard as I tried, that girl behind the line kept crying out to me. My heart continued to ache more and more for the broken girl I once was and the choices I'd made that I regretted over and over again. The reality of what I had done filled my heart with deep grief and sickness that overwhelmed me. I couldn't hold the secret within me much longer, and it was tormenting me to the point of falling into a deep depression. It kept building up and up until I couldn't bear it any longer; it was killing me inside. I prayed for God to help me, to forgive me, to heal me. I kept hearing him tell me that he had forgiven me, but did I forgive myself? And if so, why was I hiding it? *That's a good question*, I thought. I had so much shame and a lack of forgiveness deep within me, and I was scared. I was scared to release it, not knowing what damage it would do when it was set free from within me. I didn't want to hurt anyone else.

There came a time when I knew I could no longer bear the secret any longer and had to tell Brad everything. I remember sitting him down, not knowing where I should begin. I fumbled around a bit, trying to find the words, then started to tell him the story.

A few of my friends and I had gone to a bar one night, which wasn't unusual. I spent much of that part of my life in bars and at parties. I had shared some of that with Brad, but not the full extent of it. Many times, my friends and I were either invited backstage to party with the band or to a party at someone's house we had just met at the bar. I was seventeen at the time, and I had many years of partying already under my belt at such a young age and was never short of friends to party with. This particular night, we were invited to a party after bar hours. I was driving, which I certainly shouldn't have been. I had been drinking and had done a few lines of coke.

I was anxious to get to the person's house we were heading to. I didn't know him but didn't care; I wanted to smoke some crack. There were a few cars packed with people following one another to the party, which was in the next town over from the bar we'd been at. We drove down the highway at about two in the morning, which meant there were not many cars out. Some of us, on a dare, decided we were going to race down the two-lane highway, stopping just before the police station. I loved dares. I wanted to prove I wasn't afraid. I liked putting my tough shell on, especially when it came to showing off to the guys. I pushed my foot down on the pedal and screamed down the highway. I loved the adrenaline. Not everyone in the car enjoyed it though. Some were screaming in fear, and some were hooting with excitement. I wasn't letting up. I was the only girl involved in this race, and I was going to win, and I did. I slowed down just as we were going to pass the police station, my heart pumping with adrenaline. "Yes!" I yelled, lifting my arms up in victory.

When we arrived at the house, it was packed with people already. After several hours, I felt myself slipping away while sitting on the couch. Next thing I knew, through my semi-state of consciousness, I felt a heaviness on top of my body. I had a difficult time breathing. I felt weak and groggy, and I had a hard time opening my eyes. I was still feeling the effects of the previous night's party. It couldn't have been too long after I passed out, I thought. I felt as though I was in a boat on the water, the waves pressing against it and thrashing me around. I was confused. As I began to slowly open my eyes a little, I could see that the room was empty and quiet except for the guy on top of me. It took me a few minutes to figure out what was going on, what he was doing. I felt the weight of his body pressing down on me, his chest against mine, one of his hands was holding my arms above my head.

I started to squirm; he was so close to my face. I felt his nasty-smelling breath on my face. His body against mine was so heavy that any movement I made was not having any effect on getting him off of me. I tried screaming, "Get off of me! Get off of me!" Then I felt his free hand slap against my mouth. I was trapped. I hardly knew what had happened; it happened so fast. I was crying under his hand and trying to squirm loose, but it only made it worse. Staring at him with my eyes, I knew him but couldn't figure out why he was doing this. He was one of the guys, part of the group we partied with for many years, and I had thought he was a friend. Sure, I thought he was attractive with shoulder-length dark brown hair, dark brown eyes, and a tan complexion, and we had teased and joked with one another in the past; but it had never amounted to anything—we were just friends. When he finally got off me, I was in shock and streams of tears flowed down my face.

I got up quickly, walked over to him and pushed him as hard as I could, "What the fuck was that about, you asshole?" I screamed loudly, wanting to beat him up.

"You know you wanted it," he said with an eerie smirk on his face.

"I wanted it? What the hell does that mean? I was passed out!" I yelled through my tears. "That's what you do when a girl passes out?" I was so disgusted with the grin on his face and his attitude that I reached out and slapped him across his cheek.

"Shut up, you know you wanted me," he said staring at me with a look of anger on his face for slapping him. He put his hand over his cheek. "Bitch," he said as he slowly began to dress himself. I punched at his chest several times, like a crazy madwoman, yelling at him, wanting to take back what he had just stolen from me as he just stood, grinning. I hated him so much at the moment. He turned around, got his boots and coat on, and walked out of the house. I stood for a long time staring at the door, trying to put all the pieces together. I sat down in the chair across from the sofa in shock. I wrapped the blanket around me, trying to stop my body from shaking. I stared for a long time at the sofa, where it had happened, trying to figure it all out, if it was a nightmare or if it had really happened. I did not know how long I sat, staring. I was in complete shock.

I did not know where my friends who had come with me were. I got up and decided to go looking for my roommate, my best friend, Sarah. Desperation filled my veins, and I needed to get out of there. I found my friend sleeping in one of the rooms. I woke her up and told her I was leaving and if she wanted a ride home, she had better get up now. We both gathered our stuff in silence and left. Sarah asked me what was going on, if I was okay. I was still in distress and did not know what to say, if I should tell her what happened. But I didn't really know what had happened, nor did I want to talk about it. Did the guy really do what I thought he might have done? I told my roommate that I was fine, just not feeling great, which could definitely be the truth after a party. We arrived at the apartment we had just moved into a few months prior.

I immediately got into the shower and tried to replay the night over in my mind. *Did I ask for this? Did I egg him on? Did I deserve this? I mean, I wasn't the "loose" type, but I sure wasn't the innocent type either. Look at my lifestyle!*

I stood in the shower for what seemed like hours, waiting for the water to wash away the filth deep inside of me, but it did not and could not. It ran too deep. I scrubbed the outside of my body, hard, hoping it would help me feel cleaner, but that did not work either. I thought about the people who had taken advantage of me as a child; was there a pattern here? I hadn't asked for this or given permission, or had I? I had come to hate the male figures in my life, all of them getting from me whatever their sickly pleasures desired. From the times in the wheat fields, stained with dirt, to now, only adding more filth inside me.

Days turned into weeks. I stayed away from him. I was embarrassed and hurt and didn't know what to do, so I did what I knew best—I hid and got high. I started to feel sick around the fifth week, throwing up and not able to keep anything down. Some of my friends at work were getting suspicious with all the trips to the bathroom I was making. I knew this wasn't good. The woman I was working with asked if I was all right, if I was pregnant. I said that I wasn't. But I knew I had to be. I waited a few weeks, hoping all this would go away, trying to drown myself with drugs—maybe that would take care of it. I was scared. I'd been raised in a Catholic home, went to church every Sunday growing up, and knew this was against everything my parents believed in.

I wasn't getting any better, so I went to the doctor, hoping he would say it was a bad case of the flu. He had been our family doctor for several years, and he was young and good-looking. He confirmed that I was indeed pregnant. I sat in his office and cried and cried and cried. I told him all that had happened and that I didn't know what to do.

"Well, you have several options. The obvious one is to keep the baby. The second option is to give the baby up for adoption, and the third option is to have an abortion," the doctor said in an order-of-business tone.

On hearing the word *abortion*, my whole body began to cringe. I could not do that. But neither could I keep the baby or give it up for adoption.

"I could recommend an adoption agency or, if you decide to abort, which I believe would be your best option, I could perform it for you at the local hospital. We'll call it another medical term, it would be covered under your parents' insurance." I was not eighteen yet. "Your parents won't even have to know anything about it." He went on to explain, in a "no big deal" manner, that I would be in the hospital for four days, then it would be done. He was very persistent in the fact that this was the best option. He had done this many times for others in the past and told me that it would be difficult to have a child at my age and under these circumstances.

I didn't speak. I couldn't believe it! It struck me that what I thought was a life-changing decision was just another day at the office for him. This was about my life, my baby. It was as if I was numb, in shock, to what my ears were hearing. I got up and left while he was still talking, telling him I would have to think about it.

I ran out of the doctor's office. I needed to talk to someone, certainly not my mom. I couldn't. There was a longing inside me to go to a church, to light up a candle, kneel, and pray. Even though I claimed to not believe, I remembered the safety and peace I felt in the church growing up. I remember going with my mom often to light a candle for someone and praying for them. I loved staring at the many candles, the light, the peace. Instead, I decided to talk to my best friend and roommate. I told her everything that happened at the party, that I was pregnant, and what the doctor suggested. She shocked me by telling me that she'd had an abortion too and that it was the best decision she could have ever made. I asked her what happened. Sarah just told me that at the time, she and her boyfriend were too young to have a baby. I couldn't help but wonder how many more girls have had abortions; it was like it was no big deal. I struggled with this for weeks. I could not get the voices out of my head . . . do it, don't do it, do it, don't do it. On and on it went . . .

I knew my parents wouldn't approve, and deep down, something was telling me not to, that it wasn't right; but on the outside, I was being pulled in the other direction—especially by my doctor. He had called several times asking what decision I had made. *No one will know. It's easy. You are too young to look after a child. Your life will change and be hard . . .* and on and on it went. I decided to listen to the voice of the doctor; it was louder than all the others. He seemed to know what was best, more than I did. He sounded confident this was the right thing to do, and I trusted him.

I took time off from work, went to the hospital, and in several hours, it was done. Just like that! I recall being semi-awake, not feeling much, kind of like getting a pap smear done. I could not see anything nor feel anything and when it was done. They wheeled me back to the room. After waking up several hours later, I laid in that hospital bed all alone staring up at the ceiling for four days as the nurses came in to get me up and move. I was numb. I couldn't comprehend what happened to me, what I had just done. I cried and cried as I laid my hand on my stomach. I could not physically feel a thing, but I was falling apart inside.

I was broken and laid there all alone; no one knew my secret. I wondered if anything would have changed if I had just gone to a church and lit a candle. I could hear children in the distance, babies crying. It seemed as if all of a sudden, I noticed them and heard them; and when I did, I wanted my baby back. People had spoken about it as if it was nothing, but no one ever prepared me beyond the physical pain that I would feel. I could not bear it. I needed to get high. Anything to get this deep feeling of guilt and excruciating pain in my heart to go away. No one had known. I had no one to talk to, just a deep secret I had to keep hidden. More dirt added to the deep pile already within me.

Every day since that day, I recalled that moment like it was yesterday. That was one of the hardest times in my life, and even now, when I remember it, my heart fills with deep sadness and regret. I think about how old my child would have been, what he or she would have looked like, and then I had to stop. The struggle within me at times was too much, but I never want to forget any of it. When I looked at my children over the years, I saw my missing child too. As time ticked on, the pain got a little less, but not the memory. I had brought it to the Lord, time and time again, lamented the loss, and repented the sin and the shame.

I knew that the blood of Jesus had covered it, and I felt forgiven, yet I never could forget what I had done. I felt like somehow, I needed to pay or make up for what I had done, which was impossible; I could never repay such a debt.

Sharing the abortion with Brad was very difficult. I had to explain what had happened to me and what had led me to the worst decision I had ever made. I cried the whole time, the pain in my heart pouring out to him. The memory was fresh in my mind, as though it had just happened to me. He was gentle with me, held me, and cried along with me, wanting to take away my pain. It felt good to release it out into the atmosphere, letting go of the hold it had on me. I would never forget, but I didn't have to live in the torment of it each day. I felt freedom to share my pain with someone, to have Brad hold some of it for me.

"I'm so sorry, Mama!" I cried into room 6. I loved my mother and wanted to share my life with her, but I also knew it would have tormented her. I wondered if I would want my children to share those kinds of things with me. I would want to know and comfort them, yet it would break my heart knowing that I was not there to protect them from everything. I wanted my children to know that they could talk to me about anything, but also through my own journey, I learned that some things were for me to work out with God and God alone.

There were things I did not want to know about my children. They each had to walk their journeys and eventually turn to God to work out their own healing with him. That was the hardest part of parenting for me. I had to know I did my best, loved them deeply, but had to let go of wanting to fix their lives, make them choose the right path, and to allow them to find their way to salvation and peace through the same God that I received mine from. Like my mom had done for her children, I too covered my children with lots of prayer. I lifted them up to my Heavenly Father and trusted that he would protect my children, his children. They were all his children. How much more would he love them, care for them, than I ever could?

Chapter 11

For everything there is a season, a time for every activity under the sun.
—Ecclesiastes 3:1

A few years into our marriage, Brad and I felt that the seasons came and went so quickly. It was a time when our lives began to really grow and weave into one another. I found myself beginning to let go of my need to control, learning to trust him and his decisions for me and our family. After my first marriage, I told myself I would never trust a man and allow him, anyone, to control my life. Slowly, as time went by and Brad proved to be a gentle, honest, and loving husband, I began to understand what a partner in life meant. We became one, talking through decisions we had to make together, praying together, looking out for one another. It was freeing to me. I didn't have to control and make all the decisions. I didn't have to do life alone. It was the two of us working together. It felt good to share the responsibility. I had lost so much of myself when I was married to Matt that being married to Brad was a whole new learning experience for me. I had to learn to trust Brad and know he was looking out for my best interest and our family. Our time together was growing, and so was our love for one another.

I smiled as I recalled the day Brad and I found out we were pregnant again, two years after Alissa was born. We walked out of the doctor's office building and started jumping up and down on the sidewalk, screaming for joy. "Ahhhhh . . . I can't believe we're having a boy!" I screamed, running and jumping into his arms.

"Oh my gosh, Sam . . ." was all Brad could say. He was choked up. He picked me up and twirled me around and around. "Wahooooooo!"

I laughed while he cried tears of joy. I loved watching him, his excitement flowing out of him when he found out he was going to have a son, a little him. It must have been more to it than I could understand. A man and his son. Was it about carrying on the family name, or was it about having someone who was the same gender and could relate to one another, man to man?

I understood it a little because the thought of having a boy terrified me. I didn't know anything about raising girls, let alone boys. But I did know more about playing house, coloring, dolls, and doing crafts than Brad did. I did not think boys could relate to those types of things. Brad didn't. Brad was good with the girls. He loved them deeply. But there were some things he could not relate to or connect with. He was all man. Fixing the girls' hair, tying ribbons, sitting around coloring—even though he did these things, you could see the awkwardness in him. It was not his cup of tea. Maybe that was something he was looking forward to with a son, another man around the house, someone helping him with the chores, looking forward to teaching him manly things.

I was so grateful for the relationship Brad and I had. He was a great husband and dad. I had watched him change from the geeky-looking guy I had met years ago to a really handsome young man. I noticed the glances from other women, and I grinned thinking of the first time I saw him standing outside my apartment door and how I was so grateful for his family's continual pestering that had led us to one another.

The pregnancy was difficult, and I was sick pretty much the whole time, like my previous pregnancy. My kiddos seemed to take up much of the space between my uterus and my ribs, right under my breasts. The little guy growing inside me seemed to be a little bully already, kicking me hard and often getting his little feet stuck underneath my rib cage. I was thankful that being this uncomfortable was temporary compared to the beautiful gift of a child in the end. Often, I heard women speak of how they loved being pregnant, feeling the baby grow inside, not having a period, eating whatever they wanted. Sure, I loved feeling my baby move and hearing his heart beat, knowing that a life was growing inside of me, but I did not like being sick for nine months. It certainly gave me more of an appreciation for those who felt sick and sore every day of their lives.

When I was eight and a half months pregnant, I had gone to the grocery store and was entering the back door of the house. I was carrying two bags in my hand. The back door led to the kitchen, which I had to climb three steps to get in. I got to the second step, and as I opened the door and put my foot on the third step, I abruptly stopped and screamed in pain. Something happened, a pop, that caused me great discomfort and made it impossible for me to move. Brad quickly came to my side to try and help me.

"What's wrong? Are you okay?" he said, worried, as he grabbed my arm to help me up the last step into the house.

"I don't know!" I yelled in a panic. "Don't move me! I hurt up in my chest. Sharp pains," I could hardly speak from being out of breath. "I can't move. It hurts so bad." The pain was shooting up into all areas of my body. I didn't want to move a muscle.

"Okay, ummm, I'm not sure what to do!" said Brad frantically.

"Me either! Just wait a minute." I stood waiting to see if the pain would subside. After several minutes, it did decrease enough for me to sit and try to catch my breath.

"I think we need to take you to the hospital," Brad said, looking very concerned as he came over to help me get up and to the car.

"Okay." I did not argue. I was in so much pain and was scared something had happened to the baby or that I was having a heart attack.

We arrived at the hospital, and upon seeing that I was pregnant, they gave me a fast pass in. The emergency room doctor came and examined me and wanted an x-ray, then possibly an ultrasound. The doctor listened for the heartbeat, and it sounded strong. We sat and waited for the results, what seemed to be a long time after the x-ray was done.

"Well, I've got some good news and bad news," said the doctor as he walked in. "I'll start with the good news. The baby is doing great. Nice and strong! As a matter of fact," said the doctor as he put the x-ray on the screen, "he's so strong that he popped one of your ribs in the upper part of your left side. Must have given you a good kick. Sign him up for soccer as soon as he's old enough," the doctor said with a chuckle.

"What? Oh my gosh, that's crazy," said Brad incredulously. "What are you going to do?"

"Nothing! Can't do a thing about broken ribs except let them repair themselves and take it easy," the doctor said.

I held my side as I burst into laughter and cried at the same time from the pain. Brad and the doctor just stared at me. "I . . . am so . . . relieved that the baaaaaby is okay," I managed to get out. And I was. Sure, I was in pain, but that would repair itself in time. The baby was all that mattered.

Wham! Another trigger for me to think about my lost child. My mind went to a place of great despair and guilt. Despair for missing my child, guilt and sorrow for what I had done, that I had robbed my child of life. Yet here I was, crying and celebrating that this child was healthy, which certainly was a cause to celebrate, but did I have a right to be happy and elated while another had not been so lucky by my own hand? This often tormented me. I really had a hard time forgiving myself. I'd often have nightmares over it, trying to find my baby. I knew that there had been many women like me who had done this, but that didn't justify or alleviate the pain though. It was more a pondering on how did all these other women process it? Or did they?

I rested for the remainder of the time until our son was born. During that time, I had to compartmentalize my thoughts and feelings so I wouldn't drown. I didn't put it away to forget about it; I could never do that. But I had to rest my mind from it taking over my every thought.

The day little Ethan decided to enter the world was the day the biggest snowstorm of the year arrived with a vengeance. We lived only a few blocks from the hospital, but my doctor, who lived a little out of town, could not get to the hospital because of the storm. Roads and highways were closed. Dr. George, who lived only a few blocks away, was the on-call doctor and could walk over to the hospital. I didn't know this doctor. I was afraid when it came to pushing because of my broken ribs. Also, I had instructed my doctor the moment I found out I was pregnant that there would be no question that I would get an epidural at the time of delivery. I wanted it but was worried because my doctor wasn't there to deliver my baby. Lauren, months ago, asked if she could be present for the delivery. Brad and I had talked about it, and since she was ten, we thought it would be a good learning experience. Homeschool lesson.

It was late afternoon when I was having serious contractions. They were coming fast and hard. We decided it was time to go to the hospital. When we arrived, I made sure that the nurses and doctor knew the plan for giving me the epidural. The doctor had not arrived yet; they would call him when it got closer to delivery. As time got closer, and I was ready to push, there was no epidural. Again, I asked the nurse while she was prepping me for delivery.

"I'm sorry, hon, it's too late for an epidural," she said. "By the way, you're doing great. It won't be long now. Hang in there." I wanted to hurt her at that moment. I could tell that the nurse did not like giving anything during the birthing process.

I grabbed her shirt, pulled her closer to me, and said, "I am not happy about this. I have a broken rib and it hurts like hell. I need an epidural *now*."

Seeing her mother in pain and hearing her acting crazy, Lauren ran out of the room crying, terrified. She no longer wanted to witness the birth of her brother. I was worried for a moment, wondering if we had scarred her for life. Maybe it was a good thing, I thought. As a teenager, maybe this moment would be so embedded in Lauren's mind that she'd keep her distance from the boys.

"I'm so sorry, ma'am, but I really can't give it to you. It's too late," the nurse kept saying.

Okay, I thought, *it's too dang late. Fine. I'll focus on getting this baby out, but she had not heard the last of it.* Little Ethan was born at 9:05 in the evening, and once again, Brad cut the umbilical cord and cried like a baby. His cry was mixed in with Ethan's cries. Ethan had some mighty strong lungs, which only grew stronger in the months that followed. He was born on the day of a bad storm and came out like a storm. He was jaundiced and colicky, and Brad and I had no place in our minds or body to focus or even think of anything else but trying to comfort and soothe this child for over a year.

Ethan did not sleep, and we were sleep deprived. The first year was kind of a blur. Brad and I played tag team, switching from watching the baby to taking care of the other kids. We couldn't take Ethan out for long periods of time without him screaming, so it was better to stay home. Ethan needed one-on-one time. I seemed to cry often from exhaustion. There were times when I would put Ethan in the car seat, put the dryer on, and placed him on top to try to bring comfort to him from the vibration of the dryer and for me to have a bit of relief as well. Other times, I would just drive around town, around and around, music blaring, to try and get him to sleep.

Thinking back now, I could laugh about it, but it was no laughing matter then. It wasn't easy. I was far away from family, and no one really came to visit or help us. We were on our own, which was pretty much my life story, having to do it all on my own. The beautiful thing was that after Ethan turned two, he was the sweetest, happiest baby. He was so beautiful, another beautiful blonde-haired towhead with blue eyes and a big smile. He would follow his dad everywhere, wanting to hammer, cut things with a saw, and ride on the tractor. He would spend hours fixing his bike, things in the house, and the cars with his little plastic tools. The girls loved playing house with him and often dressed him up in dresses, put make-up on him, and painted his nails. Brad got mad; he didn't like seeing his son being dressed up like a girl. But Ethan was all boy. As he grew into a young boy, seven or eight, he got some of his own real tools. His grandma got him a real drill. He was so excited about that. Ethan and his dad built birdhouses and a tree house, and Ethan would create his own things with scrap wood and steel.

These times were times of great growth. I was moving further and further away from the "then" times. The "then" was becoming more and more of a past memory, a whole other lifetime ago. These times kept me so busy that I didn't have time for past memories to invade my space. I moved forward, determined to do this right, to be a good person, and to focus on my tasks ahead and on my family. The past was exactly that, the past, and I was proud of myself for being strong and leaving it there. There was no sense in dwelling on things you couldn't change; it was what it was, better left behind. Besides, I was walking in faith. I loved the Lord, and a lot of things were changing within me. I was starting to be more comfortable with myself, enjoying the better me. I felt peace and joy. I had a great husband and beautiful children.

Brad and I made the decision to homeschool the kids, which I loved. We pulled Lauren out of school after the third grade. In my heart, I wanted to be with my children and have them close to me as long as I could. I could not stop staring at them and breathing in their scent, listening to their sweet little voices. I didn't want them to experience what I had—the lack of a mother. I needed to protect them and make sure they had a good, safe childhood.

First thing in the morning, after breakfast together and seeing Brad off to work, the kids and I would cuddle and read. Then we would look at the weather patterns and chart them. We'd practice their printing and writing, create science experiments, and learn history, and do geography projects. In the afternoons, we learned how to cook and bake. We'd decide on a meal, go shopping for the ingredients, and work together to make Brad dinner. We would have theme parties, dressing up like the people we were studying, making the food from that culture, and invite people over to join us and to teach them what we learned. We joined a homeschool group and went often on field trips together. We also went on weekend trips camping or in the winter skiing. I was feeling like my life was coming together. I was filled with love and surrounded by the love of my children and husband. I felt that I was being who I was meant to be.

Nothing was without its challenges though, and sometimes, the kids were in their little moods and didn't feel like doing what I asked them to, but overall, it was worth it. I knew I was teaching them skills they wouldn't get at school—cooking, sewing, and knitting. Most of all, the time with them was irreplaceable. We were so close in those days. When we watched a movie, all five of us would sit on the same couch together. We'd cuddle and eat popcorn. We had story time in our bedroom.

With homeschooling, we could protect them from what the world wanted to teach them, even if it was for a short time. The early days of teaching the kids were not just about academics but also about character, integrity, honesty, and self-awareness. Not to say they didn't have their inner struggles as they got older, but they knew who they were, and they were secure in that. The world would try to do enough damage on them as they grew older, but for the time being, Brad and I had more control over what their little ears heard and what was being taught.

Every week, on Tuesdays, we'd do an act of kindness. We had to either go help someone in person, or we wrote them a card. This taught each of us to stop, think outside of ourselves, and think of others. The kids enjoyed helping and making others feel loved. They shared stories of what God was doing through them, feeling like they were making a difference. They also loved visiting old people in the nursing home, reading them stories and bringing them treats. Ms. Stella, an old lady who attended the same church we went to and lived across the street, was someone the kids loved to visit. They would ride their bikes to her house, and she often baked cookies for them and gave them candy. They would come home to share the stories Ms. Stella told them, often the same ones over and over again, but they loved her and she loved them. One day, they came storming through the garage door, full of excitement, after visiting Ms. Stella's.

"Mom, Dad, guess what Ms. Stella showed us?" Ethan said, huffing and puffing, a big grin on his face.

"What is it, Ethan?" I asked, smiling at the excitement on his face. He was so cute with his almost white blond hair and shiny blue eyes. They seemed to sparkle more when he was excited.

"She showed us how to catch a gopher," said Alissa quickly.

"Aww, Alissa, I wanted to tell her!" Ethan said, looking at his sister with disappointment.

"Well, you can tell her how. Sorry!" Alissa said with a sorry look on her face. She didn't like hurting her brother, but sometimes, she couldn't help herself from blurting out an interesting part of the story. Ethan and Alissa were very close, even though there was a little less than three years between them. Everywhere we went, people often asked if they were twins; they looked so much alike. Alissa was a little smaller for her age, and Ethan was a little bigger for his. Alissa was always watching out for her little brother.

"Okay . . . so you get an empty milk jug and fill with water. Then pour the water down the gopher hole. Mom, you gotta be ready 'cause the gopher will jump out and into the milk jug," explained Ethan, flailing his arms and doing the motions as if he were actually catching a gopher.

"So the gopher fits in the small hole of the milk jug?" I asked, knowing the answer but wanting Ethan to continue telling the story in more detail. He was so adorable!

"Oh, you have to cut the hole a little bigger, but not much. The gophers are pretty small! It's so cool! Ms. Stella is the coolest old lady I know. But then she tells us the story of her falling off her dad's horse wagon way back in the olden days . . . like . . . every time we go. I'm kind of sick of that one, but I just listen anyway 'cause she's old, right? Like she can't remember much, right? Right, Mom?"

"Right, Ethan. So what happens to the gopher?" I asked him, smiling. I loved how excited he got when he told stories.

"Ummmm, Ms. Stella dumps it in a large bucket of water and puts a lid on it. That's the not so nice part. It drowns," Ethan said with a sad face.

"Well, that's quite the lesson Ms. Stella taught you. If we ever have a gopher, we can try it," I said, getting up and giving Ethan a hug. "Thanks for visiting Ms. Stella."

"I don't think I wanna do that, Mom. It was kind of sad seeing the gopher get dumped into the water knowing it was going to drown. I couldn't do it." Ethan was so cute. I was so proud of him. My heart was filled with admiration. He was such a shy boy, but he loved telling stories. I remember his little tales about having bees in his ears and monsters in his bed and all sorts of other stories he'd make up.

Lauren was the big sister who made everyone follow her and do what she wanted. She loved reading and sports. Alissa and Ethan adored her. Alissa was more the thinker, book smart. She loved playing but wasn't too coordinated in sports—it was like she had two left feet. She too was a leader, directing Ethan and telling him what to do when Lauren was not around. It was so amazing to me how different and unique they were from each other. Each one had their own gifts and talents, and I loved watching them develop. I wanted so much for them but was also scared of failing as a mom. A lot of the time, I didn't know what I was doing. Often, I would lie in bed wondering many times if I made the right decisions in certain situations or if I was too harsh or too lenient. Every day, I prayed for wisdom and guidance to be the best mom I could be. I wanted to give them so much of what I didn't get as a child, especially safety and protection.

Sometimes the fear of things happening to them, like when I was young, would steer me to make decisions out of fear. I did not like my kids sleeping over at anyone's houses. Sometimes I allowed it but not very often. It made me stay up all night worrying. I did not trust people. In my past, I had trusted people who looked trustworthy, who seemed nice and kind, but it turned out they were not. How could anyone tell the truth about a person from the outside? It seemed too easy to fool people, making them believe you are a good person, yet you have evil intentions. Even knowing someone after a long time did not mean they were trustworthy. You hear often of outstanding citizens, even about a Christian radio guy, who did some crazy, awful things to kids. I had also experienced it myself. Even though I had told no one, it still lingered in my mind. It was the wheat fields that cried out to me, calling me, following me each day of my life. It was a part of me that would not let go of me, and each time it came to the forefront of my mind, I shook my head to push it back, back to the dark cavern of my memory. Those were the memories that made me not trust anyone with my own kids. I had to protect them. I would die if anything like that had happened to them. That was something that hurt me to the depth of my core, thinking about the fact that no one had come to my rescue.

Chapter 12

Therefore I will not keep silent; I will speak out in the anguish of my spirit, I will complain in the bitterness of my soul.
—Job 7:11

She's standing in the wheat field, walking, but she keeps looking back. Each time, thinking that this time, she would see something different, but it's not. It's the same. An area is flat. The area is dark, and she saw impressions of bodies lying beside one another. She feels sick inside. She hates that spot and wishes it would grow like the rest of the field, tall and swaying back and forth with the wind, beautiful. But it doesn't. It is dead. She wants to feel whole, clean, done with it, but the spot continues to look back at her. Tormenting her. She wants to spit at it. She hates it. It has affected every part of her life. What would it be like without it? She doesn't know because it has been there most of her life. She reflects on all that has happened, years of turmoil because of it, this one spot. It has tainted her life, everything pointing back to the one spot. She wants to rake it, clean it, plant new seed, but she also wants to stay far away from it. She wants to bury it, burn it. She wants to be free of it, but it is etched in every fiber of her being. It has followed her everywhere, in her addiction, in every relationship, in her identity, in the depths of her soul.

She tries to hide from it, to run from it; but it is always right behind her, taunting her. It's a part of her she doesn't want, but it wants her. She feels sick. She wants to throw up all that is in her that binds her to it. No matter how hard she tries, how much she begs for it to go away, it never leaves. She takes a step, and it takes a step. She turns a corner, and it turns a corner. She runs, and it runs. She hides, and it hides behind her. She screams at it, and it looks silently at her, not needing to say a word. It doesn't have to. She says, "You've done enough damage. Now leave me alone!" But when she looks back, it's still there, and she screams in defeat.

Chapter 13

*Wise words are like deep waters; wisdom flows
from the wise like a bubbling brook.*
—Proverbs 18:4

The farm life was a new adventure for us all. I had been brought up in the country for the first part of my life, but the only animals we ever had was a cat and a dog for a short while. When I moved out at seventeen, I went to live in the city. At seventeen, I loved the hustle and bustle of the city, and there was so much more to do there. Being young draws you in to the things that seem exciting and happening. Also, the fact that one can easily hide among the masses of people was extremely attractive to me. I wanted to blend in with the masses, unnoticed. It seemed like, until then, I had been an open target for others to use me whenever they wanted.

As maturity set in, marriage and kids came into the picture, and my perspective changed, and my desire to be in the midst of the drama or lost in the crowds shifted. My heart and mind longed for simplicity and peace. My longing to get away, to begin a whole new life, to leave my old self behind, tugged deep within me. I was so desperate to rid myself of my old life. Farming? I knew nothing about it, yet an excitement grew inside of me. When Lauren was seven years old, she started taking horseback riding lessons, and just recently, we had purchased a horse named Lucky. I had no experience with horses; they were big and scary. It was a whole new adventure and life ahead, so contrary to where I had come from. I wanted to experience nature and life, breathe in the fresh air, and soak up the moment. I was tired of running. I wanted to stop running. Halt. Get to know my surroundings and who I really was.

Brad grew up in the country too, but not on a farm. He also had no clue about living on a farm. Initially, we had no intentions of ever moving away from town, from being one block away from the lake and a few blocks from the downtown area. We lived within walking distance from all the conveniences of a small tourist town and never dreamed of being anywhere else. After a few years of being so close to the neighbors, to the right and left and two behind us, Brad was getting annoyed. Listening to their noises and hearing them complaining every time he had projects fixing things around the house or having people over during the daytime for a barbeque. One of the neighbors would stick her head over the fence and say, "Are you almost done making all that noise?" Brad would smile back, stomp in the house, and grumble like a bear. The space around us seemed to close in, get smaller and smaller, until we felt like we were being choked. One day, Brad came home from work and told me that we were all going for a drive.

"Where are we going?" I asked, eyebrows raised in question.

"Wait and see. It's a surprise," he said with a mischievous smirk on his face. I knew he was up to something but had no clue what it was.

"Not even a clue?" I poked, making my sad puppy-eyed face and pouted lips.

"That won't work, Sam. You'll have to wait and see. It's not far," Brad said as he turned away from me, trying to ignore my pleas for a little hint. Deep down, I liked surprises and adventures. Lauren was ten, Alissa was three, and Ethan was eight months. Lauren was curious too; she kept asking her dad where we were going.

"You guys don't have any patience. It wouldn't be a surprise if I told you," said Brad with a little chuckle as he walked out the door.

I sat on the passenger side looking out the window of the truck as Brad drove out of town. As we drove farther away from town, there were fewer and fewer houses, more land and trees. I felt myself relax, feeling the outside come into the truck, even when the window was closed. Nature was surrounding me with its beauty and peace. Several miles out, Brad turned right on a country road, down a few miles, then turned right again into a field, literally.

"Where are you going? This isn't even a road," I asked, confused.

"I know. I asked the owner, and he said it was okay," Brad answered with a sigh.

"Dad, this is cool. It's like going four wheeling," said Lauren as the kids were bouncing around in the back. Brad was still driving the gray, beat-up Ford truck that he had when we first met. He loved that truck, even though there was no suspension. I thought I was going to get sick, but the kids were having a blast.

"Without the four-wheel drive part, it's only two-wheel drive," replied Brad with a chuckle.

We drove down what looked like a farm tractor track in between two fields for quite a way back. I could not figure out where on earth we were going. All I could see were farm fields and a forest ahead. Brad drove to the end of the field, butting up to the edge of the forest where he could go no further and stopped.

"Let's get out!" he said with excitement in his voice as he shut the engine off.

"Like here? What are you going to do to us?" I asked with a little worried look on my face.

"Follow me. It's an adventure," Brad said as he got the car seat out with Ethan and began to walk into the thick, dense woods covered with vines and prickles everywhere. Lauren followed Brad while Alissa held my hand and trailed sideways as I tried to protect her from the thistles and branches swinging out at her. Brad stopped in the middle of the woods.

"This is it!" he said, spreading his arms and looking at me.

"This is whaaat?" I asked, looking into his eyes for an answer.

"This is where we are going to build a house," Brad said, smiling at me as if saying, *Trust me.*

"What? What are you talking about? This is in the middle of nowhere. And who said we want to move?" I asked totally confused as I picked Alissa up.

"We do," said Brad. "Imagine this cleared up. Come, follow me," as he swung his arm inviting us to follow him.

I rolled my eyes and sighed in defiance as we followed him further into the woods until we reached the edge before it dropped off into a deep and wide ravine. It was the Black River. My eyes opened wide to the open scenery that surrounded me. It was beautiful! I looked at Brad with a questioning look on my face. "But how? I mean how are we going to afford this?"

"We'll sell our house. We should make a profit. We've been there for five years, and it's around the corner from the lake. We can get a loan to purchase the land now," he said. It sounded like he had thought this all through. "I can do some of the work too, which will save us a lot of money. I have some building experience."

"It is a beautiful spot, complete with a beautiful ravine. Plus, I do hate being so close to the neighbors, and I'm tired of their complaining every time you work on something. But I will miss the lake only a block away. We need to go home and think about it," I said, thinking about what it would be like to build a house in this spot, looking over the ravine, away from people. I envisioned the kids exploring in the woods.

"At some point, we could build a barn and bring Lucky home," Brad said with excitement in his eyes as he looked at Lauren and winked.

"Yeah, can we, Mom? That'd be so great! I could ride whenever I wanted to. Please, Mom?" Lauren said, putting her hands together in pleading mode and looking at me with twinkly eyes. I smiled and looked at Brad. I really liked that idea. I had often thought about living on a farm, living out in the country, and having chickens. I don't know what it was about chickens, but that was the first thing that came to my mind when I thought about farms. I didn't know anything about farming, but it would be a fun adventure, and it's good for the kids to experience. A lot of room to explore and play.

I turned to Lauren and put my arm around her. "We'll have to think about it, okay? We have to see if we can make it work."

We went home, looked at some numbers, and within a week, we decided to take a leap of faith and go for it. We began building in December, and by June the next year, we were moving into our new home. We had done a lot of work, but it was a long six months. Brad had been at the house many nights working late while I looked after the kids. On weekends, I would bring the kids down, and we would work on gathering and burning sticks and cleaning the property. Within a year of moving in, the barn was built, and we brought our first horse home. As the years went by, we had chickens, sheep, rabbits, dogs, and cats and added more horses. We even planted a garden for a school project. But after several years of battling the weeds and tomato worms, we gave that up.

We had a good time. The girls showed horses at the county fair every year along with sheep, and as they grew older, they had attained my competitiveness and showed on the bigger horse circuits. The kids had to do plenty of chores and learned many lessons about responsibility. Those lessons were difficult ones. They learned that they had to work hard to get better at riding. They also had to look after their animals, which was a daily responsibility; the animals did not clean or feed themselves. They also loved having barn cats that kept multiplying quickly, but the kids had a blast with them. They would spend hours upon hours playing with them.

The boys, Brad and Ethan, didn't like the horses so much. Ethan rode a little, and Brad was not comfortable around them, so instead, they got dirt bikes, made tracks and ramps around the property, and rode around. Ethan was only three when he would go over ramps with his little 50cc mini bike Brad found. Ethan loved it, and he had no fear, just like his dad. It was Brad who showed Ethan how to make ramps and jump over them, not me. It was also Brad who showed the kids how to ride bikes, running behind them and letting go as they peddled away. I hid inside the house when it came to doing those sorts of things, just thinking of my kids falling over made my skin crawl and filled me with dread.

Brad and I returned home from a week's vacation to find a dozen chickens in our dining room, thanks to grandma and grandpa, my parents, who babysat. Brad and I didn't know a thing about how to raise chickens. Brad built an area in the horse barn for them with a fence and little houses for them to lie in. They were not laying hens but chickens to kill and eat. We were all so excited when it was time to kill and eat them. The chicks were cute when they were small, but as they grew, they became noisy and smelly. We had someone come and take them away to kill, pluck, and clean them. I was excited to roast a couple of our own raised chickens, and we placed the remaining chickens in the freezer. I made mashed potatoes, gravy, green bean casserole and stuffing to go along with the chicken. Brad blessed the food, and we began to eat.

"Mom, this chicken is gross. I can't even chew it," said Ethan spitting it out.

"Ethan, that's disgusting. It can't be that bad," said Brad as he took a bite of his chicken. He made a funny face as he chewed and chewed. Then he too spit it out on his napkin. "What on earth is wrong with this chicken?"

"See, Dad, I told you," Ethan said laughing. "That's gross, Dad!"

I was scared to try a piece, but as I put it in my mouth it felt like I was chewing a piece of rubber that tasted nasty. I too spit it out on my napkin as I began to laugh hysterically. The rest of the gang joined in. We laughed so hard, we were all crying. Brad later called the man who butchered and cleaned the chickens to tell him about the awful-tasting chickens. The man asked Brad a few questions to discover that we were supposed to contain the chickens in a small tight enclosed area, so they didn't have much room to move and get too tough. That was our first and last experiment with raising chickens.

We all had a good laugh about the chickens for years, those "tough" chickens we would say. Our friends, the DeRoses, had funny stories about their experiences on the farm too. We loved hearing their funny farm stories. They were city folks from New Jersey who moved to the country, wanting to be farmers, just like Brad and I. They had cows, pigs, and chickens in their farming days. Once they had bought a dozen chicks and brought them home. They put out two pans, one filled with food, the other with water.

One day, they came home, and the chicks were covered with food all over their bodies. They had gotten wet from being in the water pan then went into the seed pan, which stuck to their little fluffy yellow bodies. Our friends decided that the best thing to do was to wash the seed off the chicks' bodies. They filled the sink up with soap and water, put the dozen chicks in the sink to wash, then rinsed them. As they placed them on the towel, their little bodies shivered from being wet and cold. Feeling sorry for the little baby chicks, they decided that they needed to warm them up. They turned the oven on low, put them on a large pan, and shut the door for a few minutes to warm up and dry. Next thing the little chicks' beautiful yellow bodies caught on fire. They quickly opened the oven and threw them back into the sink filled with water and individually dried them off with a towel the best they could. When it was time to kill and eat them, they defeathered them and noticed that their skin was all spotted black from catching on fire.

My family too had our share of funny stories of horses running through fences and chasing them down the road. Sheep head-butting the kids and knocking them down—that was Ethan's funny story. We had gotten Alissa two sheep to show at the fair. We bought them when they were little, raised them for six months, then brought them to the fair to show and auction off. This entailed feeding them, taking care of them, and walking them so they became comfortable with us. Quickly, we learned that sheep were timid, stupid, and spooked easily. They were scared of their own shadows. Brad had built them a house with a six-foot fence around it and a gate to go in and out. They may have been stupid, but they were so cute! For the first several weeks, every time Alissa or anyone would walk toward them, they would get scared and slam their body into the fence over and over again to try to get away. She would have to talk to them gently to quiet them down. They were like sheep on way too much caffeine, hyper and crazy. When Alissa tried to walk them around the yard, she would have to drag them as they'd often plop their bodies on the ground, scared to move.

One day, Brad, the kids, and I were out in the sheep pen, putting logs down for the sheep to jump over; they loved to jump. Ethan was bending over, putting a log in place when the sheep put his head down and gently head-butted him. Ethan laughed and bent down again to see if the sheep would do it again, and it did, but harder, which knocked him off his feet. They did this a few times until Brad and I noticed the sheep backing up and looking more intense, while Ethan was ready for the next head-butt but couldn't see what the sheep was doing. It pawed at the ground several times, getting ready to run toward Ethan. Brad grabbed Ethan and pulled him out of the way just in time. The sheep hit the fence with a slam.

Often, during our morning devotions, we talked about the sheep; they had many questions about why God referred to people as his sheep when sheep were so dumb. They'd ask, Was God saying humans were dumb? Why would he call them dumb when he was the one who created them?

"Wellllll," I said, "maybe not dumb but not so bright. Slow to understand maybe."

"No, we are dumb!" Ethan said, pointing to the side of his head.

"We are," said Alissa. "But through God we can be smart."

"Well . . . what do you mean?" asked Ethan, looking intently at her.

"Like the other day, you were building a ramp to jump over with your bike, but Dad ran out and told you to stop. Why? Because you'd built it wrong and you would hurt yourself, but you didn't know that 'cause you are not smart yet. You're not dumb. You just don't know the right way, but Dad does. So he showed you how to fix it so you wouldn't slam your face down on it. I'm thinking that's kind of what God's saying, to trust in him, follow him 'cause he knows the right way," explained Alissa.

"Wow, that was deep," said Lauren, looking at Alissa with an impressed expression on her face.

"Yeah, Alissa, thanks. Let me add to that: Dad loves Ethan and doesn't want him to get hurt. Ethan could have ignored Dad and done it anyway. What would have been the consequence?" I asked, looking at each one as they thought about my question.

"I could have slammed my face, maybe broke something," answered Ethan, after a long, thoughtful moment.

"Yup. Soooo . . . as a shepherd that looks after his not-so-smart sheep, God loves us so much He wants to look after us. He knows what's best for each of us, more than we do, but we need to let him, trust him. If not, he will not make us follow him, but he allows us to choose his way or ours," I said as I looked at each one of them with so much love, hoping that they understood the metaphor.

I understood it more, deeper, as their mom. I was learning that Lauren, Alissa, and Ethan were each unique, different from each other, even though they all came from my body. As much as I wanted them to be the best they could be, to live to the fullest, I couldn't make them do anything. They had to make choices and learn for themselves; that was the hard part about parenting—letting them make the final decision, as long as it wasn't life threatening, letting them learn from it. Finally, teaching them how to get back up, brush it off, learn from their mistake and keep moving forward.

I was surprised and shocked that such wisdom came out of my kids. I admired them all, and they were so sweet and intelligent. I thanked God often for allowing me to have eyes to see my beautiful children for who they were. At times, it was hard to know if they understood life and its complexities. If they understood that things were not always as they seemed and faith was largely a practice of believing in the unseen. Yet to me, there was proof of it all around me. In the creation, in my children, in my trials, in my quiet times with God, in the strange encounters I had almost daily with people and events that could only be ordained by God. I wanted my kids to see it, to experience his presence too. I knew I would not have survived this long without him, with all I had seen and experienced in my life. I would have overdosed, jumped off a cliff, been institutionalized, or who knows what.

Living on the farm was a lot of work, but there were a lot of rich lessons with what the kids experienced that would forever stay with them all their lives. Brad and I devoted much of our time on the farm raising our children and sacrificing much of our time for them. We also received so much back, learning many lessons about parenting and the important things in life through our experiences on the farm. Life was precious, and spending time with our children was so worth it to us. We tried to soak in every moment. Often, I'd watch my kids care for the animals, mucking out the stalls, carrying heavy buckets of water, helping Brad bail and stack the hay. I couldn't help but feel so much pride for them. I was so glad that we decided to homeschool the children and move to the country. We had grown so much closer as a family in those times.

I was on a constant high. I never imagined that my life could have been this good. I loved every moment with my children at home, being so close to them. And my husband was amazing. He could pretty much do anything, a jack-of-all-trades, and to me, he was growing stronger and more handsome with each passing day. We would often finish each other's sentences or nod in agreement without a word being said. It felt as though time and life experiences were bringing us closer to being one. Life with Brad became more and more comfortable, and we seemed to be the perfect match.

At times, it seemed too perfect, like something bad was going to happen. I knew I did not deserve this life I now led, and I often had a feeling that the plug would soon be pulled on my "perfect" life. That I would eventually have to pay for my past. But I wanted to stay in this world I had carefully created for myself and not allow the past to come into it and infect it and fill it with its disease. I still struggled with the belief that I needed to be punished, that something was not right. A mistake was made in allowing me to be happy, to have a relationship with a man that was deep and special, that I could be so blessed in having three beautiful, healthy children.

I remembered the day of my encounter with Jesus as though it was yesterday, the love and healing I had felt. Yet it was still difficult accepting the fact that my Heavenly Father loved me despite my past, failures, and mistakes. The bad I had done often seemed to overpower the good. I heard and read in his word many, many times how Jesus's blood was shed for *all* my hurts and pains. It was difficult for me to really grasp that idea, to think I could ever feel the freedom of forgiveness, freedom from shame and guilt, freedom from the past that seemed to continually haunt me, follow me, remind me of who I was and possibly still am, pulling me back to the "then." Missing me. Telling me I did not belong in this place, with this "perfect" family. I knew it wasn't perfect in the sense that no one ever did any wrong or challenged me, but it was my perfect place of fulfillment, of love and peace, of contentment, my chance to be a good mom and wife. Eventually, I thought, I would have to pay for the wrong I had done.

Chapter 14

Don't just pretend to love others. Really love them. Hate what is wrong. Hold tightly to what is good.
—Romans 12:9

I hated thinking about my teen years; it was such a crazy, chaotic mess. I was glad to be done with those years and wanted to stay far away from that part of my life. I was walking further and further away from my past, from my youth. I was growing deeper in my relationship with God. I attended a little church in the middle of nowhere and helped minister to young children. I loved working with them. They were so innocent and sweet, their minds wanted to learn, and they actually liked being around adults. I was in my early thirties and feeling more comfortable with my life and where it was going. But this comfortable place that I was in would soon change, and one day, our pastor, Ed, called Brad and I into his office.

"Hey, Sam, Brad," the pastor waved as we walked into his office, "have a seat."

We sat down, a little nervous about what it was all about. I always had that feeling that I was going to the principal's office, that I had done something wrong.

"I'll get right to the point. The youth leader is leaving. He's moving, and we need someone to take over the teen ministry until we find a replacement. We all thought, the steering committee, that you two would be a great replacement. What do you think? Just until we find someone," he said as he leaned back in his chair and waited for us to respond to his offer.

"Wow, umm, this is a bit of a shock. We've never led a ministry before, let alone teens," Brad said as he turned his head to look at me with a question in his eyes.

"I don't even like teenagers!" I blurted out, thinking of my own teenage years, cringing. Teens were much too complicated for me. How could I be of any help to burgeoning young minds when my own teenage years had been such a mess?

"Well . . . we think you two would be great. We've prayed about it and really feel God wants to use you guys in ways you never thought. You guys are great with not just kids but people. You're young and fun too. Plus, we see you growing so much in your faith and your love for God," Pastor said, leaning forward and looking at us more intently.

"We'll have to think about it. When do you want an answer?" Brad asked.

"Tomorrow," Pastor said. "Just kidding." He chuckled. "How about in the next two weeks?"

"Sounds good," said Brad as he stood up and reached to shake pastor's hand.

"I'm not interested," I said, shaking my head in defiance as we walked out of his office and out to the car.

"Well, let's not make a quick decision. Let's take our time, pray about it together, and see what happens," said Brad, putting his arm around me as he led me to the passenger side and opened the door.

"You're not seriously thinking about it, are you? I hate teens. I hated my teen years, and I can't stand being around them," I said as I looked at him before getting into the car. Just thinking about it gave me anxiety. I really didn't want to be around them. They reminded me of the years I wanted to forget.

"I don't know. Something just stirred in me a bit, so I just wanna wait a bit before making a decision," said Brad. There was compassion in his voice. He got into the driver's side of the car. He reached over and touched my hand that was resting on my lap and looked at me. "Please, Sam, give it time and see what God wants us to do."

I looked at him and turned my head toward the window. I was worried. Brad was acting strange. It surprised me that he was even considering it. He probably would be good at it, but not me. I was not changing my mind.

I laugh every time I recall the memory of that conversation because something did happen to me. My heart changed. I hate to admit it, but Brad was right. I do not know what made me change my mind, to agree to minister to teenagers, but something, God most likely, changed it. I started to pray about it and thought maybe I might be okay doing it for a while since I did understand about the many issues they dealt with: broken relationships, addiction, suicide, loneliness, abortion. Maybe I could be helpful and compassionate. Besides, it was only for a short period of time, I told myself.

We had a small group of kids to begin with, about five. We connected with the kids so well that the kids ended up inviting friends, who invited friends, and next thing we knew, there were twenty kids in our youth group. That was a lot for a little church of under a hundred people. The kids were from the outback, beyond the city limits into the country where kids ran wild and parents would hide from the law or child protective services. Many of them lived in poor conditions, some in abusive homes, many single parent homes, some were cutters, many were abused; it was a mixture of mess.

But our hearts went out to them. We grew to love them and to minister to their hearts, to be there for them, to talk to them, to teach them God's word, to pour love into them and listen to them. We brought them to concerts, on mission trips, and did many service projects around the neighborhood. We grew as a team, and what was meant to be temporary stretched across fifteen years.

It was tough, seeing and hearing what some of the kids lived through without being able to fix it. Brad and I learned that truth the hard way. We had a few teens stay with us for periods of time due to bad situations at home, and we believed if we just put them in a better environment, the children would heal and flourish. But it wasn't that simple, nor did it work that way. You would think many of their past issues would go away because you place them in a different environment, give them a safe place to live and opportunities, but their brains were traumatized and taught a different way of living and thinking. They had little to no motivation; they did not know how to pick up after themselves, make rational decisions, or understand consequences or boundaries. Brad and I couldn't hammer it into them over time. Several times, we had to find different alternatives for them because it was too much for our family to deal with.

There were two young teens who showed up at youth group, Jake and Cristy, for the first time. They were brother and sister, and the church bus had picked them up for church, and I clearly remember how dirty and smelly they were. They were both shy and reserved. Their words were broken and difficult to understand as though they had just come out of living in the jungle all their lives. I could tell that there was more behind the scenes with these two; I knew some of the signs. I was learning that I had a gift of discernment. I sensed when things were not right or when someone was hiding something or not telling the truth. Sometimes I would tell Brad, "There's something up with that person. Something is not right," when the person seemed fine to everyone else. Brad, at first, would say that I was worrying too much, maybe pre-judging them. I wasn't. I just felt something was askew. After some time, Brad trusted my discernment. It wasn't intuition; it was something inside of me telling me to keep my eyes open, that there was more to that person, to pray for them, and to be wise in my interactions with them.

Brad, the pastor, and I would stop over at Jake and Cristy's home once in a while. I had never seen anything like it. I didn't think anyone lived in such conditions in America. They lived in a run-down trailer with a few smashed windows, garbage all over the yard and inside, with several dogs roaming in and out of the house. One was tied up beside the house, and no one would dare approach it. I wondered how they could live in such poverty yet feed all the dogs.

When Jake opened the door to let us in, the smell hit me. it was so strong and almost knocked me out. I tried hard to hold my breath as much as I could without instinctively putting my hand over my mouth and nose. As I looked around, there was feces everywhere. There was one couch, with cushions that sunk into it, and there was no way someone could actually sit on it without sinking into it and hitting their butt on the floor. The kitchen counter was stacked with opened cans of food, and other stuff I could not identify. Jake was standing in the kitchen eating something out of a can with a plastic fork; when he finished, he just chucked the can out the window. I tried not to react. I stared at Jake in utter shock, trying to figure out why he had just done that. He seemed not to be bothered by it at all! I watched his face as he looked at me, not even noticing that he had done something unusual. I smiled at him; that's all I could figure out to do. It wasn't his fault; it's what he was taught to do. It was probably common practice and something he thought everyone did. Inside me, my heart ached at seeing the condition of their home. I wanted so badly to rescue them. I wanted to take them both home at that moment and clean them up. They lived like animals.

Over the next few years that Cristy and Jake were at youth group, Brad and I tried to teach them life skills, like how to cook and clean up after themselves, hoping that maybe they would begin to have a sense of pride that they could do something themselves to change their circumstances, even a little. But it seemed the old habits, the old ways, kept calling them back. They struggled because our way was so foreign to them; they just couldn't grasp it. It taught us that the ways you were taught, the conditions you were brought up in, were embedded deeply. It was the only way they knew how to live. Brad and I thought about trying to bring them to our house to live, but we learned that if we did, Jake and Cristy wouldn't be comfortable. Even if the conditions were way better, it was a foreign land for them and would lead to culture shock. Eventually, because of child protective services being on their heels, the family up and left one night, and we never saw them again.

There were many situations like that that broke our hearts. There was a girl who struggled with cutting due to the physical, sexual, and mental abuse she received at home. There was another girl who was severely sexually abused, another who was anorexic, and the list went on. There was no way Brad and I could ever come close to fixing any of their problems. Many nights, we cried for the kids and lamented over their broken lives. It was difficult, heart-wrenching, but we continued to stand strong, to be people the kids could trust and come to, to talk with when they needed it, and to show them the love and hope of Christ. At times, it was hard to feel any hope for these kids, but we learned that we had to leave it in God's hands and do what God was calling us to do right in the moment. That is what we hung on to or else Brad and I would have drowned in the midst of it all. Trying to help and fix the troubled lives that surrounded us was too much for us, or anyone for that matter, to bear or to even try to fix. There were too many and much too complicated. That's why we had to learn to trust in God to guide them through it all.

I would often reflect back on my teenage years and the struggles I'd had. People often looked at our life and commented on how easy we had it, that we had a nice home, a "perfect" family, and it angered me at times because they did not know me. They didn't know my past, the journey I had walked, and the pain I was still dealing with because of it. I was certainly grateful for my life now and considered myself blessed, but it did not come without a cost, and it frustrated me that people would judge me from my outside appearance.

I knew all too well that my new journey didn't erase the past, nor did it exempt me from future storms. My faith allowed me to see life with different eyes and obtain strength from God to endure. It taught me not to judge people. My mother had often said, "Don't judge a book by its cover," and I was truly beginning to understand what she meant by that. When you only looked at the exterior, you didn't see the journey someone had walked and what they'd gone through and experienced. I was learning to listen and to love people where they were at and to allow God to do the fixing.

We really wanted to help the kids that came into our lives. I understood more than anyone the inner struggle and torment some of these kids were dealing with. Brad was great with them too, and even though he hadn't gone through the things I had, he saw them deeper through my eyes. We started taking them on mission trips. Each year, the kids had an opportunity to go if they pitched in to raise money, and we would travel to different areas in the United States and Canada, giving them the chance to experience life beyond their four walls.

On one trip, we went to the mountains of Missouri where we camped at a camp for city kids whose parent or parents were behind bars. The group helped fix things around the camp and acted as counselors to the kids for the week. The food was scarce; we were given kid-sized portions, and at some point, in the middle of the week, Brad and I snuck out to get the teens more food. The weather was hot, over a hundred degrees, and the spot we camped on the property was hilly and very lumpy. It was a good lesson for all of us on enduring tough living conditions. But through it all, the youth felt good doing something that made a difference in other people's lives, and it gave them a sense of worth.

We also went to the inner city of Toronto several times to serve the homeless meals, work in the homeless shelters, and help in some of the ministries across town. On one trip, my group of four went to a home where a woman was dying of AIDS. She had three children—five, ten, and fourteen. That was one of my hardest, most memorable missions. We painted their kitchen and fixed up the small basement into a playroom for the youngest daughter, who was five. As we worked every day for a week, we got to know the family. The mother shared her story and how she came to Christ. She touched my heart, and I know she made an impact on the youth. My group surprised the little girl by painting a mural of Tweety Bird on one of the walls. It was the girl's favorite character, and she was so excited when she saw it. That filled the youth with such joy that they could put a smile on the face of little girl and her dying mother.

Before going to the home, we had to go to a class to learn about HIV and how it was and wasn't transmitted. The reality of it all was that the lady was dying. We were told not to get too close and not to exchange personal information. It was part of the organization's rule when we went to people's home so as not to get too emotionally attached. But it was difficult not to. Our hearts opened up and soaked in the memories, and we all cried when it was time to say good-bye. Each trip made an imprint on my heart that opened my eyes more to understanding life in a deeper, more spiritual way. That there was a short distance between life and death and how you lived the in between.

On the same trip, we arrived on the day of the Gay Pride parade. The mission team, which consisted of over fifty kids plus their leaders from all over, had a fun day planned to do a scavenger hunt around the city. The teams were given a list of things to look for and a camera. Once we found an item in the city that was on the list, the team had to take a picture with it. Our theme for the week was "No Shame, No Shame, No Shame" to signify that we weren't ashamed of the gospel. This slogan was printed on the back of the T-shirts we wore when we went out as a group. We didn't put two and two together; my team were working on our scavenger hunt and trying to avoid the parade, which was not an easy task since they traveled down every main road of the city. The first time we had to cross the parade's path, my group of eight teens plus myself were stopped by a group of guys.

"Hey, we just wanted to say thanks for supporting us!" they said as they raised their hands to give us all high fives. As the guys walked away from us, I looked at my group, confused. We weren't there supporting them. Why would they think that? We looked at one another and shrugged in confusion and continued on our way. Then, one of the girls in the group stopped and started to laugh hysterically. She was pointing at everyone barely able to speak.

"The . . . shirts!" she said, bending over and holding onto her stomach.

"Huh?" replied some of the kids together staring at her in confusion.

"The shirts . . . look at the back . . . of our shirts," she said, pointing.

We all reread the back of each other's shirt, which said, "No Shame, No Shame, No Shame." I think all at the same time, the light bulb went on and we suddenly got it, and we started to laugh. The guys we met thought we were saying there was no shame in what they were doing. We laughed so hard when we understood why someone would think that. Inside of me there was a battle going on. I struggled with how to love others that lived a life that was contrary to what was pleasing to God although I myself had lived a life contrary to God for a long time too.

I was beginning to understand what my choices cost me, that my God was a loving God and the perfect father, who loved me enough to pursue me all those years and never gave up. I began to understand that God wanted something different for me. How could I accept others yet not agree with the choices they made that would lead them to destruction? My heart longed for all to know the love of the Father and to be free from the burden of sin. Jesus said not to judge those that did not know him or his ways for they live in ignorance (Eph. 4:18). How do I love but not necessarily agree with them? How do I have patience and compassion but not fix them? I had much to learn about the balance of the two, to love, to guide, and to disciple while allowing God to work through me into their hearts. I had much to learn about how to live out my own testimony of salvation and new life without scaring others away.

During our time in the city, we saw homeless people bathing in water fountains in the park. We fed hundreds of homeless at the shelters and handed out sack lunches on the streets. Our team also had the privilege of sitting down with the homeless to share a meal. We listened to their life stories, what they once were—musicians, physicians, teachers, engineers—until a life situation happened that changed the course of their lives and caused them to end up on the streets. A wife leaving for another man, a child's death, gambling, alcohol, drug addiction, bankruptcy, there was a story behind every face.

All my misconceptions that homeless people were largely unintelligent, poor, and unable to take care of themselves were shattered. I learned that they were some of the most intelligent, compassionate people I would ever meet. Life just happened, knocked them off track, and they could not get back on. One of the men I sat with said he was a famous pianist once. As I sat listening, I couldn't help but wonder if he was telling the truth. I asked him if he would play for us, I wanted to see if he could actually play like he said he could. He said he would be honored, got up, marched over to the grand piano on the stage at the church's auditorium where we were at and played a piece by Mozart. He played as though he was Mozart himself, without any sheet music in front of him. My jaw fell open, as did most of the team helping, and tears filled my eyes as I listened. I felt the beautiful music in my soul along with the man's pain, connect, for a moment, and dance together as I closed my eyes.

Yes, there were mentally ill people too, but whatever their circumstance was, they were people. They were God's people who deserved compassion and love. The trips were an open door to the world around us. Even if we didn't travel far, it was still a life-changing experience. We encountered young people from all over with different backgrounds and life struggles. We served people from all different walks of life, and each path we crossed was a story to tell. From a youth removing the socks from his feet to give to a homeless person who had none to a wooden cross necklace given to a priest who needed encouragement, needing to know that God was there with him.

With each trip, Brad and I saw a difference in each of the youth after the week was over. The worship times and the messages given were always a time of growth and to connect with the young people. It opened doors for opportunities to share and go deeper in their spiritual walk and be open about their struggles. I saw hope. When there did not seem to be any, I saw glimpses of it here and there. I saw joy rise up in them, maybe because they were doing something to help others when they didn't know how to help themselves. They saw life beyond themselves, beyond their own lives. Maybe it was an escape from life even if it was only for a week, leaving it behind for a little while to do something for others, realizing that they could accomplish something in life and that they did matter.

Some stayed in our youth group through their teen years, but many came and went. I remember them all and often think about them and pray for them. Some have come back and connected with Brad and me, and I checked in with them, trying to give them encouragement. There were many whom I hadn't seen in years, and I didn't know where they were or how they were doing. My heart yearned for a better life for them, a life of love, peace, and joy within themselves, to find who they were in Christ and he in them. That is where the true meaning of life is, within. I could only hold on to the hope I had experienced myself and know that I had done what God had called me to do—and that had to count for something.

Chapter 15

I will not leave them as orphans; I will come to you.
—John 14:18

    I had many dreams, and most didn't become reality. I knew it was my lack of confidence in myself, as well as my fear. I had never felt confident enough or intelligent enough to take risks or try new things because the fear of failure was stronger than the risk. But God was really doing a work in me. He opened my eyes to the world around me and healed my inner wounds. I still struggled with people, with communicating, and with feeling inferior around them. I preferred spending time at home with my family to hide from my insecurities, yet there was a longing inside me. I wanted friends. I needed friends. I wanted to be able to have close relationships with other women like my mom did.

    God continued to push me to work on my fears and insecurities, helping me to do things that were hard for me. Like talking in front of people and putting me in leadership positions. I allowed him to push me beyond my four walls, physically beyond the walls of my home and spiritually beyond the walls of my mind. The many years working with teens helped me to discover who I was and what I believed. They also showed me about life beyond my hiding place, thinking I was the only one who felt shame, who felt lost and broken at times. They showed me that everyone in some way was broken and in need of love, compassion, and understanding.

    One of my dreams was to help others, connect, and build relationships. I dreamed of a place where people could come and feel like it was a home away from home or even a needed place away from home. I thought often about the show *Cheers*, a bar where people came and shared their day, struggles, and challenges, and they felt like they were a family.

> Sometimes you wanna go where everybody knows
> your name
> and they're always glad you came
> You wanna be where you can see
> our troubles are all the same.
> You wanna be where everybody knows your name

Something about that theme song always warmed my heart. It was not necessarily about the bar, I did not want to open a bar, but I loved the thought of a welcoming and inviting atmosphere where people felt like it was a home away from home. Maybe something like a coffee shop, most people liked coffee, and it was something that brought people together. I liked that thought. I envisioned lots of books, a variety of coffee, a chalkboard, and a beautiful, comfy furniture. I didn't know where or how, but it was a dream that kept growing and gnawing at me. I wanted people to feel his comfort and his love in a non-threatening environment. I prayed about it. I wanted people to find peace and joy in the midst of their chaotic lives, a safe place. I did not know if that was just a dream that would always be a dream or if God had something in mind. The thought kept popping up in my mind, so I kept dreaming the dream, and if it was meant to be, God would have to make it happen.

I loved where my life was going, which was so different from where I had been. My oldest child, after many years of struggling, had joined the army and was living her life and discovering herself. I knew there were some things that Lauren struggled with: insecurity, partying, wanting to fit in, but I also knew that she had to walk her own journey and figure life out as I and many others before her had to do. It was not easy for me to let go. I often envisioned seeing Lauren in the driver's side mirror running down the driveway, screaming, as I drove the truck and horse trailer without her. Lauren had been giving me a hard time all morning, talking back to me and cussing. I had warned her if she did not stop, she would be left behind. Lauren did not stop. I had to follow through with my threat and left her behind. That was one of the hardest things I had to do, disciplining my children.

When things got out of hand with Lauren, when she'd sneak out of the house in the middle of the night, skip school, lie, be disrespectful, we would send her out of town on a mission trip with Youth Unlimited. When Lauren came back, there was a change in her for several months after, until life settled back in, and slowly she would start getting into her old habits. There were times of deep prayer and crying out to God for her, for all of my children. I just wanted them to follow him. Life was already full of trials, they would all face them throughout their lives; but if they had God to lean on, call on, trust, and have faith in, I knew they would be okay. I was finding out that the true test of faith was when my children grew; they wanted more independence and wanted to make their own choices, which were not always good and the way I liked, but I had to let go and allow them to find their way, to walk their own journey.

Another deep desire implanted in me was to foster teens. Brad and I had teens live on and off in our home, but we felt we needed to make it official in case someone needed a long-term place to stay. We signed up to become foster parents and took the necessary classes to qualify, and in six months, we accomplished all the requirements and received our license to foster. While we were taking our classes, we were shocked to find out that in the state of Michigan, there were over five thousand children waiting for permanent homes, not including those needing foster care. That broke our hearts; we didn't realize there were so many kids without homes, and we wanted to be part of the solution.

In the videos, we saw some hardcore behavioral issues and difficult situations where kids came from, but with a little tender loving care, the video said they would eventually come around. The families on the video had lots of patience with the foster kids, talking with them about the different ways the kids could deal with their issues. Sure, there was a period where things would be difficult, but if you stuck with it, said the video, you would all become a family, and they would quickly acclimate. Brad and I talked about it over and over. We believed we had a good strong family. We had room in our home. We had love, compassion, and patience. We had gained some wisdom working with teens and raising three kids of our own.

We filled out an application that asked many questions: What age group would we like to have a child, how many, and on a scale from one to ten, the severity of their problems. Brad and I had marked that we would like one child, ten to sixteen years old, gender did not matter, with mild issues since we had two children still at home, who aged ten and twelve. Several days after completing the forms and the needed classes, we received our first call from the foster care/adoption agency.

"Hi, Mrs. Davis. My name is Sarah from the foster care adoption agency. We are calling to inform you that we have a possible child placement for you," she said with great enthusiasm in her voice.

"Oh really?" I couldn't believe it was so soon. "Can you tell me about the child?" I asked with much curiosity.

"Of course, but . . . it's actually two boys," the lady began to say, but I had to cut her off.

"Wait, we only wanted one child," I said, my body stiffening up in a panic. I didn't want two kids. Didn't they read our forms? We said one!

"Yes, I see that, but let me tell you about these two boys first, then you can think about it and decide. The youngest is twenty months and the oldest is nine. The parental rights have been terminated. They are on the mild end of the scale in regards to having any issues. The older one is on ADHD medication but is doing well," she said with such tenderness in her voice.

"Sorry, I don't even know what ADHD is, let alone want a twenty-month-old. I don't think I can start all over with a toddler," I said, wondering why she was calling me about this in the first place. I was getting a little frustrated with her because it was not what we had asked for.

"Sam, they are really good kids, honestly. Just come meet them," Sarah said, pleadingly.

"I'll talk to Brad. I just don't know if I can deal with two kids, especially a toddler," I said, feeling a little anxious thinking about two kids, especially a twenty-month-old.

"The truth is, many people want the baby, but not the older one," she said, her tone was sad and desperate.

"Well, if someone wants to take the younger one, we can consider taking the older one," I said, which sounded like a better solution. There was no way I wanted to start all over with a toddler. I was done with that stage. Besides, I was in my forties, too old to be chasing a little kid.

"We can't. We prefer to keep sibling groups together. Besides, if you do decide to take them, there is a lot of help and resources available. You don't have to do it on your own," she said, trying to convince me this was a good idea.

"Okay, I'll talk to Brad. Is there anything else we need to know about them?" I asked, sensing that the lady on the other end was not telling me everything.

"Well, the little one was born testing positive for opiates, which they really don't have enough evidence on the real long-term effects. He is a little behind for his age, but he is a sweet, smart boy and will soon catch up. Sam, they truly are wonderful boys. We all love them here at the center." There she was again, repeating about the boys being so wonderful; it sounded like she was trying to sell me on the idea of taking the boys, trying to make it sound like we are getting the best deal.

"Wow, I don't even know what ADHD is or opiates. I'll have to look it up. There are a lot of things we need to consider. I'll get back to you. Thanks." I said my good-byes and thought about the many children out there in Michigan alone that needed a home. Maybe this was a sign from God. I did not know what to do. I had a lot of thinking to do and needed to talk to Brad and the kids.

I spent time researching and reading a few books on ADHD and opiates. The solution for attention deficit hyper disorder was medication. With medication, the disorder could be controlled. As for opiates, I didn't find too much information on the long-term effects of a child who was born positive. I checked with the foster mom who had them, and she said they were good boys. Not much information there. All I kept hearing was that they were good boys. Brad and I talked about the possibility of two kids, one being a toddler, and if we were ready for that. It was not in our plan, but maybe it was where God was leading us.

It was difficult knowing what the right thing to do was. It would have been nice if a clear written sign had been given to us. One of the advantages was that our youngest biological child was soon to be twelve, so they could all help with the care of the little one; they would be great older siblings. I loved my children; they were so sweet. We were all so close as a family since we spent lots of time together. Homeschooling was a huge part of that.

It was a tough decision. Besides that, our first grandchild was soon to arrive in a few months. Lauren had met someone in the army, and they were having their first child. The agent from the adoption agency called to see what we had decided because they needed to find a home for these children. Brad and I were not ready yet to make a decision; we needed more time but thought maybe we could just go meet the kids to see what they were like. That too felt weird, like shopping for kids, yet it was a scary thing not knowing what kind of people we were possibly going to welcome into our family. We heard about others adopting and returning the children, and that certainly was not an option for us. That would be so cruel. I didn't understand how anyone could do that.

Our kids seemed okay with whatever we decided. They seemed a little excited at first to have more siblings, maybe thinking we would all be a big happy family. Our home had an open-door policy with our kids' friends and the kids we ministered to at youth group that they could hang out at the house, so the house was full of life, and we all enjoyed that.

The initial plan was for us to go and meet the kids, then pray and decide if it was a good fit. This was far from our original plan of just one child and fostering teens, but so was everything else in our lives that had turned out totally different. Nothing seemed to go according to our plans. I remember when I first walked toward the visiting room door at the adoption agency offices. Seeing through the window of the door, the baby was sitting and playing with toys. The little guy was cute; blond hair, nice round little face. I looked over to where the older boy was sitting at the table by the wall holding a deck of cards. He had dark hair, looked like a normal nine-year-old. They were adorable and cute, which was a positive thing. They did not look alike, maybe because there was such an age difference. But their eyes looked kind, and their smiles were inviting. I watched them through the window for a while; the nine-year-old kept shuffling the cards he had in his hand, over and over again, as if he was nervous. The little one was playing as though he didn't have a care in the world.

I was nervous. We entered and introduced ourselves; I sat on the couch next to the toddler, Aster. Brad went to the table where the young boy, Alex, sat. Aster was looking at me with his big blue eyes and bringing me toys. He crawled over to me. I began to play with him. He seemed sweet. I helped him up on his feet to see if he could walk; he was able to but was very unstable on his tippy toes with his hands up in the air needing to balance himself.

I looked over at Brad and the young boy. Brad was leaning in as they chatted and discussed what game to play as the boy nervously shuffled the deck of cards. He seemed talkative and personable. There was a little bit of a distracted look to his eyes, but I passed it off as nervousness. Who wouldn't be in this situation? How could parents choose to live a life separate from their children? I could not understand that a parent wouldn't fight and do anything for their family, their children. The boys' parents had chosen a path in life that was unhealthy for their children, so the state took custody of them. Apparently, they had given them almost two years to get clean, giving them opportunity after opportunity through programs that would help them with rehabilitation, parenting, and job training. Unfortunately choosing their own path leaving the children in the government system, which was not always the better option. What child would want to be separated from their parents? But the children were not given a choice.

After a little time, Brad and I switched places so we could have time with each child. I sat down across from the young boy.

"Hey, my name is Sam. Nice to meet you. Do you want to play a game of cards?" I asked Alex as he fiddled around with the cards not looking at me.

"Sure, can we play fish?" he asked, looking up at me for a moment then looking back down at the cards. He was cute, with beautiful hazel eyes, yet he had difficulty looking me in the eyes.

"Ah, yeah, I love playing fish. Played it a lot when I was young. Pass the cards around, and let's do it," I said. As I watched him, I concluded that he was having a hard time shuffling and figuring out how many cards should be given out. I also noticed his distraction, but aside from that, he seemed like a nice boy. We visited for an hour, then went to the counselor's office to discuss our thoughts.

"Do you have any questions, or would you like to share any observations or thoughts you have?" the caseworker asked, looking at us with curiosity. Her eyes were piercing mine as though she was trying hard to see in further as to what I was thinking.

Brad spoke first. "Well, they seem nice and all. It's just hard to know with one visit. I mean I certainly feel for their situation. There were just minor things that I saw, like the young boy being easily distracted. Is that because he was nervous or because of his ADHD?" he asked as he ran his fingers through his hair. He did that when he was in deep thought. I looked over at him and smiled; I thought it was sexy when he did that. I felt so lucky to have such a smart, good-looking guy. He blushed when he noticed that familiar smile. "And the little guy, he seems very unstable on his feet and doesn't seem to say any words."

"Alex, I'm sure, was very nervous so it probably was a combination of that and his ADHD. He has medicine to control a lot of that. He does fairly well. Aster is just a few months behind with his developmental stages, but he is doing well too, and we believe he will catch up quickly," she said as she opened the file on her desk and turned a few pages over. "Listen, the older one has seen many things he should not have seen for his age." She paused, pronouncing her words clearly and shaking her head, trying to collect herself enough to go on. "He tends to try to be an adult, yet he's only a child. He's mostly been around adults that did not filter their conversations. He has been in counseling since he was taken away from his parents. We recommend he continue to do so if you choose to take them, but he is a good kid and in time will adjust fine. The younger one doesn't remember anything but the foster home he is in, which is a good home, and tends to think they are his parents. The reality is that they need a forever home. They need love and stability," the counselor, Sarah, said.

"Why are their foster parents not keeping them? And wouldn't removing a toddler from the only home he knows be a bad idea?" I asked, twirling the ends of my hair with my fingers. I was trying to figure out why other family members would not step up and take them. It broke my heart thinking about these kids not having any family.

"The foster parents are in their late sixties. They have fostered many children but do not want to adopt. None of the boys' family members are in any physical or mental shape to adopt. The grandfather that Alex spent time with is physically incapable. Aster also has therapy for his motor skills and speech, and they will come to the house to do these things with him. We believe children are very resilient and will adjust to their new home in time. These two are some of the better-behaved children I have seen in a while. We cannot separate sibling groups. They must stay together," she said as she continued to shuffle the papers around in the file. I'm not sure if she was really doing anything with them. She hadn't written anything down or shared anything with us.

Brad looked at Sarah for a few minutes as if he was trying to figure out what he was going to say. "Well, thank you for your time. It's a big decision. We will have to go home to talk about it, and we will get back to you by the end of the week," he said. He got up from his chair and looked at me, indicating he was ready to go.

We walked out and got into the car. We sat for a while and were silent, both in our own thoughts. Brad made no attempt to start the car. I said, "Brad, it's so sad. We can't just walk away and not do anything."

He turned his head and looked at me with concern in his eyes. "I don't know, Sam. Two kids, a toddler. I don't know if I can do this. Maybe one, the older one. But both?" Brad responded.

"I know. I keep going back and forth in my head. I want to, I don't want to. I'm scared of failing, not being able to give them what they need. But then I remember too that the older kids can help. Plus, Lauren is having a baby. They will be close in age. We can all help. I mean I can't just leave them without a home. They can't find one because of their age difference, yet they won't separate them. Then, I think in time, like the caseworker said, they will acclimate and become part of the family with a little TLC," I said, feeling the tears run down my cheeks. I was confused too. I didn't know what the right thing to do was.

"I hear ya. Your heart goes out to them. But it's a huge deal, Sam. Our youngest is almost twelve. Do we really want to start again? I can see having a nine-year-old, but a toddler," Brad said, his tone clearly indicating that he was leaning toward not going through with it.

"Yeah, I know," I said as I stared out the window at nothing in particular lost in thought. I was torn.

The thought that they had no "forever" home tugged at my heart. I had a home with plenty of space for them. I had worked with kids, troubled kids too, for many years. Could we not do this for the betterment of these kids, give them a "forever" home? Two fewer kids the government had to find a home for. I missed the years when my kids were young; besides I had a few friends who had "ooopsies" in their forties, and they managed just fine. I could have play dates with them, and they would help. I felt I had gained more wisdom over the years, more patience, and felt not so uptight about the little things in life, more relaxed about things. I would have to convince Brad.

*****

"Sarah . . . we decided to take the two boys," I said excitedly into the phone, my heart beating fast. After two weeks of back and forth with Brad, we had made our decision. It was not easy, but I convinced him that we could do this with plenty of help. I know he was still not a hundred percent convinced, but he saw how determined I was to help them.

"Really? Wow, that's great! We will let them know and get all the paperwork signed, and we will begin with weekend visits to start," Sarah said. I could feel the relief in her voice that Alex and Aster would have a family.

"Okay, sounds good. How soon do you think we can start the weekend visitations?" I asked, anxious to begin the process of getting to know them and for them to move in.

"How about next weekend?" Sarah asked.

"Wow, okay, since we committed and are doing this, might as well start right away," I said. We made arrangements for weekend visitations and said our good-byes.

I sat down with a calendar and began to mark down the dates the boys would visit. I was nervous but excited. I didn't know where to start to prepare for them to come. I had to get beds, prepare their rooms, and get everything else ready for them. I didn't know what they liked to eat, if they had any allergies, or anything! I had a lot to learn. Apparently, they would come with no belongings. I put my pen down on the desk and put my head in my hands. "God, are we making the right decision?" I hoped we weren't going to regret this.

Chapter 16

Faith is the confidence that what we hope for will actually happen; it gives us assurance about things we cannot see.
—Hebrews 11:1

"Honey, please could you come home and relieve me for a bit? I can't hold him anymore," I cried into the phone over the screams of the child. I wasn't sure how much more I could handle. It had been over an hour since Aster had started his tantrum. He was kicking, screaming, thrashing his arms trying to hit me, head-butting, and spitting at me. Screaming and screaming and screaming. I sat, holding him firmly in a basket weave hold that the therapist had taught me when he threw a tantrum, which seemed like all the time. I tried hard to keep him from hitting me with his head, my hands far enough from his mouth so he could not bite me and leaning forward enough to keep his legs from kicking. I didn't know where the other kids had gone, probably hiding in their rooms again to get away from the chaos; it seemed to be part of our daily lives now.

In just a few more hours I would need to go pick up Alex from school. I didn't know how I was going to do that with my inability to control Aster. The foster care law said that one could not homeschool foster children until we officially adopted them, making it as though they had never belonged to anyone else. Erased. The past all erased on paper. But the past could never be erased from their minds. At the time, that was fine with me; there was no way I could homeschool him. I could barely homeschool my other kids anymore with all the turmoil of two more children who were not easily acclimating to the family.

Brad and I kept believing over time that it would get better, once it was legal and Alex and Aster knew that they were here to stay. We hoped much of their negative behavior would stop. But that did not come true after the adoption went through. It did not improve at all but seemed to continue to get worse. Then any help we received prior to the adoption went away. Why? Because we were now the legal parents as though I had given birth to both of them. It was as though Brad and I had done this to them, as if it was all our fault they had issues. The biological parents had been set free now, and they had no more responsibility to their own blood.

Brad quickly got home and took over holding Aster. If we let him go, he would throw himself against the wall over and over again. We could not allow him to do that. I had to step outside—I had to go for a run, something I had never done before in my life prior to the new kids moving in. I hated running until then.

I grabbed my iPod, stuck the headphones on, turned up the volume, and began my run. I did not have time to warm up. I was already pumped up from trying to hold Aster down. I ran and ran and ran, three miles, four miles, five miles, screaming into the air as the songs pounded into my ears. "Be strong in the Lord . . . He never lets go . . . don't give up . . . great and merciful God . . . bring all your troubles to the table . . . " and on and on. I was trying to let the words soak into me, wanting to feel the strength of the Lord fill me once again. I was glad we lived in the country because I was sure I looked like a lunatic runner screaming out to God, crying in agony at the heavy cross I was carrying.

I had begun running while on our vacation in the Caribbean Islands during Christmas break. Aster had screamed and kicked the entire five hours on the plane. Brad and I tried our best to try to distract him, to stop his screaming, and wanted so badly to avoid the stares and whispers from the people around us. I wanted to scream too and say, "He's adopted. It's not our fault he has issues. We are doing the best we can." It was horrible. Early in the mornings, I would sneak out to the beach to have some quiet time with God. I'd beg him to take this from me. "If the kids can't change, then do something in me so I could tolerate all this, so I could be a better mom and handle the situation better." Alex too. He asked a million and one questions about random things while bouncing off every solid object he could find. His attention span for anything was five minutes, at the most. Once, at a hockey game, he climbed up on top of the pop machine and began to jump up and down on it yelling and screaming at some kid.

When I got to the beach, I decided to take a walk. I took my shoes off, feeling the warm sand beneath my feet. I placed my towel and shoes on one of the chairs, stuck my headphones in my ears to try and drown the noises in my head and began to walk down the beach. Then I began to run slowly, then I quickened my pace, huffing and puffing, harder and harder, crying harder and harder. Anger was giving me momentum to go faster and further until I fell face first into the sand and lay there for a long time, not wanting to go back, not wanting to face what was behind me. I couldn't do it one more day.

Every part of me longed for the days before all this. When peace filled my being. When I felt like a good mom. When I felt better about myself. I hated the person I was becoming. I was depressed and hated my life. I wanted to run away because of the failure I had become. I was not able to take care of two broken children who needed me, yet it took very little time before I would lose it with them. The longing in my heart ached for my biological children, the times we had cuddling in front of the television. The games we played and the adventures we went on. I yearned to have those days back. I felt bitterness filling my veins; I was angry at what I had lost.

How many times in one day did Aster throw a tantrum, not a normal one, but a full-blown, out-of-body-and-mind tantrum? Screaming like he was possessed, kicking, spitting, biting and trying to head butt me. Once his behavior crossed the line, there was no going back, no reasoning with him. How many times did we have to leave an event due to another tantrum, having to carry him to the car, screaming and kicking? The stares, the faces, I learned not to look. I just looked straight ahead because I could not deal with one more disgusted look and the whispers. Guilt, shame, and failure became part of the continual voices in my head. I couldn't recall the number of times I had to clean feces smeared all over the bathroom walls or pick up pieces of broken toys. Slowly, our world became smaller as the exclusion grew. Not many people could deal with the chaos of our lives, the screaming and inability to control our children. We were included less and less in family and friend gatherings. I felt so disconnected from the world, from life. Our focus was day-by-day survival to keep us from losing our minds.

Our world changed drastically over a short period of time. I remember how strong I felt at the beginning, that we could do this, that the kids needed us, needed the whole family. Yet we were all unprepared for what had happened. Therapy sessions twice a week for each one, night after night sleeping in Aster's room on a mattress set on the floor beside his crib, my hand between the bars to comfort him as he screamed and thrashed his body all night as he tried to sleep. This went on for almost the first four years. There were many times where he sat in the corner hitting himself, talking to himself.

Brad and I, mostly me, felt hopeless, helpless. There was nothing we could do to change Aster's behavior because his brain was broken, and there was no repairing it. None of this seemed to have been noticeable when we first met or during the first few visits. I don't know if it was because of being pulled away from another home, the only mother he knew? I just know he hated touch as time went on, like it hurt, so we had to brush his skin with a sensory brush several times a day. We bounced him up and down on the floor so the pounding of his feet would bring a tingly feeling throughout his body, like electrical circuits moving all around to stimulate him.

Brad came home one day to find Aster screaming in the living room, throwing things, and I was hunched down on the floor in the kitchen crying.

"Sam, are you okay?" Brad asked as he crouched down to look at me. He swept the strands of hair out of my eyes.

"I can't, Brad. I just can't do this anymore. I can't handle it. He won't stop screaming. Every little thing sets him off," I said in a whisper, barely able to speak through my sobbing. I could not bear to look at Brad. I was so ashamed of him seeing me like that.

Brad sat down next to me, Aster screaming in the background. He put his arm around me, pulling me to himself. "Oh, Sam, there just has to be an answer to all this. We can't live like this. As much as we know it's not their fault, it's in them and we can't seem to fix it," he said with deep concern in his voice, his voice cracking. By the sound of his voice, I knew he was trying to hold it in, trying to be strong for me.

"Brad, I'm losing it. I have done everything I can. I feel like I am really losing my mind," I said, finally looking up at him into his eyes. I knew I looked like a complete mess. I couldn't help but feel such deep shame and guilt for failing.

"Sam, this is so hard. I too feel at times that I can't go one more day. I feel we've neglected our other children. We've put them in school after homeschooling them after—"

"Brad, I'm so sorry for that. I couldn't do it all!" I cried, feeling like he was finally putting the blame where it belonged, on me. I moved out of his embrace and put my head on my knees. I had begged him, convinced him, that taking two kids would be good. Regret penetrated through every bone in my body.

"No, no, please, Sam," he said, sliding his body in front of mine and grabbing onto my arms. "Look at me!" he pleaded. I raised my head a little, enough to lift my eyes to his. "I'm not blaming you. I'm not saying it's your fault. I'm just saying I myself feel overwhelmed and disconnected to them all. We've spent so much time with Aster and Alex and their issues that I don't have as much time, or little time, for the others. I feel so guilty about it and miss what our family was," Brad said. I could hear the bitterness in his voice, choking up, trying to keep it in. "Sam, we need to find a doctor for Aster that can help us. He needs to be put on meds."

I knew he was right. I was on the verge of losing my mind. "I agree, but none of the doctors we've been to will put him on medication until he's at least six," I said, feeling hopeless that we will ever have peace again in our home.

"I know, which doesn't make any sense, 'cause is he really better off in this state without it? He can't deal with life, and they are worried about altering his young brain. Really? It's messed up already. I don't mean that in a mean way, but geez, he's suffering. Look at him," he said as he pointed to Aster who was still in the midst of his full-blown tantrum.

This was true. I begged God to help us, to connect us with someone who could help the kids and us all. Something needed to be done, or I would have to take something to calm my nerves. I knew a lady in town who was raising her grandson who had issues as well—maybe I would ask her if she knew a good doctor who could help us. Someone who knew what the best therapy and medication that could help him. We had gone to so many doctors and specialists, and we were given so many labels, sensory issues, OCD, ODD, PTSD, on and on. But that didn't help him—no one could help him. He was in play therapy, but it made no difference. We could not reason with him; his mind was so irrational, like his brother's. His brother was similar but a little milder compared to Aster. He was not easy either, yet more tolerable. We received many calls from the school too for Alex. He cannot pay attention, is always out of his seat, blurting out and interrupting in class, constantly talking, etc. He was in therapy and on medication to help him, but it did not take away all of his issues. Constantly setting boundaries was important to keep some sanity because neither boy could figure things out on his own.

In the midst of it all, I tried to take my biological kids out on dates individually to try and stay connected to them. Once, I was on a date with my son Ethan. We were driving to Walmart to pick up a few things. He was very quiet on the way, looking out the passenger window. Then he turned to me and asked, "Mom, why are we doing this again? It's hard, and I miss our old life." He may have been thirteen at the time. He looked a lot like his dad when he was Ethan's age, but he was taller than Brad at thirteen. That wasn't too difficult since Brad was only five feet, seven inches.

I could not speak with the big lump in my throat. Looking at the road ahead, I too wondered why. I once knew, but now I had forgotten. "I'm sorry, buddy. I don't know, but what I do know is that I love you and God loves us all. So I gotta put my trust in believing he knows what he's doing." I glanced over at him as he watched me with his big beautiful sad eyes. I saw in him the desire to do the right thing, the kind thing, to help others, but this was tough for him, for all of us. I wished I could make it better, calm the waters, but I couldn't. I wanted to stop the car, reach over, and hug him so tight, protecting, comfort him, comfort myself.

That was all I could come up with. Did I believe that myself? I had begged for an answer. I had begged for a miracle. I had begged him to block my mind and heart from the hurts, to allow me to just go through the motions because it was too hard.

After speaking to my friend who was raising her grandson, she gave me the information and number for the doctor they used. We called and got an appointment for Aster. Doctor Slogan looked like Einstein: tall, slightly disheveled white hair. He was very kind and spoke with passion about all he knew about the function of the brain and what happens when it is broken. He talked a lot, but he certainly knew his stuff. I liked him. He was friendly and tried to explain to us in layman's term so we could follow along. He looked carefully at all of Aster's history and asked lots of questions. He also did some tests because he had a suspicion that Aster had fetal alcohol syndrome along with brain damage due to a positive diagnosis of opiates at birth, which caused premature birth and respiratory issues. Dr. Slogan started with a few mild doses of medication, which made a huge difference in only two days. It was a huge relief for Brad and me, even though there were still many challenges ahead of us. It seemed, though, that the tantrums where a little less, and Aster could sleep better at night. We did not like the thought of having to give him medication but understood that, without it, Aster was unable to function. In kindergarten through third grade, we received a call at least once a week to pick Aster up from school because he had been aggressive and had to be put in the safe room. Besides that, constant communication and an IEP, individual education plan, and meetings were a big part of our lives.

There were a few trips to the hospital where Aster had to be strapped down and injected with a drug to calm him down. We had many challenges with the Department of Health and Services trying to get the proper help at school and home. Not many understood the effects of FAS and how it affected families. Many suggested taking parenting classes to learn to be better parents. Many sent behavior specialists to try another behavior modification method along with the dozens we had already tried. It was a full-time, everyday struggle for us to keep things sane, to keep myself from falling apart. One more thing I had to do better, one more thing I failed at, until resentment grew in the depths of my soul. Every little scream made me scream as though I was feeling every pinprick when a potential meltdown from Aster would begin. I felt like I had OCD or PTSD, anxious and nervous at the possibility of something major happening, especially when I had to use the word *no* or take them out somewhere.

A lot of time was spent writing in my journal, praying, and reading my Bible in the early morning hours, 5:00 a.m., in the privacy of my closet. I needed an escape, an alone time. Why wasn't there intervention or healing after all the things we had gone through and endured? But I noticed that our faith grew and became stronger, and peace began to seep into us in the midst of the chaos when we let go and gave it to God. It was strange. It did not take away the difficult days, but it changed, taking one day at a time. Learning to put my trust in God no matter if I couldn't see or understand the situation or outcome. He still loved us, despite our failures, cared for us and would work all things out. I had to believe that, and through it, I felt closer to God. There were many times I yelled at him, lamented, and begged for him to remove the thorn from my side, yet I felt his arm reach out and tuck me under the shadow of his wing where I felt safe.

We also met some wonderful people, people who understood our challenges and who came alongside of us to help and encourage us. There were still many times when Brad and I wondered if we could go on doing this and times when we felt deep hopelessness and despair, but over time, we began to recover our strength to press on and hope would once again fill our souls. The mountains didn't seem so high and impossible, and the valleys didn't seem so low.

That was our journey, learning to release control of what we could not control and take one step forward, knowing that God had gone ahead of us to prepare the way. He did not expect perfection. He knew we were human and incapable, but his desire was for us to trust him and have faith.

Six years from the time Alex and Aster came to our home, and the year my mother died, my dream of a coffee shop became a reality. It was crazy how it all came to be. Being at the right place at the right time, connections, and stepping out of my comfort zone into God's will.

It came at the right time, separating my home life of raising kids to working in a coffee shop ministry serving God and people from our community and beyond. We're situated in a tourist town, which means people from all over the world come and go. We only had the three boys left at home. Lauren was living in North Carolina near the army base with her husband and two kids. Alissa was going to college in Texas. So that left Ethan, who was a senior in high school, Alex who was sixteen, and Aster who was eight. I felt such a deep desire, a calling, to build relationships within our community and what better way than through coffee? Most people liked coffee or lattes or tea, and it brought people together. What made this coffee shop different from others is that we have a presence in the community that's intended to connect with the people and offer them coffee in a comfortable environment that showed love and compassion. The atmosphere and people were inviting, which made everyone who came in feel welcomed and special.

It was a time in my life where I needed to feel like I was doing something productive instead of feeling failure. I felt like I was coming full circle in my faith in certain areas, knowing who I was and my identity. My faith was sweet and my identity solid. I had lived and endured so much in my life that I felt I could connect with many people going through many different challenges and to point them to Christ, the one who could bring healing to their broken hearts. I learned to be a better listener, not a solver, but a connector. I knew I could not solve anyone's problems, but I knew who to point them to him. I prayed that each person who entered the cafe would encounter him in some way. Even if his name was not mentioned, they felt a warmth, a welcoming, a peace like no other when they came in, and I wanted to be part of that.

I felt so fulfilled. I felt useful and purposeful. I had not felt like that in a long time. I loved being at the coffee shop. Even though it filled my days, it filled me. For a season, it was my escape from the insane world at home. I met so many people from different walks of life and had the opportunity to listen to others and to share some of my testimony. Brad and I also began to minister to couples in our home, and I began ministering to women. I felt a peace within me that helped me realize my worth once again. Even though I still felt some failure as a mother and continued to struggle with our adopted boys, I at least felt useful somewhere else, ministering outside of the challenges at home.

CHAPTER 17

I lie down and sleep; I wake again, because the Lord sustains me.
—Psalm 3:5

I wondered how I could be lying in my mother's bed when the last time I saw my mother was in this very spot. Yet being at the very place that my mother last lay comforted me. There was more than just death in this room. There was life. There was joy and healing in the midst of the pain and brokenness. Here was the very place that my mother's story began to unravel day by day. The unlikeliest place you would imagine that it would happen, a nursing home.

Yet it was the place many lived their final years before dying. It was the place where you pondered over what your whole life was about. Where memories would invade your mind, good and bad. Where you fought demons and won victories. Where you asked yourself many questions and wondered if you had done enough: Did my life matter? Did I make a difference? And where you wondered if you could have done more, done better. It was also a place where many cared to forget the life they had led, wanting to forget and live their remaining years locked away, grumpy and miserable, drugged out on medication to alleviate not only their physical pains but also their mental pains, the memories. For my mom, it was a place of escape, tucked away from the pain that lay on the other side of the walls she lived within.

I recalled the Wednesday morning when I finally reached my mother by phone. We normally spoke almost every morning around eight, but the last week, I could not reach her. I was worried. I continued to try, and on this particular Wednesday morning, my mom answered the phone. My sister had told me that our mother had been sick with the flu, and the doctors had put her on oxygen, which was a first for our mom. Besides, in the nursing home, the flu could kill.

When I heard my mom's voice, it was soft and distant. I could barely hear her. I spoke to her, telling her that it was okay if she did not want to talk. I would do the talking for her. I just wanted to make sure she was okay. In a quiet raspy voice, my mom said that she missed me. She wished I could be there with her; she said she was not feeling very well. Next, the phone went dead, and I knew she had hung up.

All day long, my spirit was not at rest, nudging me to go to my mom. I wasn't sure what to do. She had been sick many times, and many times I had gone to be with her, asking each time if this time was different. She'd had a few near-death experiences in the past but had recovered. The urgency to go this time kept building up in me until I finally spoke to Brad and asked if I could go.

"Yes, absolutely, you know I'm always supportive of you visiting your mom. We just don't know how much time she has. Make arrangements to go this weekend, and I'll take care of everything here."

"Brad, I honestly don't think she has until the weekend. I don't know. My gut instinct is telling me to go as soon as I can," I said with urgency in my voice.

"Wow, really? Well, you know you have always had strong instincts about things, so if you think you need to go now, then go," Brad said with such compassion in his voice that it tore at my heart a little.

"Thanks, hon, I really appreciate it. I'll get things organized with the kids and see if I can pull it off." I was so thankful for this wonderful man in my life. He was so loving and compassionate.

It was not the ideal time to leave. It was exam week for the kids, and their schedules were all over the place. My friends volunteered to pitch in and help pick the kids up here and there and to babysit the youngest, who was only seven. The other challenge was the weather, which had been bad lately, and so much snow had fallen, causing school cancellations. The next morning, day of departure, bad weather arrived with a vengeance. A severe winter snowstorm was pounding southwest Michigan. Schools were closed, and many accidents were reported as well as roads being closed. I was not sure if I should risk driving. Brad checked the weather and said it was only supposed to be bad in the southwest area of the state, because of the lake effect, and that all looked clear elsewhere. He told me to head to Kalamazoo instead of the Grand Rapids way and that I should be fine. I promised if there were any problems, if it did not clear up, I would stop somewhere to sleep and stay safe. He reassured me all would be fine at home and not to worry.

I headed out but needed to stop at the gas station first to fill up. It took a long time just to go five miles to the station, and visibility was difficult. After filling up, I went into the store to get a few drinks and snacks for the trip.

"I hope you're not going too far. It's pretty nasty out," the lady at the gas station said.

"Wellll . . . as a matter of fact, I am heading to Ontario, Canada. My mom is really sick, and I need to go and be with her," I said, shrugging.

"Oh, wow, that sucks. Both for you and your mom, having to travel in this weather. Be careful and traveling mercies to you," she said.

"Thanks so much, I appreciate it," I said, and I really did. I needed all the prayers I could get for so many areas of my life.

God, please let me know if this is a bad idea; otherwise, watch over me, I prayed, but my spirit kept nudging me to go on. In the past, I had asked God that when it was time for my momma to go to be with him, to please grant me the deepest desire of my heart to be right by her side, holding her hand, as she passed from this world into his arms. I felt that tug now. I was certain that this was it; this was the time. I sensed his presence in the car, pushing me forward, giving me permission to carry on and not turn back. *Jesus, take the wheel*, I prayed.

Carefully and slowly I drove, passing many cars in the ditch, through whiteout conditions. At times, I could barely see several feet in front of me, wondering if the car was moving at all. A mile seemed like several, but I kept pressing forward, remembering a Disney book

I often read to my children where Goofy was racing someone to the next town. Goofy said, "Slow and steady, steady and slow, that's the way to go." *Yes*, I thought, chuckling to myself at the oddity of this popping into my head, *slow and steady, steady and slow.*

An hour later, twenty miles from town, I came to the next town. As I passed through, I could see bits of blue sky ahead. I smiled and kept my eyes focused in front of me, hoping to see bluer sky and less white. The sky began to open up more and more the further away from home I got. It was like going through a wall of two seasons. *Thank you, Jesus.*

The rest of the way, six hours of driving, was clear as though no storm had ever crossed my path. As I pondered this, looking behind from my driver's side mirror, moving away from the white blur behind me, I thought about my life, the storms that had raged across my path with destruction in their winds. At times, I had gotten myself right in the eye of the storm, unable to see anything but the storm, feeling no hope of blue skies ahead. Many times, giving up hope, not believing that maybe the storm would end and a new clear day would arrive. Storms had struck my life, and many times, I allowed myself to give into it, not having the strength to fight, time after time being spit out after it sucked all hope and energy from me.

But as I drove on, I realized that God was always there with me. It was I who had given up, who had laid down my sword too soon, the sword too heavy for me to fight back. He wanted to show me the blue skies. He wanted for me to press on, to surrender to him, to allow him to fight the storm for me. I did not know how I had always done it, life, on my own. I did not know how to surrender it all over to him.

This journey through the real storm brought another revelation to my soul. Even though I could not see where the storm ended, he could. I had to trust him, stand in faith, and follow his lead through it. Like the storm, I did not see what was to come in my life, but he knew and he was right there with me. I just needed to trust him. When I had gotten on the other side of the storm, I felt victory! Only moments earlier, I had felt fear. I was afraid but kept asking God to help me to keep going, to let me know when I needed to do something different. When I saw glimpses of blue, I began to smile, and my heart began to fill with excitement and hope. I was going to make it.

I arrived at the nursing home at seven in the evening. As I walked in and greeted the nurses, the supervisor called me over. She looked worried. She loved my mom and said she had never seen her like this. She did not think it was going to be long. There seemed to be a heaviness permeating the hallways, something in the atmosphere that felt sad, a loss. As I entered room 6, I waved to Sharon, my mom's roommate, who was lying in her bed tucked in for the night. Sharon had had a stroke. She was confined to the wheelchair or her bed. She spoke softly through one side of her mouth, not able to use much of the other side due to the damage from the stroke. She also loved to paint, and she was glad she could still use her right hand.

"Your mom's not well," she said, trying to be heard over her usual low, soft voice. "I'm scared." She looked at me with sad eyes.

I walked over to the side of her bed. "Yeah, I know," I said as I placed my hand on Sharon's cheek feeling her sadness and trying to comfort her.

I walked around the curtain to my mother's side. Tears pushed their way out as I stared at the woman in the bed. The respiratory machine was hooked up in her nose. She lay on her back, eyes closed, mouth open, breathing loudly, in and out, in and out. I pulled the chair close to her and sat down. I grabbed her hand and rested my forehead on it and cried. I knew this time would come. No one was exempt from death. My mom was eighty years old now. She had lived longer than everyone ever expected. But no one could ever be fully prepared for a moment like this, especially when it was your own mother. I stayed by her side until late. At one time, I got in the bed with her and held her, like I had done many times in the past. What would I do without this woman? I wondered. I knew that I could always come into this room and lay with my mom when I needed to, but what now? That night, I left my mother's side tired but content that I could be here with her.

That night, I didn't sleep well. I was thinking about my mom all alone in her bed, feeling as though her time to go was soon. I thought often to get up, get dressed, and go down to the nursing home to be with her. I should never have left her alone. This brought tears to my eyes. I had prepared for this moment but still felt unprepared. I wanted to talk to my mother, to hear her voice, feel her touch upon my skin. Was I really ready to say good-bye to my mommy? Of course not, but I had to.

The next day, Friday, I headed back to my mom's early in the morning, afraid of missing the moment she passed. She was in the same state, incoherent and sleeping. Again, I sat by her side. While I sat, many of the staff came by to visit. I knew this was different, and everyone seemed to have felt it too. I sat, soaking in every moment, listening to her breathing, as their memories flooded my mind. With tears in their eyes, the people shared stories about my mom, how she was such an inspiration to them and to many of the patients. She made each person there feel so special, and each had their own special bond with her. Her love for them was deep and sincere, completely unconditional.

Throughout the seven years at Grace Villa, I knew that my mom had made many friends there. She spoke about them often. Until this moment, I had not realized how many people loved and cared for her. How many lives she had touched in this place filled with physical and mental sickness but more so with broken hearts and lives. She brought love and hope to a place where people were sick, dying, hopeless, and lonely.

My mother sat with the dying and shared the gospel of salvation. She had prayed that they would give their lives to Christ, feel his love, before they took their last breath. These were her people, and her love for them ran deep. It was not only the residents that she made an impact on, but the workers too. They came in her room with broken hearts, broken marriages, kid problems, and barren wombs to sit while she loved on them and prayed, no matter if they were believers or not. They'd pour out their lives before her, share secrets and pains that ran so deep only she knew about. She held them in her heart, laying each before the Lord.

I listened as one by one they came into the room to share their story about my mom, their voices cracking with pain seeing her slipping away. I saw the pain in their eyes knowing that their beautiful friend was not going to be there much longer. My heart grieved for each of them, for they shared the same love that I had for my mom. Even though I had her for much longer, they had spent the last seven years with her through her physical pain, caring for her and being there when she had her moments of darkness too. I was jealous in a way because they knew another side of her that I was not able to get to. I knew that even though my mom ministered to them, listened to them, loved them, they too were there for her. She told them things that I would never know. She shared her life with them during bath time, the deep secrets that she wouldn't even reveal to her own daughters. I knew that God had healed her, but the memories of the emotional pain she endured throughout her life still lingered deep within her.

One nurse told a story about how one day, a lady they refer to as "the grumpy lady," who always had a sour look on her face and barked at everyone, was in the hallway sitting in her wheelchair yelling at one of the nurses. My mom, feeble and barely able to walk, got out of her bed and went to the woman. She bent down, pointed at the lady's heart, and said, "You may have a black heart, but I still love you. God loves you and wants to give you a white heart." She kissed the woman on the forehead and returned back to her bed. The lady sat in her wheelchair for a long time, outside my mother's room, just staring at her, her face in shock. The nurse said that, in the days that followed, she would go to my mom's room and made sure to wave to her. She seemed to have turned a corner and made an effort to not be so mean and always looked out for my mom. It seemed as though Grumpy Lady had a bond with my mom. My mom loved her despite her meanness.

Growing up, moments like these were a common occurrence in my life. I heard someone say once that if you make a one-degree shift in a direction, it would change the course of your life, good or bad. That stuck with me, not only for my life, but if I, through my words and actions, could influence another person's life by one degree, that could have a huge impact on someone's life, good or bad. I hadn't really thought of it like that before, the idea that one small act of kindness could change a life. My mom's little words and actions had a huge impact on people's lives, and she had influenced the lady's attitude in the wheelchair with one simple action. She influenced the workers by simply listening to them, giving herself to them, mimicking Jesus's actions of compassion and love. It was not a matter of how much money she had, what school she went to, who her friends were, for she had very little of that influence left in her final years. She was in a little ten-by-ten-foot area along with a roommate. She had a bed, a dresser, end table, memories on the wall, and a body that was rotting inside. Yet she had it all, more than many other people would ever have. She had a heart that longed to love others, for them to find God and the healing power he had to mend their broken hearts, just like he had done for my mom and me for that matter. I knew my mom was special. But that day I saw her more closely, deeply, intimately as though her heart was pouring out to me without her even being able to speak a word.

The most precious moment was when she opened her eyes and looked at me, staring in confusion, as if wondering why I was sitting there. I didn't know if my mother ever really knew I'd been there or not. As recognition worked its way into her mind, a big smile formed on her face. I moved in closer, putting my face only inches away from hers. As tears flowed out of my eyes and onto my mother's hand, which rested on the bed just below my chin, I looked into her eyes and said, "Hi, Mom, it's me . . . *mouche a merde*." My mom and aunts called me that when I was little since I was so shy. When my mom was around, I stuck to her like flies stick to poop, and that's what the saying means in French. Of course, it sounds better in French—almost everything does. My mom looked at me with such joy, as though she had won the biggest prize in the world. She took my hands in hers and made the sign of the cross, head, chest, left arm, right arm, then placed her hands on my face and told me she loved me and that she was proud of me. Then she closed her eyes and went back to her place of sleep as though she had never woken up.

"Mom? Mooom," I yelled, wanting her to hear me. "Wake up, Mom, please." I laid my head beside hers and cried and cried. I wanted my mother back, yet I knew God had just given me a gift, a treasured moment with my mom that no one could ever take away. My soul was screaming inside. I wanted my mom forever, always to be by my side. No matter how much I failed in life, my mom always said she loved me and that she was proud of me. I needed her to be with me through all the joys in my life and all the hardships to cheer me on. I slipped into bed with her, feeling the warmth of her body beside me and the soft pink flannel pajamas she had on. I put my face close to hers, listening to her breathing the way I had done so many times to my children when they were small. The sound of life. *How can I live without her*, I wondered as I lay there, *my mom who loved me like no other?*

Chapter 18

Then the angel showed me the river of the water of life, as clear as crystal, flowing from the throne of God and of the Lamb down the middle of the great street in the City.
—Revelation 22:1–2

Coming to understand how sick my mother was over the years helped me to understand why prayer had become such an intricate part of her life. Her sickness ruled her; it took away her freedom, her ability to be a mother, a wife, a friend, the way she wanted to. She could not give herself to others as she desired. She was continually in a battle against the enemies raging through her body and mind. She was afraid to give into it and lose more of herself, so she fought her battle through prayer. My mother was a strong woman, that's what I saw—a woman with so much against her but time and time again getting back up and fighting. Many did not see her pain, hear her cries, or the strength it took for her to fight these battles.

While spending time with my mom, something happened inside of me. I had not completely understood her journey as she struggled with her sickness and pain. I had been so wrapped up in my own needs, my own pain. I was angry at the times my mom had been absent from my own life because of her sickness. I had been mad at my mom for so many years, thinking that much of my pain could have possibly been avoided if my mom hadn't been absent because of her illness.

But maybe I wasn't so much mad at my mom but at the sickness itself that took her physical presence away from me and my siblings over the years. I wept over my selfishness and immaturity. How could I not have seen her suffering? My mother had tried so hard to be strong. She hid her physical and emotional pain. She carried the sorrow and guilt for not being able to tend to her children like she wanted to. I knew she wanted to be more involved in our lives, but she couldn't. That day, by my mother's side, I wept and grieved on her behalf for all that she wanted but lost. My mom gave all that she could of herself. She did her best. I realized too that the only way my mom survived this long was by her faith. The strength to persevere, to keep going through it all, came from God. Her faith was so deep, so strong, that even though her body had failed her, her inner strength was a powerhouse.

Friday afternoon, my dad came to visit Mom. Normally, when I was visiting, he gave me the space to be with mom by myself. But my sister, Rachael, who was the eldest, six years older than me, looked more like our mom and was only five feet two but had more of our dad's personality. Hard, stubborn. We told our dad that he needed to come spend some time with mom. He sat holding her hand as tears streamed down his face, not quite able to grasp the fact that she would not be with us much longer. I wondered what was going through his mind at that moment. Fifty years with this woman to come to this point. How does one let go? Go on? At eighty-six years old, how would he manage on his own? We knew without a doubt that she would be free, in a better place with God. No more pain or sorrow . . . exchanging a life here for a life in heaven with the One she loved more than anything—a life filled with singing, dancing, peace, and love. But he would be left behind to grieve a great loss yet celebrate the gift that she was to us and so many. It was bittersweet.

If I were only allowed to use one word to describe my mom, it would be *selfless*. All her life, she put others before her. I remember often coming home from school and there would be another straggler living in our basement or a friend on the couch needing rest from their broken life . . . if only for a day or so. My mom would serve them, hold them, and love them, never judging. She would say often to us kids not to judge others, for you just didn't know where they'd been, what pain lay deep within. I knew my mom had not had an easy life herself. She had struggled with feeling unloved, unwanted by her father, enduring many hardships; but oh if my mom only knew how much she was deeply loved, how she would take a part of so many people's hearts when she took her last breath . . .

Those close to my mom questioned why, if there was a God, he would allow her to suffer so much for so long. I asked this question often too. I remember a time when we talked about this, my mom and I. My mom said, "Sam, God is not the one who makes people suffer. He is all good. This is how the world has become through our own doing: sin. Don't blame God. He has given his people free will and through their choices, beginning with Adam and Eve. We have brought sickness, suffering, and brokenness into this world. God created everything perfect. Besides . . . he has healed me. I am no longer sick inside. Only my natural body is failing."

With tears in her eyes, she placed her hand upon her chest, which lay flat from surgery, rubbing her hand over her heart. "Healing within is worth all the physical suffering." As she took my hand and looked into my eyes, she continued, "There are many people who look good and healthy on the outside but their insides are all broken up." Then she shared the verse that she clung to all her life, Philippians 4:13, "I can do all things through Christ who gives me strength."

Watching my father that day with my mom, he was so different from the man I remembered during my childhood, much softer and filled with emotions he did not often express. I pitied him more than anything. He seemed like a lost child without a mother. She was more like a mother to him than a wife. My dad struggled with making decisions, and he was afraid of everything.

I remember that every summer, we went camping for two weeks with a big tent that fit the whole family, and one night, when we were in the tent, a thunderstorm began, the trees cracking in the wind, the tent swaying back and forth, and my dad cowardly hid under the covers, scared. The wind managed to pull up one of the corner tent pegs, causing part of the tent to collapse. My mom was the one who went outside to fix it and made sure everything else was secured and intact. If we heard strange noises outside, it was my mom who investigated. She calmed the waters when things were in disarray.

She soothed his fears, set his clothes out, and made sure he had clean underwear. What would he do without her?

In my younger years, I resented my father. I didn't understand him, nor did I have a relationship with him. Again, it was not being able to see beyond the man in front of me, to the pages in between. I did not know his journey, the things that happened that caused him to be so afraid, to be so withdrawn from his own kids. I always felt that he just hated me, that I was just a problem in his life. He spent his time trying to be as far away from us kids, his children, as possible. He was more like an alien to us than a father, and I yearned deep in my heart for a father-daughter relationship. As a child, I dreamed of sitting on his lap with the warmth of his arms wrapped around my body, feeling safe and secure in a world that I was very afraid of. I would make up stories of the perfect dad, making him my hero.

When I had my kids, my father seemed to wake up from his stupor and lavished his love on them. I saw the tenderness in him toward each one. His grandkids adored him and could do anything with him. They would play cowboy, he would be the cow, and they would practice roping him. He and Ethan would go on bike rides and build stuff with wood. Brad and I would invite him on our family vacations, and he was like a kid in a candy store, as though he just had realized that there was a whole world around him that he had never seen. He was like one of them, "Sam . . . look at that! Wow, dat was so neat!" He became the dad that I dreamed about to my children. The grandkids experienced a different man than I ever did, and I was grateful for it.

As I watched him there by my mother's bedside, I saw his tender heart. I saw a man who loved a woman in a way that I could not fully comprehend. He had his own love language that only he could fully understand. His heart spilled out of his eyes onto the sheets of her bed. He held her hands, stared into her face, and allowed his fear of losing her to fill the room. There was no doubt in my mind at that moment, that my dad deeply loved his wife, my mom. Even though I did not understand him, I knew that he loved his wife the best he knew how.

My sister, Rachael, and I decided that we would stay the night with our mom. The nurses had wheeled an extra lounger in the room with some extra pillows and blankets. Later on in the evening, they also brought in a tray with cookies, coffee, tea, and juice. They took such good care of us, trying to bring as much comfort to our souls as possible and making these last moments a little easier.

Rachael and I sat on each side of Mom, each holding her hand. We opened our Bibles and took turns reading verses to her about the river of life flowing from God's throne, the golden streets, the angelical angels singing, and bright light coming from the face of God that lit up the entire heavens waiting to receive her. Of the people who had gone before her, her own mother and father, and many loved ones. They would be waiting at the gate to celebrate her entry. Sometimes, the emotions cohabitating in the room became overwhelmingly heavy, so much so that we could not speak a word but just sat and allowed the sadness to flow from our eyes. We thanked our mom for the life she had given us and the love she poured into us. We laughed about the crazy things our mother did to lighten the loads of our lives. She had a way of bringing hope to what seemed at times to be a hopeless situation.

When we were little, if we misbehaved at the store, our mom would dance and sing at the top of her lungs, which she was terrible at. We would be mortified and immediately stopped misbehaving, embarrassed. Once Brad and I went away for a week while my mom and dad babysat our three children. When we returned, there was a large box in their dining room with a heat lamp and dozen little chicks in it. "They were so cute," she said. "We couldn't resist." *Yeah, who's the one who couldn't resist?* My mom loved playing pranks, especially on our dad because he would get so mad. In the midst of heavy trials, hardship, and being sick most of her life, my mom tried to put lightness into all situations, even when we knew she was hurting inside.

Rachael and I had grown closer in the last ten or so years, but this time was different. We were sharing a time in our lives that was so intimate and would forever change us. The atmosphere in our mother's room was peaceful. Even in these hours full of death, we felt the pure, holy presence of the Lord.

It was strange. I felt so much joy and celebration in my heart when only hours earlier I didn't think I could do it. It was like the heavens were opening up and getting ready to receive my mom. As her breath became more labored, I said to Rachael that I believed these were her final breaths, that she was getting close. It was hard for me to say, but I just knew it was close. We played worship music. The song "Beautiful Exchange" was playing, and we encouraged her to let go, that it was time and Jesus was waiting. Our mother took a few deep breaths, and then her breathing stopped.

I held my own breath for a long time, waiting for my mom to breathe out. I put my ear to her mouth, but heard nothing. I let out all that air I had held in, laid my head on my mother's chest and cried and cried. There were no words to describe the feeling, the emotions I felt watching my mom take her last breath, an experience that could have two different outcomes, being with God or being separated from him. Knowing that my mother was a woman who loved God with all her heart, I had the assurance that she was going to spend eternity with her Savior. No more tears, no more sorrows, and in his presence.

As I stared at her body, an empty shell now, I waited for something to happen, an earthquake, a bright light, a small breeze. But nothing. What I felt was an amazing sweet presence of the Holy Spirit washing over me, lifting me up into a place of absolute peace that would carry me through the next several weeks. Rachael said she experienced the same thing. It was hard for us both to describe. I lay beside my mother, holding her slowly cooling body, knowing that she was no longer with us but with Jesus. Even though I knew this, I still couldn't let her go. This was my mommy—the one who wiped my tears, kissed my booboos, went to war for me. From the deep pit within me, I let out a cry, emptied my soul, and said good-bye. A huge part of me went with my mom that day. I was the youngest of four, her baby. I was so attached to her in many ways, and I knew that a part of my heart had broken off in that moment.

After my mom passed away, the nurses came in, and we were asked to leave the room so they could clean our mother up and prepare her for the funeral home to pick her up. While the two nurses were in the room cleaning and changing our mom's clothes, laying her flat down in the bed, a third nurse walked down the hall and into room 6, retrieving the bed alarm pad situated under my mom's mattress, and on her way out, she picked up the alarm device that sat outside her room. The nurse turned back around and headed back to the nurses' station while removing the batteries from inside the alarm.

Several months ago, when I was visiting my mom, she was all black and blue from a fall. The last year or so, my mom had been feeling weaker and had trouble getting up without falling. The nurses were very concerned, for good reason, because she would slip and hurt herself and bruise all over her body. The insurance company purchased a wheelchair besides the walker she already had, for her to get around in. My mom was a tad stubborn and wouldn't use it. The nurses kept warning her to use her wheelchair if she wanted to go anywhere. My mother would ignore them and would continue to use the walker, or nothing at all, which caused several falls and weeks in bed. One afternoon when I was there, a nurse whom my mom called Curly—he was European with a cute little accent and lots of dark curly hair—ran into the room excited. I asked, "What are you so excited about?"

He looked at my mom then back at me with this mischievous smile and said, "I have the solution to all of our problems."

"Oh boy, I have a feeling she's not going to like this," I pointed, pointing to my mother, who was staring at Curly with her big beady green eyes. I was laughing inside; I knew this was going to be good.

He picked up my mother's frail, light body and placed her into the wheelchair. She yelled at him, worried about what he was about to do. "What are you doing, Curly?"

He placed a large square pad, maybe two feet by two feet, underneath the first mattress. He picked Mom up again and placed her back into bed, covered her up, and tucked her in while she continued to eye him with curiosity. He then explained as he held a small box in his hand, "This is a bed alarm. Every time you lift your body out of bed, the alarm will go off. This box will be placed outside your door. The minute we hear this alarm go off, one of us will run down the hall to spank you and put you back into your bed."

"Curly, this is a genius idea!" I said as I smirked at my mother.

My mom stuck her tongue out at us like a defiant child and said, "You two are mean. Why are you doing this to me? Don't you like me anymore?"

"We love you, that's why we're doing it," Curly said to her.

Curly and I laughed so hard, but Mom did not think it was funny at all. She tried to say that this wasn't fair, that she had the freedom to get up and go as she wanted, and I knew this war was not over yet for Curly or the other nurses. As expected, my mom tried to get out of bed in the months that followed. She would even try to move fast to get to the hallway outside her door to try and turn the alarm off, but the nurses were too quick for her. My mom was stubborn. She continued to try to get rid of the alarm, so it was an ongoing game between her and the nurses. But deep down, I believe it was her way of saying she didn't want to get to a place of total dependency on others. She still wanted her freedom, but it was being taken from her, and she didn't like it. I couldn't imagine how that must have felt, always reliant on other people, even needing help to go to the bathroom. She had no privacy, her dignity taken away.

When the nurses finished cleaning my mom up and laid her flat, they came to get Rachael and me to let us know we could go back in the room. They told us to take as much time as we needed to be with our mom. The funeral home would only pick her up in the morning. Five minutes later, I heard some commotion going on down the hall. Two nurses came running into my mom's room laughing with excitement and the alarm going off in their hand. We were taken aback that these nurses were smiling and laughing while we were sitting with our dead mother.

"You won't believe what just happened. When we returned to the nurses' station, the alarm kept going off, even though the batteries had been removed. There are no batteries in this alarm, and we cannot shut it off," the nurse said, shocked.

Rachael and I looked at each other with big smiles. We all knew that our mother was having the last laugh in this one. It brought tears to our eyes. God is so precious, how he gives laughter in the midst of difficult, sad times. He wants to bring laughter and joy to our hearts, a sense of connection, in deep moments of sorrow. I knew my mom and Jesus were laughing together. This brought joy to my heart. In the next weeks, there were many moments like this. God had planted little bits of my mom all around me that brought comfort and healing to my soul.

We ran into Curly at the nursing home several days later. He was filled with awe about the alarm and said that it had been going on and off ever since my mom passed and he had to call someone in to repair it. He also shared how special Mom was to him. He often gave her baths; my mom loved baths. While washing her frail, torn-up body, she would ask him about his life. He said the workers were not supposed to share personal information with the residents but that, "you just couldn't help it with her." He said she showed so much love and compassion to everyone that you just ended up spilling things out to her that you had no intention of sharing. He also said she too shared secrets she could not keep inside, secrets that if shared with us may hurt too much.

I was certain there were many secrets hidden within the walls of that bathroom, between her and the nurses who cared for her. Curly, as well as many other residents in the home, asked my mother where she got her strength, how she could carry on through all her pain and still smile and care for others. I asked Curly how she answered that. He said that she would point up to heaven and say, "God is my strength."

As tears rolled down his face, he shared with us how our mom had witnessed to him of God's love and strength. He knew her favorite Bible verse, Philippians 4:13, "I can do all things through Christ who gives me strength." He did not know of this God that our mom was so close to, but ever since he'd met her, he began to feel it within himself. He said there were days when he would come in depressed and in a bad mood and make his way down to our mom's room. The minute she saw him, a smile would form on her face. She would say, "Hi, Curly," and in that moment, his mood would change.

The love she poured out to everyone who came into her room lifted up the weight that sat upon their soul and filled them with a renewed sense of peace and strength. My heart swelled. I knew it was the presence of God. Just in the last several days, I had learned so much more about my mother than I had in all the years I had known her.

CHAPTER 19

See, the Lord your God has given you the land. Go up and take possession of it as the Lord, the God of your ancestors, told you. Do not be afraid; do not be discouraged.
—Deuteronomy 1:21

It was time for me to leave the safety of room 6. I had gone through much of my memory bank and relived much of my past that I now had to go and live out my future. I got up from the bed and looked out the window of my mother's room one last time. I said my good-byes and turned from the window. I passed by Sharon's side of the room and waved good-bye, stepped out into the hall, and looked back once more to take it all in. I then turned and walked out of Grace Villa nursing home. The time I spent in room 6, I felt much of my mother's life transformed into my own. Intertwined as though her legacy would live on in me, like a baton in a race being passed continuing the journey of faith. I was able to release her, to say my good-byes, bringing closure to her death that would allow me to move on to deeper healing that I could not do while she was alive.

As time went on, I knew there was still some land to claim, a big piece of land within me that had been stolen long ago, right in the center of my soul. It had followed me around, tormenting me for much too long. It did not go away just because I told it to. I had to stop running, turn around, and face it, not allowing it to own me anymore. As much as I grew, I faced some difficult issues in my past and healed from many hurts, but there was still a wheat field and a little girl who kept calling me back. I would see her everywhere, me as a child with almost white hair, beautiful yet sad, sitting in a field all alone. The wheat was high, but where the girl sat, the wheat was flat and packed down. No one could see her sitting there but me.

When I passed any field, I would see the little girl sitting, staring back at me. I dreamed of her, the little girl, trying to reach out to me. But I would not reach out to her. She had been waiting for me in that same spot for a long time, waiting for me to come and rescue her. I tried so hard to remove her from my mind, my thoughts, but a picture of her kept flashing and kept flashing until the thought of her consumed me. *No*, I would say, *I don't want to go there. It's too hard. The past is the past, and I've had enough of it.*

Yet it kept one step behind me. Everywhere I went something would remind me of the little girl left in the field. I had to go back and rescue her, but how? I did not want to face those hard times, yet I wanted to connect with the little girl, to become one with her. Most of my life, I was disconnected from her, abandoning her to the past. This part of my past seemed to be the final piece to claim but the hardest. The missing piece of my wholeness.

I was involved in an inner healing journey group since last fall, two and a half years after my mother's death. I had gone for training and now was participating in one to learn more about it so I could also begin to facilitate a group. Many of the women I ministered to could benefit from doing some soul searching and inner healing of long ago wounds. I had already dealt with many wounds of worthlessness, drug addiction, promiscuity, abortion, and guilt. But apparently, these were secondary behaviors from a more underlying wound. Something that went deeper that led me to run away and go down a difficult road. I was beginning to understand that more now, but there was too much pain and anger that I didn't want to stir up, so much anger of what happened to the little girl in the wheat field. When it would invade my mind, I was afraid of the anger and the hate that followed, hate for those who had hurt me, not to mention feeling sick to my stomach at the thought of it all.

In my training group, we started with the first layers and made our way down to the deep wounds. I learned that we all had core longings of wanting to be safe, have self-worth, be unique, loved, nurtured, and appreciated. I learned that from the beginning, there was a false interpretation of what love was through what I had experienced in my life. I had never felt safe or worthy or unique. I felt love from my mother and being nurtured, but I also felt abandoned. I also received love from the wrong people, love that broke me. The wounds of my past lay deep within me, and I worked hard to hide them by believing lies, reacting to the lies through emotional upheavals and dysfunctional behaviors that brought me to the life situations I found myself in. Broken marriage, addiction, anger, anxiety, promiscuity, and worthlessness.

It was almost a year-long journey to inner healing, asking God to come into my wounds, even though he knew everything about me. He wanted me to come to him, trust in him to surrendering it all, and allow him to heal me. On week fifteen, in the spring of 2016, just months before turning fifty, there was a lament. I was lamenting the wound that had been controlling me all my life. By then, I knew it was time, no matter how difficult it was, to cross over the line into my childhood and into those dark places. I had to be in a place of healing and peace, that this no longer could have a hold on me.

The day of the lamenting came. I was scared, nervous, but ready to get this off my chest once and for all. I had never talked about it until this moment. I sat in the chair across from the facilitator.

"Do you want to be close together, or do you need a little space?" she asked with gentleness in her voice. I had come to know her and trust her through the healing group. I felt comfortable with her.

"Can we get as close as we can? I need to feel safe," I asked as I scooted my chair closer to hers until our knees touched and I felt the warm of her touch on my hand.

"Just know that this is a safe place, and I'm here if you need anything, and most of all, God is with you. We will pray for the Holy Spirit to be present and guide you through your lament." I closed my eyes as she began to pray and guide me to a safe place with Jesus. We had been working on safe places in our time together. It was a place you could imagine that you felt comfortable, safe. It could be a favorite spot in a park, on the beach, or at home. Then you would ask Jesus into your safe place with you to talk. This helped to ease any anxiety you felt so you could better connect with Jesus uninterrupted.

My place, most days, was room 6 at the nursing home where my mom lived for the last six years of her life, a place where I felt safe. There were others too, on a park bench, on the beach, at home by the fireplace. I knew Jesus was with me always, but in these places were where I liked to go and talk to him. Once, God brought a memory of when I was a child riding in the boat with my dad on the Atlantic Ocean, going to check the lobster traps. Now, I was brought back to that time because I loved the very few times I spent with my dad, that we were alone in the very place my dad loved the most, in the boat on the water. In my mind, I could still feel the wind blowing my soft, blond curly hair.

I could see the coat I wore, a white shiny rain coat with colorful polka dots, my dad in his fishing gear, the waves of the water, the smell of the salty ocean air, as if I really was there. It soothed me, comforted me. I felt my mouth forming a smile while my eyes were closed living in the memory. When I invited Jesus into my memory, I looked over to where my father was and instead saw Jesus steering the boat and laughing into the wind. I hung on as we went faster, and I began to laugh along with him. I loved being there with him. I felt the warmth of his love caressing me.

I was then asked by the facilitator to share my wound through a lament, which was to express my grief and loss of something of great sorrow. I then opened my eyes, still feeling the warmth of Jesus's presence. That comforted me because I knew this was going to be difficult to do. Bringing up something from way back from in my past. Crossing the line to "then," which grew like a cancer over time and had affected many things in my life. Yet, I desperately wanted to bring healing deep within me, so it would no longer have a hold on me and I would no longer be running and hiding from it. What would that feel like? I wondered.

I began. As my past unfolded in the words I wrote on the pages in front of me, I envisioned myself as a little girl back in the boat, not with my dad, but with Jesus. I spoke to him about the sexual abuse that happened in the wheat field. How I did not want to do the things I was told to do. How I was confused and ashamed, a river of tears mixing with the wind as the boat went faster and faster. I screamed my pain into the wind at Jesus, describing to him the things that happened to me, many times feeling the bile from deep within me wanting to spew out my mouth.

I was angry. I asked him where he was, how he could allow that to happen when I was just a child, seven, and for many years after. All the years that the wheat fields had followed me, all the shame, pain. and self-hate I felt seep into every relationship, every addiction, every wrong turn, as I tried to run and hide from it, drown it, crush it. But there it was, following me, tormenting me. Jesus kept driving the boat as I released it all, screaming how I hated the feeling, how it made me sick, and yet how I allowed it to continue.

The wind carried my words with it, twirling them around and throwing them into the air. Jesus kept driving as I continued to release all that had been hidden deep within the crevices of my soul. The mold that layered the pain came undone as the truth within me began to rise, my body feeling the release of all the years of hiding. I was feeling lighter and lighter as more was released into the wind and carried away. It felt good, so good. I realized that I had so many layers after years and years of trying to run away from it, thinking that the past was the past, better left behind. Yet it felt so good to say it, to speak it, to finally share my deep secret, to release it all to Jesus and into the wind.

The boat began to slow down. I sat down, exhausted. The boat stopped, and Jesus sat beside me and pulled me to him. I could not see his face or the form of his body, but I felt his presence. I felt him tucking me under his huge arm. I felt the warmth of him envelope me and his love fill me as I cried into him. *Where were you?* I whispered. I felt the question float through the air. *What did it cost you?*

I laughed. *Are you kidding me? It cost me everything! I gave myself to whoever wanted me because I felt ugly, used, dirty, and I never felt clean or whole. No matter how much you told me I was yours, how beautiful I am in your eyes, that You created me, knit me in my mother's womb, had a plan for me, a purpose . . . I never felt good enough! That innocent little girl was left in the field. I lost her. I miss her. I want her back . . . whole.*

It cost me a pure relationship with my husband. I hid myself from him because I was afraid he would see my dirt, the filth beneath my skin. There are things I couldn't give him because it reminded me of things I had to do as a young child. My identity, that I never even got to know, was stolen from me at a young age. It filled me with fear, not allowing my kids out of my sight, not wanting them to ever experience what I had, yet not being able to save them from everything. Everyone was suspect in my eyes because no one was safe enough for me. I was afraid to tell, afraid what people would think of me. So I told no one. The secret invaded every part of my life. Funny how I thought keeping it a secret would save me from shame, yet it only grew deeper. What did it cost me? Being a beautiful bride in white! I longed for that, and I grieve that loss, and so much more . . .

The scene changed in my mind. I was back to myself, my age now, and Jesus and I are walking in the wheat field where it all began. He is holding tight to my hand. I did not feel afraid, just anxious. We came to an opening, the flattened ground where the young Sam sat. We both sat down with her. Jesus had my blanket, my childhood blanket that was my security then, my hiding place. He covered us all with it; the blanket grew enough to make a tent over us all, and a bright light shone around us.

The light enveloped us in his love and peace that only could come from the light. Jesus blew into us his healing breath, and the blanket danced above our heads. Laughter filled the air as I wrapped my arms around my child self. I hugged her and kissed her and told her how beautiful she was. I felt the joy fill me up as we connected and became one. I heard Jesus say, *I have always loved you. I have always been here with you.*

As he stood up with a pitcher in his hand, He tilted it and began to pour water over me. Then the water turned into blood. *There was a cost, and I paid the price. For you and for all. The world is broken, but in me you are whole. My blood was shed for you, for all of you. I put you back together. You are my bride, my pure and beautiful bride.* I felt the water and blood flow through me, like the day He appeared to me twenty-nine years ago, washing all the impurities and the pain from inside of me. I was being made whole. *Your land belongs entirely to me. You are mine, and I am yours.* I got up, and we danced, Jesus and me, in the wheat field. I laughed and cried and felt the healing rains wash away my pain.

When I opened my eyes, I laughed for joy what Jesus had just done for me. I felt so good, so light and free. When I went home that night, I knew, as exhausted as I was, that I needed to share the truth with Brad. He knew there was something I was hiding, had seen the pain in me throughout my journey, but did not know what it was.

As I told him my story, I wept through it all, as he did. I was always afraid that he would be angry with me because of all the lies or untold truths. I had never lied. I just didn't tell him what had happened, but I felt I was the lie because he had married someone he did not fully know, that I had never told him my whole story. My past had begun to unravel over the last few years, a past he had never known existed.

When I had finished, he held me and wept with me. I felt his tears against the skin on my neck. "I love you, Sam," he whispered as he caressed my head. "You are so brave and courageous," he said, pulling himself away and facing me. "I would like to wash you in the bath. Would you let me?" he said looking into my eyes.

"Ummm, why?" I asked, turning my eyes away from his. It was hard for me. I now felt exposed, naked. I felt really strange.

He put his hands on my knee, "Please don't think that I think you are dirty. I want to do it for you. I want to, as your husband, wash you as a symbol of how Jesus sees you and how I see you. I couldn't save you then, but I can protect you now. I already see you clean, but by doing this, I want you to know it absolutely." Brad was so passionate and tender in the way he touched me and spoke to me. I felt his deep love for me.

"Okay," I said, still feeling a little awkward. It was so hard for me to be bare before him without the lights being off and under the covers. I also felt so relieved that he still loved me and wanted to do such an intimate thing.

He filled up the bath with warm water, the way I like it. He left the bathroom so I could get undressed and get in the tub. He then came back in with a face cloth in his hand. He put soap on it and began to gently wash my skin. I felt his love and forgiveness as he washed me, the silence speaking its words of peace within my very being. Once again, the cleansing water purified my soul.

"I will always love you, Sam." He stood, bent over, and kissed my forehead. "I will always be by your side, through thick and thin, sickness and in health, hardships and joys. I love you with all that I am." Brad reassured me as the tears ran down his cheeks into the bath water. "The pain that runs deep within me is that I wasn't there to protect you. I want to protect you, Sam."

It was a difficult journey to travel. So many bends, circles, and backtracks; yet with each step, I felt freer. I was able to use what happened to me to begin the healing journey for others as well. I went to Peru shortly after, which gave me many opportunities to speak to the young ladies about my journey, which in some way was similar to many of their stories. There were many tears that were shed as I held each of them, and they released their pain into the light. The darkness no longer had a hold of them. They had been brought into God's light, and he was healing them—and me.

I had known for many years that I was a child of God, that I was loved by him and had felt him with me, his strong presence inside of me. Yet for some reason, I was afraid to let him see that part of me, even though I knew full well that he knew what it was. He knew everything about me. But I did not want him to see my shame. I felt dirty and wanted to hide, like Adam and Eve in the garden after they had sinned. Now, I wondered why I believed that lie. Why I believed something I knew was not true. Once it was all out, no one had anything else on me. No more secrets! All the land inside me, every part of me, belonged to him.

Chapter 20

We now have this light shining in our hearts, but we ourselves are like fragile clay jars containing this great treasure. This makes it clear that our great power is from God, not from ourselves.
—2 Corinthians 4:7

Since I was no longer a child, my feet could reach closer to the sky as I swung, pumping my feet up and down. The swing rose high, very high, and the wind would catch my long blond hair that covered the aging gray. It felt good! Not just the wind against my face and the way the swing made me feel, but the lightness and freedom I felt within me. I was no longer haunted by the "then." I was no longer hiding. I felt the little girl inside of me, happy and carefree. Sure, I still had a journey to walk, I was not done yet, but I knew that with my Jesus, I could live a life of peace no matter what lay ahead. The world was broken, but I was no longer broken in Jesus. I stood on his firm foundation, on his love, word and promises. His truths melted into me, telling me who I was in him; a child of the one true king, an heir to his kingdom, a child set free from the bondage that once held me captive. As my legs pumped and I swung higher into the wind, I sang my victory song:

Oh, victory in Jesus,
My Savior, forever.
He sought me and bought me
with His redeeming blood;
He loved me ere I knew Him
And all my love is due Him,
He plunged me to victory,
Beneath the cleansing flood.

About the Author

Lucie lives in Southwest Michigan with her husband and the youngest of her five children. She enjoys spending time with her children and grandchildren, traveling the world doing missionary work. She is living her dream by managing a coffee shop ministry where she gets to enjoy a variety of specialty drinks but most of all extending a rich and satisfying life in Christ to all who enter the café. This is her first novel.